The Lilac Tree

a novel by
Nicolette Maleckar ❧

Ben Yehuda Press

Published by Ben Yehuda Press, L.L.C.
430 Kensington Road
Teaneck, NJ 07666
http://www.BenYehudaPress.com

Ben Yehuda Press books may be purchased for educational, business or sales promotional use.
For information, please contact:
Special Markets, Ben Yehuda Press, 430 Kensington Road, Teaneck, NJ 07666.
Email: markets@BenYehudaPress.com.

ISBN 0-9769862-2-1
Library of Congress Control Number: 2005935388

First Edition: November 1987
Second Revised Edition: April 2006
06 07 08 09 10   / 10 9 8 7 6 5 4 3 2 1

Introduction

I left Germany on one of the last children's transports to England in August, 1939, and came back in November, 1945 as a civilian employee of the American army. My aim when applying for the job was the crazy hope that I might find surviving family members. Amazingly, my mother had survived due to her gritty determination, the heroic efforts of friends, and a great deal of luck.

Lilac Tree grew out of my admittedly selective memories of a surreal experience. The Berlin I had left was cruel and frightening: It had been hard to find anyone who had a kind word for Jews. I came back six years later to a pile of rubble with small enclaves of normalcy. The hatred towards Jews was still palpable, but nicely hidden under the requisite protestations of hatred for the Nazis.

The plight of the Berliners in their unheated, bomb-damaged homes was heartbreaking. You could smell their hunger. Hunger had a distinct smell and it was everywhere. And there I was, well-dressed in a marvelous American uniform, better fed than I had been in years. The PX made available unbelievable luxuries, including two cartons of cigarettes a week. A non-smoker, I found myself rich. Cigarettes could buy anything. I knew one fellow who bought an excellent piano for twelve cartons of Lucky Strikes.

The spectacular ball gown I acquired for three cartons came in handy later, when I was back in England, performing in a theatrical repertory company, a career gravely hampered by my total lack of acting talent. But that is another story.

My hitch with the American army had one lasting side effect. I fell in love with Americans—not one particular American, but Americans as a whole; their warmth, their openness, their humor, and their kindness. I knew that I wanted to live among these people, that I would finally feel at home.

In May 1949, I stepped off the Queen Mary, and submitted my belongings to a custom officer, a huge fatherly man. When he finished, he patted my hand and said, "You are going to be very happy here."

He was right.

❧ *Chapter 1*

In the late fall of 1945, Berlin was not a comfortable town, even for the victors. Few buildings were intact, and there was a makeshift quality about life. Everything seemed to be held together with make-believe.

The city had been divided into sectors, each supervised by one occupying power. Russia had the east end, which housed all the museums, the finest theaters, and the great national library. France had the north, which was mostly factories and slums. England had the west end, with its pathetic remnants of fashionable shops and nightclubs. America controlled the southwest, a collection of pretty suburbs, partially intact.

Surrounding the city was the Russian zone, not easy to get in or out of, and the few overcrowded trains that managed to get through disgorged a pitiful ragtag collection of humanity. There were the returned prisoners of war and the Berliners who had escaped from the air raids and were now trying to find their homes among the rubble. And then there were the children.

No one knew where they came from. They were dirty and secretive and streetwise. They begged and stole, and for every one who found a home, there were ten more who tumbled off the train.

They were pitiful, their noses pressed against the windows, wanting in. And they were everywhere.

To the good, kindly, conscientious people who had come to try to bring order to this disaster area, the children were the ultimate challenge—and the inevitable defeat. You rescued a hundred, and there were a thousand more.

Some became sharks.

They had been children once, but they'd had the breaks—and the smarts—to come out on top. And they all came to Berlin, because that's where the pickings were best.

Paul Karinof looked marvelous in his American uniform; it went particularly well with his dark hair and eyes. One of the finest tailors in Berlin was responsible for that flawless fit. For all that, the uniform was deceiving. It lacked the brass buttons and the insignia of the real thing, but many people didn't notice that. Paul was just a civilian in uniform, an employee of OMGUS, the American Military Government, who enjoyed being saluted.

Officially he was an interpreter, and a very good one. He spoke excellent English, French, German, and Russian. It made a good cover for his other, more interesting activities. He loved Berlin. He had come a long way to get there, a long, rocky road, all the way from the slums of Vienna.

He didn't often think about his earlier life. There was too much pain there— the death of his lovely, gentle mother, the lonely, cold years, and then the final shambles when the Nazis took over. But he was all right now. Each blow had contributed to his education. Though nothing could make up for the pain he'd experienced, there was a certain satisfaction in surveying the path he'd traveled to reach his current, enviable position. Paul Karinof, the poor stateless outcast, had it made.

Being posted to Berlin was pure good luck. No other place would have offered him such scope, and there his White Russian connections were most useful. It was almost like coming home, and the job suited him. It didn't pay much, but gave him plenty of free time for more profitable activities. Most interpreters had to live by the clock, trudging off to work every morning, but Paul managed to arrange a flexible schedule for himself. As long as he did his work—and he did it superbly—his time was his own.

He made it a rule never to breakfast before ten. By then, the morning rush was over at the officers' mess. There were several advantages to this. Paul enjoyed a civilized, leisurely meal. More important, the high-ranking officers always came in late. He had managed to meet some useful people that way.

The mess had been a restaurant. It was elegant in a very Germanic fashion, all ornate chrome and massive plate glass, a style Paul had privately dubbed "Third Reich Plebeian." He disliked the huge windows that gave you the feeling of practically sitting in the street. The tables he preferred were at a safe distance from the glass, where hungry children's faces were pressed with painful attention. Those were memories he could do without. But this morning, the table by the window was the only one left.

"I don't understand why we can't feed them," the major sitting across from Paul said indignantly, while the MPs made their usual, hopeless pretense of chasing the children away. "When I think of the food that's being wasted in the kitchen every day, it's too much to bear. Look at that little fellow on crutches, with the stump not even properly wrapped against the cold."

The third man at the table was older and rather tired-looking. "Would you believe that I took that very child to the Zehlendorf Hospital and had him fitted with a prosthesis?"

"I'm sure you do what you can, Doc," the major said, frowning. "But if he has a wooden leg, why isn't he wearing it?"

"Wooden nothing." The doctor grinned. "Pure aluminum, adjustable, light-weight, finest kind. I asked him myself why he wasn't wearing it. He was perfectly willing to tell me. Seems he is the sole support of two women, mother and aunt, the men missing or dead, who knows? When he wears the prosthesis nobody gives him a crumb. So Tante and Mutti have taken it away, and only let him have it back after he's finished his stint of begging for the day."

"Disgusting," the major said, flushing. He turned to Paul. "We should take the children away from people like that and see to it that they're brought up decently."

"Isn't that the way the Nazis solved problems?" Paul asked innocently. The major got even redder in the face, and glared.

"Nazis and communists," he huffed, which caused the doctor to raise his eyebrows and wink at Paul.

Lingering at the table enjoying his last cup of coffee alone, Paul gradually became aware of an uneasy feeling. Looking down, he saw a face practically pressed against his shoulder, separated only by the pane of glass. He drew away instinctively and stared into the unwinking eyes of an odd-looking urchin.

The child was dirty beyond belief, and his nose flattened against the pane gave him a froglike look. A shapeless knitted cap was pulled down low over his forehead and ears. He was not so much dressed as packaged in an assortment of sweaters and shawls. It was impossible to guess his age. He could have been anything from six to sixteen, an anonymous lump of misery.

Definitely not an attractive child, Paul thought, and drew fastidiously away from the glass. Still, there was something fascinating about that unblinking stare. It would not be ignored.

Suddenly it came to him. It was like looking into a time-warp mirror: Paul Karinof that last year in Vienna, dirty, hungry, and lost but fiercely determined to survive.

Experimentally, Paul picked up a slice of bread and with ostentatious care buttered and folded it. The eyes never left his hands. He wrapped the sandwich in a paper napkin and slipped it into his pocket. The child stared. Paul gathered up a few more items of food and then made a slight motion with his head toward the side of the building where the garbage cans were lined up. The enormous eyes widened even more. For a moment the child stood frozen, then melted away.

Paul sauntered out of the mess hall, past the MPs whose unlovely job it was to make sure no one took food out to the beggars. Both MPs seemed to have poor eyesight. They appeared quite unaware that the pockets of Paul's uniform were bulging, not only with bread and butter, but with an apple, two oranges, and a hardboiled egg someone had ordered and not eaten. He swung his greatcoat over his shoulders, which hid some of the bulges, and proceeded toward the alley in a leisurely way, shaking his head at the children who gathered hopefully around him. They stepped back just enough to let him get by, then closed ranks behind him.

He found his particular urchin sitting on a garbage can, watching his approach with the same wide-eyed intent that had first caught his attention.

Paul handed over the bread and for a moment thought the kid would grab it and run. If he had such an idea, he wisely discarded it. There were too many competitors crowded around the mouth of the alley. Paul watched the bread disappear.

"Still hungry?" A nod.

He gave him the apple. The child weighed it in his hand and looked around at the hopeful crowd waiting for scraps. His eyes narrowed thoughtfully. Obviously he wanted to save the apple for later but had no way to safeguard it. The other children were coming closer in a surreptitious but steady shuffle. Paul knew exactly what would happen the moment he turned his back. It had happened to him, too.

"All right, then, come along," he said irritably. "You can eat at my place and clean up. It's warm and you'll be able to eat in peace. Okay?"

The bundle of rags slid down from the trash barrel and followed him with prompt obedience.

For once he was glad to have an open jeep. He suspected that that smell in an enclosed space would have been more than he could stand. The boy climbed into the back without a word and sat quietly. Something about his obedient passivity infuriated Paul. The kid was too trusting for his own good. However, this time the small idiot was in luck. Paul hardly considered himself a pattern of morality, but messing with children was not his weakness. His taste ran to women, grown-up women. The kid was safe with him.

He took an indirect route, using side streets, because what he was doing was not only stupid but quite illegal. He cursed himself for his charitable impulse. He really had no idea why he was doing it. He had no use for the boy, and taking German nationals home to one's billet was strictly against the rules. It came under the heading of fraternizing with the enemy.

Luckily, his street was empty. He hustled the child into the house and made a quick phone call to his office, explaining that he had a sore throat. The boy waited quietly while Paul pulled the curtains. So far so good.

He now turned his attention to the child. "Okay, kid! Get out of those rags. You smell to high heaven. You understand? Smell. Stink. You're filthy. Take a bath, Use lots of soap. Oh, hell, take two baths. You can eat while you're soaking." He pointed him toward the stairs. "Bathroom's up there. I'll find you something to wear. Take those things home with you and delouse them at your leisure. Meanwhile, you can put on my dressing gown. But make damn sure you're clean before you touch it."

The splashing in the bathroom went on for a long time, long enough for Paul to wonder what he had gotten into.

If the boy was anything like himself at fifteen, it would be best to get rid of him quickly. Kids like that weren't safe to keep around. They didn't care how they survived. They just did.

That, after all, was what he had done when he took to the streets—survive. He had tried his hand at many things—not begging, he drew the line at that. But he certainly stole when and what he could, ran errands for the prostitutes, and sold useful bits of information. He wondered if this urchin had been living the same way. If so, he wasn't very good at it. But then, he himself had had to be rescued in the end.

A Quaker field worker had found him beaten up in an alley one particularly unsuccessful night. The Quakers took pity on him. He was thrown in with a group of younger children and shipped to the States. At that point he was too sunk in misery to care one way or another. At least it was better than getting picked up by the Gestapo.

He had not been a pleasant child and had no idea how to mask his rage against the world. The good people at the Children's Home did their best to reach him. In the end they threw up their hands in despair and turned him over to a state agency. Nobody wanted him.

It was the lowest point of his life. He was nobody, nothing. It was a kind of death.

And then he made a marvelous discovery. He realized that he was smarter than they were. It was glorious. Overnight the problem child turned into a model teen-ager. All these people were stupid. He could think rings around them. All he had to do was figure out what they wanted to hear and give it to them. It was that easy. He was back in control, and the payoff was great.

That was a memory he could savor. Suddenly, he was everybody's fair-haired boy. A sponsor was found for him, and he was sent off to college. In eighteen months he earned a two-year degree, and that was just the beginning. The war was over by then, and there was a crying need for interpreters.

His thoughts were interrupted by a timid knock, and a very damp, sparklingly clean person stood in the doorway, rather fetching in his bathrobe, which was ridiculously large on that small body. Paul stared at the transformation. His grubby urchin looked remarkably like a girl.

"What shall I do with my old clothes?" she asked. There could be no doubt. It was a girl. "Shall I put them to soak in the bathtub?"

Paul started to laugh. "Do you think you can get them clean?"

She laughed, too, displaying marvelously regular, white teeth. She was a dish, he realized with amazement. Rather small and thin, and much too young to be really interesting, though older than he had thought at first. But the creature had possibilities with those cheekbones and that slightly pointed chin, that big luscious mouth and those eyes, a velvety brown and framed by thick, gold-tipped lashes. The hair, now hanging in wet, toffee-colored strands, would probably dry to a wonderful color, too. He'd found himself a pocket Venus.

"If I scrubbed from now 'til spring," she said in her odd accent, "I don't think I could get them anywhere near clean."

"Let's toss 'em," he suggested.

"Tossem?" Her English was quite good, of the high school variety, but it was obvious that she had not caught on to American yet.

"Throw 'em out. Burn 'em. Give 'em to the deserving poor."

She laughed again. "But I *am* the deserving poor," she said. "You won't find anyone poorer or more deserving than me in all of Berlin today."

Paul eyed her curiously, and that dependable little alarm system in his head gave a click. Useful!

He looked at her with a new attentiveness. She really was surprisingly pretty, and judging by her voice and manner, she came from a good background. Paul had a strong sense of caste. After all, the blood of princes ran in his veins. Background meant quite a bit.

He had no clear-cut idea as yet how the child could be utilized, but that would come to him in time. Women were always useful—if not as lovers, then as contacts, as go-betweens, for convenience, and sometimes just for show.

"Sit down and dry your hair," he suggested. "You can eat some of the peanuts in that bowl. Just don't drop the shells all over the carpet. I'm going to get rid of your rags, and then I'll get you something to wear before you go home. You do have a home, don't you?"

"Well, actually, no," she said.

He frowned irritably. He hadn't counted on being stuck with the child before he had decided how to make use of her. "You must have started someplace."

"Well, I did, but I ran away. The nuns said run, so I ran. Sister Celestine gave me money for the train and some for Irma."

"Irma?"

"She was the other girl. All the rest of the children in the home were safe, because they were boys and much younger. The German army had already taken all the older boys and the other girls. The nuns were hiding Irma and me, because we're Jewish—sort of."

"Sort of? Usually people are or not." He was both amused and irritated by her story.

"Well, Irma is Catholic but one hundred percent Jewish, and I'm half-and-half. My mother was Aryan."

"Why did the nuns throw you out?"

"The Russians were coming. I was glad, but the nuns thought we wouldn't be safe." She shook her head seriously. "That's the trouble with nuns. They are very good women and all that, but they do seem to expect the worst of everyone else. I mean, really, if the Russians went about raping every woman they see, they'd never have had time to win the war. I suspect it's all quite exaggerated, don't you?'

Paul sidestepped the comment.

"So you got on the train. But why Berlin? Of all the places in Germany, you could hardly have picked worse."

"Well, that's where the train stopped. It didn't seem to be going anyplace." She shrugged philosophically. "I was on that train for three days. It broke down twice, and once it got shunted onto a siding. We stayed there all night. The toilets didn't work, and it got awfully cold. And I was hungry. I spent the last of the money on a bowl of soup yesterday, and a girl gave me a piece of bread and that shawl in exchange for my boots. It wasn't much, but I couldn't wear the boots anyway. They pinched."

"So you tumbled off the train and found yourself a bathroom. Then what?"

"There was a lady giving out cups of cocoa just outside the station, but that ran out before it was my turn. While we waited, though, I overheard a boy behind me talking about getting food from the Americans, so I followed him."

Paul watched her with delight. Every movement of her head set that glorious mop of honey-colored hair into shimmering motion. The kid might be a phenomenal liar, but what a beauty!

"And what are your plans now?"

She sat back and bit her lip. "I don't quite know. When I got off the train this morning I would have said, 'Just to get something to eat, and get warm and clean.' It's strange the way one's requirements expand, isn't it?" She smiled delightfully. "Now I want to go on being warm, clean, and full."

"Very greedy of you," he agreed. "You have a rotten character. What's your name, by the way?"

"The nuns called me Maria Weber, but my real name is Hanne Goldschmidt. That was too Jewish, so they changed it. For my own good, of course, but I think I'll go back to my real name now."

She had made herself comfortable, tucking her bare feet under her for warmth. Paul looked at her thoughtfully. "Tell me, have you any plans—other than begging?"

"I am certainly not going to go on begging," she protested indignantly. "I only did that this morning for the first time. it was something of an emergency, you must admit."

"Well, and now that the emergency is temporarily over, what do you propose to do?"

She counted off her priorities on her fingers. "First, I have to borrow something to wear, and then I must go to the Chariteéé Hospital. The nuns there will take me in and give me work."

He grinned at the idea of her turning up on the doorstep of the Catholic hospital in a borrowed American army bathrobe. She faced his mocking eye with the same unwinking stare that had first caught his attention.

"Look," he said. "You don't really want to scrub urinals in a hospital, do you?"

"Well, no," she admitted, chewing on a strand of hair. "But I don't have much choice, do I? Of course, I suppose I could become a courtesan, but I don't know how."

"A courtesan?"

"You know, a bad woman, a whore. I understand they earn very good money."

"Some do," Paul agreed, stunned. "But I'm not sure that's the right job for you."

She nodded gravely. "Yes, I know. It must be very hard work, and probably requires special training."

Paul cleared his throat, "Look, I might be able to find something for you later on. What languages do you speak?"

"German, English, and French." She counted off on her fingers. "I started Latin, but I never was good at it."

"You won't need Latin. Russian would be perfect. but French and English will do. Now listen. You can't stay here. But I have a friend who'll put you up for a while. She'll find you some clothes and you can help around the house to pay for your keep, cleaning and stuff."

"Will you come and visit me?" Hanne said in a very small voice.

Paul glared at her. "Let's get one thing quite straight. We can have business dealings. We may get to be friends. We will never be lovers, okay? You get that? No romance, no deep meaningful sighs, no tears in the night. Let me catch just one soulful sniff, and you are out on your ear and on your way to the urinals of the Charité."

Hanne sniffed. "What's wrong with me? I'm not ugly."

"You're extremely pretty," Paul snapped. "But there's something you'd better know about me. First of all, I'm Russian."

"Aren't you an American officer?"

"American Russian and not an officer, not even a soldier. I'm a civilian employee. Now, there's one thing your good sisters did not tell you about Russians. It's even worse than they thought. We are most unnatural in our sexual habits—horses, sheep, canaries, anything."

She stopped sulking and started to laugh.

"So, being a Russian, I have this odd preference, I go for grown-up women."

"I'm grown up," she protested. "I'm eighteen."

He looked at her very hard.

"Well, almost eighteen. Seventeen and five-sixths. Honest."

"Good," Paul said decisively. "When you get to be thirty, maybe I'll take another look at you."

"You're in love with someone else," she said sadly.

"Right," Paul agreed promptly. "So, shall we get you dressed and go to see the Princess Lydia lvanovna?"

Hanne nodded.

Getting her dressed was easier than he had anticipated. She was imaginative, displaying a natural flair. He had provided her with a set of fatigues and a parka. By pulling the pants up under her armpits and doing an ingenious wrapping job with the jacket, she managed to cover herself quite becomingly. Feet were a problem. She had developed chilblains on the train, and the idea of putting boots over her poor swollen feet did not appeal to her.

"They hurt, you know. That's why I used the rags."

"Well, I'm not introducing you to Lydia lvanovna with rags on your feet. Try several pairs of socks and my tennis shoes. They'll be so big on you, you'll never feel them."

It worked, after a fashion, and having peered through the pulled curtains to make sure the coast was clear, he put her into the jeep, in the front seat this time.

"What if the princess does not want to give me a job?" Hanne's voice was quite small and pathetic.

"The princess will be tickled pink to give you a job. She needs you, though she may not realize it just yet. But don't you worry your pretty little head—the princess will thank us both when all's said and done."

ᕤ *Chapter 2*

Hanne sat on the stairs outside the princess's apartment and listened to the voices inside. The voices were loud and emphatic, but they were speaking in Russian, so it didn't help her any.

The princess had a deep, hoarse voice, and Hanne had her doubts about staying with her. One did not like to even think such a thing about an aristocratic lady, but she did sound drunk.

The apartment house was not exactly what she had expected, either. Charlottenburg had been a fairly elegant district in its time, but now the few buildings not bombed out were dim and shabby. The staircase had a dank, unlovely smell about it, suggestive of bad drains and cabbage. Hanne's courage, which had been so high at first, because she was clean and well fed, now started to sink. She wished she could stay with the beautiful young man. She wondered if he knew she had lied to him. She sighed. It was almost impossible to be completely honest all the time, and it wasn't as if she had lied altogether. Just a little bit, about the nuns actually giving her the money and telling her to run. Of course, Sister Celestine had left the money lying there, as if to encourage her to take it, and if the Russians had been coming, she surely would have wanted her to run away. She took off the borrowed tennis shoes and gently rubbed her toes. They felt worse now. For the first time in months, she thought she was going to cry, and she had promised herself that she would do that again.

She was saved from such indignity by the opening of the apartment door. Paul stepped out and beckoned her.

"Come on in. The princess will talk to you now. Address her as 'Excellency.' She's not entitled to it, but it makes her feel good."

Hanne straggled in after him, and found herself in a long, dark corridor, where the smell of cabbage was even more pronounced.

"I want to leave," she whispered fiercely.

"Be brave, little one," he said, holding her hand. "You'll have the silly old bat eating out of your hand in no time."

The room at the end of the corridor was huge, with a very high ceiling, and every inch of space was crowded with heavy, rather splendid furniture that all seemed to be falling apart. There were oil paintings with crumbling frames and sofas with rich brocades that had split to display wads of stuffing. An enormous chandelier hung from the ceiling, but the only source of light was a dim little bulb dangling just under its dusty splendor. Hanne looked around in amazement and finally identified the princess among her possessions. She almost laughed.

Princess Lydia Ivanovna was enormously fat. She was wedged into an armchair as if inserted by means of a shoehorn. Hanne stared at her in wonder. Her face was grotesquely painted, with very red lips, heavy black lines around her eyes, and two round spots of rouge in the middle of floury-white cheeks. Her hair, which was thin and straight, was dyed an unlikely glossy black and sleeked into a skimpy knot on top of her head, skewered by massive golden hairpins. She wore a gown that appeared to have been constructed from dark red curtain material. It billowed stiffly from her monstrous shoulders, obscuring everything except tiny feet in felt slippers and small fat hands loaded down with rings. She did not look unkind—or drunk.

"Your Excellency?" Hanne said and dropped a curtsy. The princess grabbed a lorgnette and examined Hanne through it. "Come closer, child," she said in her hoarse voice. "Let's have a look at you."

Hanne approached her curiously. She wondered for a moment where in the whole of Berlin anyone could find enough food to stay so very fat.

"My friend Paul tells me you would like to come and keep me company."

Paul waved his hand as if Hanne were a rabbit he had just drawn out of a hat. "Meet Honey Goldsmith."

"No, your Excellency, it's Hanne Goldschmidt—or Maria Weber, if you prefer."

"Don't you believe her," Paul insisted. "Look at that hair—honey, pure honey."

The old woman laughed delightedly "Aha, I have a choice. I like that. I will call you Honey. It sounds so pleasant."

"As you wish," Hanne agreed politely.

"Paul says you will run errands for me and take some of the housekeeping chores off my shoulders. As you see, I'm not as strong as I used to be, And I have always been a rather spoiled woman."

That, Hanne could believe easily, but she failed to understand the note of satisfaction in the old woman's voice. She knew that being spoiled put a person at a terrible disadvantage. It was hardly something to boast about.

"Well, then, it's all settled. You can have the maid's room. I haven't had a maid for a long time, not since Katya left, poor girl."

She turned to Paul and said querulously, "The girl needs clothes. She can't go around like this."

Paul was lounging on a sofa, looking utterly relaxed and comfortable. Hanne wondered if he ever got flustered or frightened. She couldn't imagine it. Personally, she rather liked the clothes she was wearing. They were clean and crisp and he had given them to her.

"Let's see," Paul said. "Petya's woman is about that size, isn't she?"

"Well, she used to be."

Hanne had to stand up and be measured. "Okay, so Mimi's a bit fatter, but close enough." The princess pursed her lips and nodded. 'Let's see what Mimi comes up with. She can be very good-natured if you approach her the right way."

Paul got up and stretched. "Well, Honey, I'll see you in a day or two. Be a good girl and do what you're told."

"You're not just leaving me here?"

"Sure. I told you I would. Now be sensible, and remember—nothing is ever exactly what it seems."

She felt sad to see him go. He was such a beautiful young man, and he had the loveliest bathroom, shiny tiles and a sunken tub, and however much hot water you used, there always seemed to be more.

She rather thought she was in love with him. But since he wanted her to stay with this funny old lady, of course she would.

She smiled tentatively. "Would you like me to clean this room? Or is there something else, you would rather have me do?"

The princess raised her lorgnette and gazed about her. "Is it very dirty? I suppose so. Katya used to clean. I don't think anyone has done it since she left. I think she used a carpet sweeper. Maybe it's still around."

"I'll look for it." Hanne felt pleased to have found some way to be useful.

The princess waved her hand carelessly. "Never mind, child. I'm quite used to it the way it is. Can you make tea?"

Hanne looked around and found the samovar. It was wedged between a pile of books and an empty candy box on top of a round table. To her eye, it was in need of a good scrubbing, like everything else in the room, but it was obvious that the princess had different priorities.

"You heat water in the big part, don't you?" Hanne poked a tentative finger at the big brass container. "And I suppose the tea goes into this little pot on top?"

The princess looked pleased. "You dear child, so clever of you. You'll find some tea in the kitchen, the third door down the corridor. There should be some charcoal, too, to heat the water. Some people use a spirit lamp, but that's a great mistake—ruins the flavor. And there should be a little jar of raspberry jam. We'll need that. And of course two spoons and glasses."

"Not cups?"

"Cups for tea? What a dreadful idea. The glasses are in the vitrine over there, the ones in the silver holders."

Hanne admired the silver filigree and promised herself to polish them beautifully as soon as she had the chance. Her spirits were rising. There was so much to do.

"And when the tea is ready," the princess said happily, "you can join me for a glass and I will tell you about my mother's tea parties. She always included one poet, one general, one member of the imperial family, and at least three handsome men. Her parties had tremendous success."

Hanne spent the afternoon listening to the princess and doing some cleaning. It was a peculiar apartment and took some getting used to.

The coals were kept on the balcony—the only safe place to keep them, the princess assured her. The larder was almost empty, but a tub under the sink was filled with wine bottles. The dining-room table, splendidly draped in stained damask, seemed to have been set up for a party.

"But of course," said the princess. "One must be prepared for guests. I've always kept open house for my friends."

Hanne thought of the empty shelves. "There's no food, Excellency."

"None?"

"Five potatoes and a package of tea."

The princess clucked her tongue. "I must send word to Petya, my nephew. He'll have to bring something. After all, people must eat. Wait a moment. We'll have the concierge deliver it." She stuffed a hastily scribbled note into an envelope and riffled through a pile of old newspapers.

"Aha!" she said, coming up with a crumpled one-mark bill. "You can give her that."

Hanne took the money and the envelope and went off in search of a messenger. On the ground floor she found a door frame marked Concierge, but there was no door, nor was there a room behind it. It simply opened onto a patch of rubble. She stepped through the hole in the wal into a small courtyard filled with debris.

"You keep out," said a voice behind her.

She turned and saw a small, tough-looking girl glaring at her. "That's my garden."

Hanne blinked. All she could see was broken bricks and glass. "You've planted something out there?"

The child looked no older than seven, and small at that. She had bare legs and feet, blue with cold, and her hands were stuck deep in the pockets of a man's thick wool jacket. She looked Hanne over with narrowed eyes. "Not yet, but I will." She squatted down and started to pick up bits of rubble, throwing them into a corner. "I don't want people stomping around on it. There's good soil underneath. In the spring I'll put in potatoes and beans."

"You know how?" Hanne was impressed.

"I got seeds," the child boasted. "And I've saved eyes from potatoes. We're going to have loads of food— potatoes, beans, carrots, maybe lettuce." Her eyes sparkled. "And enormous tomatoes."

Hanne was enchanted. "What about flowers?"

The little girl sneered. "Nah. Flowers are for rich people. Are you a soldier?"

Hanne shook her head.

"Pity! I thought you might have cigarettes. You got that uniform from your boyfriend? Doesn't he give you cigarettes?"

Hanne went on shaking her head. The child sighed. "You're dumb. Even my aunt gets cigarettes from soldiers and she's old. I bet you could, too."

Hanne decided to ignore this bit of advice. She pulled out the note and the one-mark bill. The child took the letter but sneered at the money.

"Nah, that's no good. Haven't you got any food to give me? This is from the crazy Russian lady, isn't it? Sometimes she has eggs."

Hanne shook her head.

The girl put her hands on her hips and glared. "Butter, then? Bacon? Apples? Well, what do you have?"

"I can give you a potato."

"Just one? I don't run errands for one lousy potato."

"It's a very nice potato," Hanne said firmly. "Take it or leave it."

The little girl weighed the letter in her hand and finally gave a brief nod. "All right, then, but I want that potato first. It'd better be a good one, big enough for me and my mother."

The potato Hanne offered was examined and approved.

"Not bad," said the child, stuffing it into the pocket of her oversized jacket. "You're all right. Tell you what—I'll let you help with my garden."

"I'd like that," said Hanne. "I've never had a garden." The little girl smiled for the first time. "We live in the back, apartment 1B. Our name's on the door—Bendel. I'm Ulrike Bendel. You can ring the bell. If nobody comes to the door, that means I'm out. My mother won't answer the bell. She doesn't pay much attention these days."

Soon after dark, the friends started arriving. The first visitor was a shabby, elderly man who sat close to the princess, clutched to his chest the glass of tea Hanne had poured for him, and started to talk quietly and passionately in Russian.

Next came two young men identically dressed in turtleneck sweaters and work pants, who kissed the princess's hand, fetched themselves a bottle of wine from the kitchen, and got into a violent argument. At least Hanne thought it was an argument. The princess smiled at them benignly and seemed quite untroubled.

Two women, mother and daughter judging by their identical high-bridged noses, brought a platter of pastries.

"Ah, cabbage pies," said the princess with a sigh of pleasure. "Nobody makes them as well as you, dear Elena Petrovna. How the taste takes me back."

Hanne passed the pastries around and everyone ate enthusiastically. The younger woman snatched the platter out of her hands the moment it was empty, wiped it with a corner of her handkerchief, and slipped it into her big handbag.

The shabby man left, and his place beside the princess was taken by a sad-looking woman who droned on in a monotone, as if continuing a story she had started a long time ago.

The princess nodded her head gravely, occasionally putting in a soothing word.

Hanne refilled the samovar and went back to the kitchen, to scrape the last of the raspberry jam onto a serving dish. It was nice to feel useful, but she could see already that keeping open house used up a lot of supplies.

When she returned with the jam, two new visitors had joined the party, a soft-looking man of uncertain age and a glamorous blond girl in a wonderful fur coat.

Hanne was introduced and found herself drawn aside and critically examined by the girl.

"Well, I for one am delighted you're here. Petya's been worried sick about his aunt living alone. She's always had a maid, of course, but the last one went into a munitions factory."

Seen at closer quarters, the girl was not very young after all, and the blond hair had brown roots, but the glamor was real enough. Hanne was quite overwhelmed by the fur coat, the silk dress, the high-heeled shoes, and great waves of a marvelous perfume.

"Honey's a funny name," said the girl, "Are you American?"

"German. Oh, I see, because of the uniform. That's not mine. I borrowed it."

The girl nodded, satisfied. "I thought so. Paul Karinof's, isn't it? Don't you have anything to wear?"

Hanne shook her head.

"Stand up. Hmm. Maybe I can let you have some of my old things. I used to be skinnier." She fell silent and looked sad.

"I think you are beautiful," Hanne said shyly.

The compliment had a magical effect. The other girl brightened and became animated. "Have you seen my pictures?"

Hanne shook her head, confused.

"None of them?" The girl seemed surprised by Hanne's lack of reaction. "I'm Mimi Krall—you know, the actress. Don't you like films?"

"I haven't seen any," Hanne admitted humbly. "It must be wonderful to be famous."

Mimi gave a deep, luxurious sigh. "I was signed up by UFA before I was sixteen," she said dreamily. "Would you believe it? I was the youngest actress under contract, Of course, for the first year they just had me playing children, but then Leni Riefenstahl herself picked me out for a lead. She was wonderful to work for—the best."

Hanne was properly impressed.

Mimi's eyes wandered away from her, and her voice became plaintive. "I do wish Petya wouldn't speak Russian all the time. He knows how I feel about it. It has an ugly sound, doesn't it? Of course, the princess likes it. It's her mother tongue and all that, but Petya was born in Yugoslavia, and he's lived in Germany most of his life. There's no reason in the world why he should talk that awful language. When I first met him, he said he was French. All his friends called him Pierre. I thought he was cute. I don't think I would have had anything to do with him if I'd known." She stared across the room at him, looking discontented, "I've never liked Russians— except the princess, of course."

Petya caught her eye and came over to them. "Are you all right, Mimi?"

He had drooping eyelids and an unhealthy complexion. There was something unpleasant about him, but his manner toward Mimi was very respectful and correct. Hanne couldn't figure out why he made her uncomfortable. He seemed like a polite, kindly sort of man.

"I get so depressed," Mimi said plaintively, "just thinking about my career." She turned to Hanne. "I haven't worked for over a year. That's very dangerous in my business. People forget your name."

"Nobody who has seen you can ever forget your name," Petya said smoothly. "Let me get you a drink."

The next day Mimi brought an armful of clothes and supervised Hanne's trying them on.

"That green looks very nice on you. Green is good for blondes like us. It's important to present yourself properly. You'll find out. I do wish the princess would take a bit more trouble with her appearance. It's all right to be comfortable, but she goes too far. Just look at that ridiculous getup."

Hanne looked at the princess in her shapeless tent garment. It did look odd, but somehow it suited her.

Mimi sighed irritably and sipped her drink. "Of course, she's a great lady. Her father, Petya's grandfather, was something or other in the Russian government—before the Revolution, of course. They lost all their money, and the title doesn't mean anything anymore. Petya says her husband really was a prince, but it's not like a German title, you know. Anyway, he got shot. Petya says she wore heavy mourning, real mourning, with a black veil over her face. Absurd, isn't it? It was years and years before she even took a lover. Still, it all happened so long ago. I think it's stupid to live in the past."

Mimi stopped and stared into her empty glass.

"Shall I get you another drink?" offered Hanne.

"Do that." Mimi thrust the glass at her. "All that talk in Russian. I get so depressed. When I think of my life...." She took the filled glass from Hanne, emptied it, and handed it back. "Wine doesn't agree with me. See if you can find some arrack."

"I don't think there is any."

Mimi drooped. "I wish Paul would come. He always brings me a bottle of arrack. He knows wine's not good for me. Have you known him a long time?"

Hanne shook her head, hoping Mimi wouldn't ask too many questions about Paul. She didn't want to talk about him. He was too special.

"I do wish he'd come," Mimi said plaintively. "At least he's not half-dead like the rest of this crowd, and he doesn't talk Russian all the time."

Hanne waited and watched for Paul, and about a week later he was back, even handsomer and more wonderful than she remembered him.

The atmosphere lightened the moment he walked in. The princess struggled to her feet and embraced him, kissing him on both cheeks. Her eyes sparkled. "Paul Denisovitch, you have been neglecting me."

He kissed her hand and then her cheek. "Not by choice, honest."

Mimi's spine had straightened. Her eyes were bright. Paul turned to her. "Hey, Mimi, how's it going?"

"Oh, you know, I'm still working in the club."

"Not for long, I bet," he said cheerfully. "Listen, I talked to someone from Hollywood the other day. He saw you in *The Golden Goose*, and he's crazy about you. Maybe you should be working on your English, just in case."

He turned to talk to someone else, but Mimi followed him hungrily. "I don't think *The Golden Goose* was one of my best movies. Did he see me in *Remembrance*? He really should see *Remembrance*. Perhaps we could arrange a private showing for him? There must be a print around somewhere. And my English is all right. I've always been good with accents."

She saw that he was not listening and turned back to Hanne. "You could improve your accent if you put your mind to it, Honey. Of course, it helps to have a good ear. Are you musical?"

"I don't think so," said Hanne. "I'd better unpack that box Mr. Karinof brought."

Mimi nodded. "See if there's a bottle of arrack."

Paul followed her into the kitchen, "Well?" he said. "Is Lydia Ivanovna treating you right?"

Hanne felt warm all over just being alone with him.

"She's so kind. And Miss Krall gave me some lovely clothes."

"Yeah. I talked to Petya about that."

"And the princess found me a pair of rubber boots so I can go outside."

He gave her a friendly nod. "Well, you're all right then. Made any friends?"

"Only a little girl who lives downstairs. She takes care of her mother. We're going to make a garden."

Paul shook his head. "Don't get mixed up with riffraff. Next thing we know, you'll have a Berlin accent."

"I'll be careful."

He grinned at her and patted her head. "See you, kid."

Hanne was content. He had not forgotten. He cared what happened to her. She unpacked the box. There was a jar of raspberry jam, cans of fruit and vegetables, a sausage, three loaves of bread, and several bottles. One of them was Mimi's arrack.

She carried it back to the salon and looked around for Paul, but he had already left.

"There was a time he'd spend an evening with us," Mimi was saying. "When he first came to Berlin and knew nobody. Petya introduced him to everyone worth knowing. But he's so high and mighty these days." She sounded huffy.

Petya turned on her with narrowed eyes. "I have no reason to regret sharing my contacts," he said sharply. "We're doing all right."

Hanne was surprised. He was usually so kind to Mimi, even though she complained all the time.

Mimi looked offended and turned to the princess. "I'm not saying anything against Paul. It's just that he doesn't visit like he used to."

"I know. They make him work so hard," said the princess. "Americans are like that—rush, rush, rush."

Hanne wanted to ask what it was that kept Paul so busy, but the princess had started speaking Russian to Petya, while Mimi turned back to her with a hair-raising description of the problems of shooting a film while air raids were going on outside.

After a few weeks, Hanne felt quite at home with the princess and became very fond of her. The princess entertained her with marvelous stories, getting as much pleasure from the telling as Hanne had in listening.

Everything she told of life on her family estates as a little girl was quite believable. It was only when she talked about her existence in Berlin that she became vague and fanciful. She never mentioned her husband at all. Hanne respected this silence. She, too, had places in her life that were off limits.

She continued her visits to the Bendels' first-floor flat. Paul hadn't really forbidden it, he said only that she shouldn't pick up the accent. Had he known more about it, he might have worried about her picking up lice. The flat was awful—cold and cluttered, and it had the sour reek of despair. Frau Bendel lay in bed most of the time, her eyes dull and blank.

"Nah, she's not sick," said Ulrike. "She's been like this ever since Vati went away the last time. She used to be all right. She used to cook and clean and do things. Sometimes she read stories to me."

Compared to her mother, Ulrike was almost clean. More important, she had energy and hope. Together she and Hanne worked at the open patch that was to be their garden, and they made glorious plans. The broken bricks were no longer thrown carelessly aside. They were now neatly stacked to form a garden wall. January brought heavy snow that slowed them up but did not stop them altogether.

There were parties almost every night. Petya and Mimi were always in attendance. The sad-looking lady frequently dropped in to continue her woeful recitation. The two young men always sounded as if they were fighting, though the princess assured Hanne that they were the best of friends. The quiet, shabby man never came back, but there were others, many others, equally shabby and just as subdued. The princess welcomed them all, beamed at her guests, and applauded and sympathized in turn.

The conversation was usually in Russian, and everyone had tea with arrack in it, and wine, and they all seemed hungry.

Paul provided food and wine, lots of it. At least once a week he came with the jeep loaded up with cases of wine and arrack, hams, loaves of bread, bags of onions and potatoes, little packages of butter and tea, and the inevitable raspberry jam. Occasionally there were magazines and records.

He would explode into the stuffy rooms like a breath of fresh air, and everyone would start to smile. He just made them feel good. He made Hanne feel good. She liked looking at him, liked to hear his voice, was ecstatic when he casually touched her. Hanne was in love.

When she thought about the wonderfulness of her life, she could barely believe her luck. There she had been, down and out and just about ready to go back to the nuns and take the consequences. She had been lost and dirty and hungry and alone. Now she was needed, she had nice clothes and food, and enough food to share with the Bendels. The princess was quite tolerant of Hanne's raids on the larder.

"One must give to the poor. It's a little difficult, of course, when we ourselves happen to be poor. But no matter, you are quite right to feed the child. We must ask Paul to bring chocolate."

There was a brief thaw in February. The snow turned to slush, then froze hard again. Hanne had her eighteenth birthday but told no one. It was nice to be older, but it was a bad time of year to be born, much too cold and dark. She thought maybe in the future she would celebrate her birthdays in June. She rather liked the idea of having no past, being free to make up her life story as she went along.

Ulrike talked about herself in a matter-of-fact manner while they scrabbled in the frozen slush. She had wonderful memories of living in a three-room apartment, with Vati coming home from work every night. That was before the bombs fell and Mutti stopped cleaning. Mutti had been great on cleaning. That's how they got the fine basement flat. Mutti took care of the entire apartment house. She scrubbed the stairs, top to bottom, every day and polished all the brass handrails. Ulrike had been small then, not yet going to school. She had liked school, but not anymore. It was too cold to sit still.

Paul brought candy bars, and Ulrike was invited upstairs to get them. The princess wanted to meet her.

"I don't know," Ulrike complained. "She's crazy, isn't she?"

"No, she's not," Hanne said severely. "She is clever and kind. Wash your hands and come along."

Ulrike grumbled a bit, but the thought of the chocolate persuaded her in the end. She knew all about American candy bars.

"So you are Ulrike," said the princess, examining her through her lorgnette. "I am most happy to meet you. Don't eat so fast, child. We won't take it away."

Ulrike tried to slow down, but her eyes were distrustful. Her attention was firmly fixed on the kitchen table, where the candy had been beautifully arranged on a plate. Ulrike would have preferred having it safely in her pocket.

"So," said the princess. "You like chocolate."

Ulrike stared. It seemed a silly thing to say, and confirmed her in her private opinion that the old Russian lady was quite mad.

"It's very good," she said politely. "My Tante Ida brought me a Zagnut bar once."

"Your aunt?" the princess looked interested. "Do you see her often?"

"Nah!" Ulrike seemed as if she might say something else, but a secretive look came into her face. She concentrated on the candy.

The princess watched her eat with satisfaction. Hanne had already noticed what great joy the old lady had in extending hospitality. This was just like one of her parties—on a smaller scale.

Finally the last crumb of chocolate had been picked up with a carefully licked forefinger, and Ulrike sat back and rewarded them with a blissful smile.

"You must come back," said the princess.

Ulrike slid down from her chair and shook her head, "Can't. I'm leaving."

Hanne was thunderstruck. "You never said a thing."

"None of your business," Ulrike said defensively, "Tante Ida's found a place for us in Glienicke, two rooms and a kitchen as well."

"That sounds splendid," the princess said heartily.

Hanne was almost in tears. "What about our garden? We've got most of the stones out of it."

Ulrike scowled, "In Glienicke I'm going to have a real garden to grow things in. This one here's just make-believe. It's nothing but a patch of stones."

"But I thought..." Hanne felt fiercely disappointed. "But we had such fine plans—the potatoes and the beans. We worked so hard. I thought we were really making a garden."

"You believe anything," Ulrike sneered. Her face was puckered with disgust. "You're dumb. You don't even get cigarettes from your American soldier. Tante Ida's smarter than you—and prettier—even if she is old. I'm glad we're going away. You're dumb."

The princess looked past the rudeness into the child's pain and confusion. "We shall miss you, too," she said.

Hanne did miss her, and she missed the thought of the garden. It was such a very cold winter. The fantasy of tending a flowering patch of ground had sustained her. She tried to go back to it after the Bendels were gone, but it was no use. Without Ulrike's forceful imagination it was just a patch of rubble. Nothing would ever grow there, neither Ulrike's potatoes nor her flowers.

Hanne filled this new hole in her life with bigger and better fantasies. Mostly they involved Paul. She expanded them and polished them into little scenarios, complete with dialogue.

He was to walk in and say, "Put on your prettiest dress, we're going dancing." She even had the dress picked out, a narrow slip of a dress, slit up on the left side, in yellow silk with a wide, shiny belt that could be wrapped very tight to make the most of her figure. Mimi had given it up rather regretfully.

"You might as well have it. I'll never fit into it again. But take good care of it. It came from Paris and cost a fortune. General von Milch got it for me. I don't care what they say about him now—he was a wonderful man."

Hanne couldn't have cared less about the general. She loved the dress.

When her big opportunity did come, it was not quite the way she had imagined it. Paul did walk in and he did invite her, but he was remote and preoccupied not his usual amiable self.

"Time for a trial run," he said.

She was puzzled. "What's that?"

"In your case, kid, it's a dance at the Femina. We're allowed to bring in Germans now. They've canceled the ban on fraternization, And there's a young lady who needs to be shown that she's not the only pebble on the beach."

"A dance!" Hanne glowed. "I'll change."

"Yeah," he said, "but make it snappy."

She brushed her hair violently and slipped into her lovely dress. She felt grown up and beautiful, until Paul burst her bubble.

"Honey, for Christ's sake. Haven't you got something decent to wear?"

She sniffed, stroking the lovely fabric. "It's my prettiest dress. Mimi says it came from Paris."

"All right, all right," he said irritably. "It's a lovely dress. Take it off. Haven't you got something simple? Like a dark skirt and a white blouse?"

"You mean like a schoolgirl?" she said sulkily. "You want me to look like a fifteen-year-old."

He took in the trembling underlip and became kind. "Look, Honey, it's not that kind of a party. You'll see. Most of the other women will be in uniform. You'd feel terribly overdressed. Okay?"

She changed into a plain blouse and skirt and felt cheated. Her script had been changed.

Sitting in the jeep for the first time in weeks, her spirits rose again. It was so wonderful just being close to him. She stole a glance at his profile. He had such a lovely face, thin and bony and distinguished. His eyebrows had a way of twitching up when he smiled. And there was a wonderful smell about him, aftershave lotion and tobacco and something else. It occurred to her that he didn't even know that she was eighteen now.

To complete her happiness, Paul threw his right arm around her and drew her close.

"Happy tonight, Pigeon?" he asked. He was thoroughly pleased with her. She was shaping up very nicely.

Hanne gazed up at him adoringly. "I've never been so happy. I just wish we could go on driving like this forever."

Paul liked adoration well enough, but his mind was on other things. He gave her shoulders a squeeze and then, to her disappointment, let go of her.

"Ever hear of the Femina? Used to be Berlin's flossiest nightclub. Now it's all ours. You'll love it. It's a gas." He sounded as if he were trying to sell her something and she felt herself withdraw a bit.

He started to explain. "I want you to get to know some of the American officers. I know you'll enjoy that."

"I don't know how to dance," she said in a small voice.

He slapped his forehead with his hand. "Of course, the nuns. Well, it doesn't matter. They'll enjoy teaching you. And the truth is quite acceptable—about the nuns." He looked at her sharply. "It is the truth, isn't it?"

"Oh, yes," she said listlessly. "The part about the nuns is quite true."

"And the rest wasn't?"

"Well, some of it was. Most of it, really."

He had already lost interest. "Never mind. Stick with the nun story and skip the bit about your arrival in Berlin. You've left the nuns and come to stay with an old friend of your mother's. Okay?"

"Can I talk about the princess?"

"Talk to your heart's content, but don't mention her name. You're living with your mother's old friend. She's sort of adopted you."

"I'm too old to be adopted. I'm eighteen."

"Are you now?" he said without interest. "You look younger. Chances are, if you tell anyone your age, they'll think you're lying."

"I'm never going to lie to you again," Hanne said solemnly, leaning against his shoulder.

"Good girl," he said, and kissed the top of her head. The Femina was a huge, ornate building, housing a cinema, a real theater, a ballroom, and several bars with and without dance floors, all being used by and made over for the American army. Hanne was impressed. So were the young officers.

Hanne felt herself open up like a flower. She was surrounded by wonderful young men who paid her extravagant compliments. And dancing was easy. There was nothing to it. Everyone was so eager to show her how. It was wonderful. And now and again, while she was feeling beautiful and clever, she felt that Paul was watching her and approving. Even while he danced with the other woman, he was watching her. It was heaven.

The other woman was in uniform. Hanne was glad now she wasn't wearing the yellow silk dress after all. Paul had been right, he was always right. She would always do exactly what he told her to do. He knew his way around and he looked out for her. He was good and handsome and clever, and she loved him madly.

She almost floated across the floor in the arms of dozens of eager, admiring young men, beautiful young men, but not one as beautiful as Paul. There was no one who could measure up to him.

Paul cornered her at last and put his arms lightly around her waist. "Having fun?"

"Oh, yes. It's wonderful."

"Good. I told you you'd like it. There's one more thing I want to show you. Come along."

She followed him down the wide, shallow, thickly carpeted stairs into a dimly lit bar.

"Well?" he demanded, standing aside to let her have the full impact. "What do you think of that?"

She stared. One entire wall was a fish tank and was lit from inside. The brightly colored fish swam around like an ever-changing mural. They were the strangest fish she had ever seen, fantastically shaped and patterned. The watery light made people's faces look green, but the effect was stunning.

"Oh, Paul, that's beautiful," she said with a sigh of satisfaction. "I'll never forget this evening as long as I live."

"Glad you had a good time. Now you can have one more Coke and then you're going home, I found a driver to take you."

The glamor went out of the evening. "You're not taking me home?"

"Not this time. But we'll do it again, okay?"

"Okay," she agreed, managing a smile. She had seen how little success poor Mimi had with pouting. She would be different—completely different. And Paul would love her.

He nodded approvingly. "You really are growing up. Six weeks ago you would have started whining. I'm proud of you."

Hanne drank as slowly as she dared. Paul waited politely, but as soon as the Coke was finished, he got up and led the way to the cloakroom.

Mimi had given her a lot of clothes, but she was still wearing Paul's parka. It was warm, light, and much too big for her—and she loved it. He watched her snuggle into it and laughed.

"Time to get you a proper winter coat, I'd say. I was wondering where that parka had gotten to. Oh, by the way, you can take this package along and give it to Petya tomorrow. Save me a trip."

"All right," she agreed, stuffing the bulky envelope into her pocket along with some packages of crackers.

He caught her wrist, his eyes narrowed.

"The kids outside," she tried to explain. "Didn't you see them? I thought maybe—"

"Forget it," he said. "You can't feed 'em all—and you don't want to draw attention to yourself. The MPs are likely to be watching."

She watched sadly as he took her crackers and threw them carelessly in a wastebasket. It was such a terrible waste.

"Never mind," he coaxed. "I'll bring you a whole case of crackers. You'll be able to feed every kid on the block."

He gave her a hug and grinned down at her.

A whole case of crackers! Hanne's heart overflowed. He was wonderful. She smiled radiantly and turned up her face to him.

He kissed her, but not the right way, not the way you kiss a woman you love.

❧ *Chapter 3*

Two weeks later not only was she wearing the yellow dress, she was back in Paul's house in Zehlendorf.

"I'm throwing a party and someone has to do the hostess bit," he had explained carelessly, as if it were the most natural thing in the world.

Hanne could hardly believe her luck. It was almost too wonderful to be true.

As the first guests began to trickle in, she had a chance to go all over the house and admire it properly; the first time she had really seen only the bathroom and the food. It was delightful, a doll house set on a tiny patch of a yard.

Paul laughed at her as she wandered around, touching every wall, every potted plant. "You really like it, don't you, Honey?"

"It's beautiful. How did you get it?"

"Luck, influence, and finagling," he admitted cheerfully. "Most of these houses go to officers. This one was up for grabs because it's on the small side."

"But it's perfect." She loved every bit of it. The first floor consisted of a huge living room with one wall entirely taken up by bookshelves. A tiny space toward the back housed a doll-sized kitchen, all shiny white and blue tiles and dark cherry wood, with—wonder of wonders—an electric stove and refrigerator. A circular staircase curled up to the second floor. Upstairs the bathroom was as wonderful as ever, with its sunken tub and the taps that still spouted unlimited supplies of hot water.

The only other room was the bedroom, not very big but leading onto a screened-in porch. You could stand there and feel you were in a forest. It was entirely enclosed by trees, which would be beautiful when spring came. All you needed was a bit of imagination.

"If I were living in this house," Hanne decided, "I'd make up a bed right there on the porch. Imagine waking up with bird sounds all around you."

Paul laughed at her. "Very romantic—the honking horns, Captain Cooley next door screaming for his cats to come in, not to mention the golden sound of Colonel Hosterly reeling home drunk and disorderly."

"Who is Colonel Hosterly?"

"A neighbor. Come on down and meet him."

The colonel, to her relief, was perfectly sober and very nice. He had brought his German girlfriend along, a leggy brunette who spoke no English. The colonel's German was minimal, but they seemed to communicate well enough on a nonverbal level. He handed her a large drink and a pack of cigarettes, pushed her down into a chair, and proceeded to talk to Hanne.

"Ingelore is a very intelligent woman," he said earnestly. "I respect that. Reminds me of my wife."

Hanne hastily masked her grin. The beautiful Ingelore might well be brilliant, but she couldn't quite see what benefit that was to the colonel since he couldn't talk to her. But he was so large and pink and serious, you just had to like him.

"My wife is supposed to be coming over soon," he explained. "Of course, it's not so simple for her. She has her profession."

Hanne nodded wisely, She knew all about women's professions by now, having listened to Mimi's monologues on the subject. "Is she in films or in the theater?"

The colonel looked offended. "Good heavens, she's not an actress. Whatever gave you that idea? Jane's a lawyer, very well thought of in her firm." He sounded proud.

"My father was a lawyer," Hanne offered conversationally. The colonel did not seem interested, but Paul was listening.

"Knock it off, will you," he said, drawing her aside. "Remember what you promised—no more lies."

"But it's true," she said, surprised. "Why should I lie about that? He was a very good lawyer. Grandmother said he would have been a judge, if the Nazis hadn't taken over."

Paul patted her. "Sorry, kid. I had no idea. Now circulate and talk to everyone. Don't let the colonel monopolize you. And whatever you do, don't go home with him."

"Why would I want to do that?" Hanne was amazed. Paul grinned. "Can't be too careful. After all, he's not bad-looking, he is a chicken colonel, and he has a reputation as one hell of a fellow with the girls."

"Nonsense. He was telling me about his wife."

"There you are. Oldest opening gambit in the world. Well, can't do more than warn you. Stick with the younger men. See that everyone has drinks, and show them where the food is."

Hanne loved playing hostess. Circulating with a jug of martinis and passing trays of fancy little sandwiches was just like being in her own home, looking after her own guests. And everyone was so nice to her, so different from the people who visited the princess. There she was just part of the background. Here she was noticed and admired. It was very exciting.

Paul was right again about the colonel. He really did get drunk and started following her around, trying to back her into a corner. The German girl stepped in with cool, practiced grace.

"I'll take him home now," she said in German, nodding at Hanne in a friendly way. "If he doesn't get to sleep soon, he'll make a fool of himself and feel bad tomorrow."

The colonel didn't want to go. He seemed prepared to argue. But the girl wrestled him into his coat with smooth efficiency, picked up his hat, and led him away.

The younger officers averted their eyes. No one laughed, so Hanne didn't dare to either, though it had been one of the funniest things she had ever seen. Colonel Hosterly was rather like a large, friendly, not very well-trained dog.

After midnight the party started petering out, and by two o'clock the last visitor had staggered off into the night. Hanne kicked off her shoes and collapsed on the couch with a tall glass of melted ice, faintly martini-flavored.

"What a lovely party," she said. "I like your friends." Paul settled close beside her and threw his arm around her shoulder.

"All my friends? Even Lieutenant Harper?"

"Which one was that?"

"Lieutenant Emily Harper, excellent nurse, great lady, and owner of the best damn legs in the American army."

"Oh, that one," Hanne said in a small voice. "She didn't stay very long, did she? Is she your girl?"

"Used to be, but no more."

"She was the one you danced with at the Femina, wasn't she?"

"Right, and that was the end of our great romance. She let me take her home, right up to her doorstep, and then she said good night, it was nice knowing you, maybe we'll see each other around from time to time and don't bother to call me."

"But she was here tonight."

Paul grinned and ruffled her hair. "Well, I said she was a great lady. She had promised to come to my party before we broke up, so she made her appearance. Admirable woman."

He hardly sounded heartbroken and Hanne was cheered. She had been only dimly aware of Emily Harper, and her impression had been of quiet, cool friendliness and a sense of distance. No threat at all.

Hanne yawned hugely.

"Good Lord, I am keeping you up past your bedtime." Paul ran his finger along her neck. "I'd better get you home."

Hanne felt very happy right where she was.

"Why bother?" she said, stifling a second yawn. "I can sleep here on the couch. You can take me back tomorrow morning."

In answer Paul bent over and kissed her, and this time it was a real kiss.

"All right, then," he said. "But you'll be much more comfortable upstairs."

Love was not quite what she had expected. It was nice, of course, to be so close to Paul, but it did hurt a bit, and he never said the things she wanted to hear. He told her she was beautiful and sexy and wonderful, but never that he loved her.

It was all right, of course. She knew that when she woke up and saw him asleep next to her. He looked so beautiful, so completely lovable. She liked seeing him naked. His body was lovely, especially his chest. It was not frizzy but smoothly copper-colored. And the black hair on it grew symmetrically in a design like a fleur-de-lys, starting from his stomach and curving in three separate, silky curls to each nipple and to the base of his throat. It was nice waking up like that. In the night she had not been quite so sure that she was doing the right thing. Sister Celestine would have been shocked. Grandmother would have been furious. But she rather thought her father would have understood.

She got out of bed carefully, so as not to wake Paul, and went to take a bath.

Soaking in the gloriously hot water reminded her of the first time she had taken a bath here. It was less than four months ago, but it seemed like a lifetime. Everything had changed. She was no longer alone and frightened. And she was no longer a child—thanks to Paul she was now a woman.

A pounding on the door brought her out of her fantasies. "Are you parked in there for life, Honey? I need to piss."

She giggled. "The door's not locked. Come in."

He came in reluctantly. "Well, how long are you going to stay in the tub?"

"Hours and hours," she said firmly. "Go ahead and do it. I won't look."

Her amusement unsettled him, and he stood there blinking. He seemed younger to her this morning and less in charge.

"I've just discovered the big difference between Europeans and Americans," she said, giggling, "We never talk about our physical functions, but we do what we have to do without a fuss. You don't mind using the words, but you'd rather burst than do it in public."

He glared at her. "Just grab a towel and get out, okay?"

She went off laughing, drying herself as she went.

Seeing him off guard like that made her happy. It was almost like being married.

Humming to herself, she went down to the kitchen to try her hand at breakfast. But she was too late. The mess from the party had been cleared away and a bony, middle-aged woman was making coffee.

"*Sprechen Sie Deutsch?*" The tone was arrogant.

Hanne nodded.

"Well, that's a relief. The others didn't, or pretended they didn't, and it makes everything so difficult. I'm Fräulein Stulp. I come in twice a week to clean." The woman had a narrow, hard face and a ropy neck. Something about her made Hanne uneasy.

Fräulein Stulp poured a cup of coffee and offered it to Hanne. If she was shocked or surprised at her presence, it did not show.

"What did you do with my robe?" Paul shouted down the stairs.

Hanne started guiltily. "I'm wearing it," she yelled back.

"Okay. I'll get dressed. Save me some of that coffee."

His appearance twenty minutes later, shaved and dapper, was intimidating. In contrast, Hanne felt untidy and childish.

"Ah. Honey, I see you've met Stulp, the woman I love best—next to you, of course." There was a hard edge to his voice. He turned to the housekeeper. "Have you emptied the ashtrays?" he asked pointedly.

Fräulein Stulp laughed without warmth. "Of course."

"Good, then you can put back the three packs you took off the coffee table. Okay?"

She flushed angrily. But after trying to stare him down for a moment, she sulkily dug into the pocket of her apron, brought out three packs of cigarettes, and laid them on the table.

"Don't get greedy," Paul said, slapping her lightly on her flat backside. "Think of the perks you have here. I bet you got a pound or more of butts."

"You're no gentleman," Fräulein Stulp said contemptuously. "To think I've come to this. Cleaning house for a gangster. If my friend knew what was going on, I don't know what he'd say."

"I can tell you what he'd say," Paul said mockingly. *"Ach mein Gott,* why was I such a fool as to join the Nazi party?"

"Do you think he had a choice?" she demanded bitterly.

"Who cares? Just git." He gave her a small push, then seemed to relent and threw a pack of cigarettes at her, which she caught deftly.

"I'll be back on Tuesday morning," she said with cold formality and bowed.

"I loathe that woman," Paul admitted, frowning after her. "Can't give up the idea that this is still her house."

Hanne was appalled. "Was it?"

"Yup. Her little love nest. The boyfriend was an architect, must have been a pretty good one. It's a nice house."

"But why does she clean for you?"

"Why not? She's got to eat, hasn't she? She cleans for five of us, three full days for the colonel and half days for the good buddies and me."

"It must be difficult for her."

"Don't weep over the Nazi bitch. She has a room in the colonel's garage. She gets to keep an eye on her house, makes sure no one burns it down, and if the boyfriend makes it back from Russia or wherever he is, and if he still wants her, they can live happily ever after."

Hanne felt chilled. Suddenly it was no longer her house. Poor ugly Miss Stulp and her Nazi boyfriend were in the room with them.

Paul stretched out luxuriously beside her, gently rubbing her back. "The fun part of it is that it's quite a joke on our colonel. He's always boasting about how clever Ingelore is. Well, she's a smart little bit all right. But his cleaning woman, Fräulein Stulp, is actually a lawyer, just like his lady wife. Think of it. Gerda Stulp, *Doktor Jur.* I saw that in a book she left behind, her ex libris decorated with the scales of justice, very fancy."

Hanne felt depressed. Some of the brightness had gone out of the day.

"Well, I'd better get back," she said glumly. "If you don't want to drive me, I can take the Stadtbahn."

Paul sipped his coffee and looked at her over the rim of the cup. "Why not stay?"

Hanne stopped breathing for a moment. "What do you mean—stay?"

"Move in, keep house for me, that sort of thing."

"But you could get fired," she said stiffly. "You said it was against the rules for me to stay here."

"That was three months ago. Fraternization's no longer a dirty word. Three months ago Colonel Hosterly couldn't have brought Ingelore to my party. Things are getting normal. Well, do you want to?"

She nodded breathlessly. Somehow everything was all right again, a bit precarious, but all right. He wanted her to live with him.

"Oh, Paul, I do love you," she said, snuggling against him. "I'm so happy. I wish everyone in the world could be as happy as I am right now. I'm so happy I could explode."

He grinned at her. "Don't do that, Honey. It would ruin the woman I love. Let's go pick up your clothes and tell the princess our happy news."

He had said it. He had used the word. He loved her.

The princess was not happy. "I will miss you, dear child. We will all miss you."

Overflowing with affection for the whole world, Hanne bent down and kissed the doughy cheek. "I'll come and visit," she promised.

"It's not the same as having you here. But I'm not thinking only of myself." She looked around for Paul, but he had gone downstairs to load her things into the jeep.

"Are you sure, Honey?"

Hanne nodded radiantly. "Oh, yes, Excellency. We love each other."

The old woman looked anxiously at the door and drew Hanne close. "There are things you should know about your Paul. He's not...."

"I'm not what?" Paul's laughing face appeared in the doorway.

The princess smiled at him, but it was not her best smile. "He's not to be trusted. He's a rascal, Honey. Don't say I didn't warn you."

Yet Hanne had an odd feeling that she had been about to say something else altogether.

She was thoughtful on the drive back to Zehlendorf. Paul looked cheerfully unconcerned, but she could not shake off the feeling that the princess had tried to tell her something and had decided against it when Paul came into the room.

"I need to know more about you," she finally said. "Why did the princess say you were a rascal?"

Paul whistled through his teeth and gave her a sideways glance. "Suspicious already? Honey, if you want to stay with me, you'll have to learn not to ask silly questions. I won't tolerate it."

"I'm not suspicious," she said. "I love you and I would like to know more about you. Is there something wrong with that?"

He ran his hand up her shoulder and grabbed her neck. It was not a caress. It hurt. "Let's get something straight, Honey," he said in a cold, quiet voice. "My life is my private business. I'll share my house, my bed, even my bathtub. Look, kid, I like you. You're great. We can have good times together. But don't try to take over. You start prying and out you go."

Honey started to cry. Her beautiful morning mood was shattered. She felt cheap and used and frightened.

Paul's touch immediately became warm, firm, and comforting. He pulled up at the curb and turned her face toward his. "Don't cry," he said softly, kissing her wet eyelids. "I'll look after you. But you mustn't ever cry over me. Okay? And you won't crowd me, will you?"

"I think I hate you," Hanne said, gulping. "You made me cry, and I promised myself that I'd never cry again."

"Did you now?" He was smiling. "Well, I promised myself I'd never lose my temper again, and look what you made me do."

"You're just trying to—to cajole me."

"Goodness. Where did you pick up that big word?" he murmured admiringly. "Cajole indeed. I wouldn't dare."

"You make fun of me and of my feelings." Hanne tried to explain herself.

"Any moment now you will say it."

"Say what?" She was startled out of her misery.

Paul assumed an air of long-suffering virtue. "Now that you have had my body," he declaimed tragically, "you no longer respect me."

Against her better judgment, Hanne started to laugh. She would not have said it that way, because it did sound stupid, but it exactly described the way she had been feeling.

Paul eyed her with approval. "I'll tell you a secret, Honey. I'll hand over the ultimate weapon you can use against me any time. When you laugh, you're irresistible. See what I've done? I have put myself in your power. Now you can train me like a seal, tell me to roll over, balance a ball on my nose. You've got me by the short hairs."

Hanne sighed. She knew she was being manipulated, but there was nothing she could do about it. Where Paul was concerned she seemed to have no defenses.

"Let's do something nice," he coaxed, "Something to make you feel good. I know what—we're going shopping."

She looked at him doubtfully. "Here? Here in Berlin?"

"Why not? Someday I'll take you shopping in Paris, but right now, yes—here in Berlin."

❧ *Chapter 4*

The Kurfurstendamm had been Berlin's most elegant shopping center. Now most of it was in ruins, but Paul took her to one of the few shops still standing. It did not look particularly promising. The shelves were empty, except for some elaborate and very ugly hats that looked as if they dated back at least to the turn of the century. The pale gray carpeting, however, was deep and soft, and the saleswoman who swam forward to welcome them was exquisitely dressed in black, with golden scissors hanging from a red cord around her neck.

Hanne was impressed. None of the women at the princess's had been as elegant as that, not even Mimi. Hanne could vaguely remember her mother having that smooth, seamless perfection. It was not a happy memory. She remembered the glossy blond hair, firmly fixed in an elaborate arrangement of waves. There had been a distinctive perfume, rich and flowery. You always knew when she came into a room, even if your eyes were closed. Hanne remembered a lot of things about her mother, but mostly the dazzling smile that never quite reached the eyes.

This woman was the same type. Her hair was swept up and twisted in a knot. Not a wisp stuck out any-where. If she wore makeup, it was done so well that it didn't show. She was tall and slender with long, lovely hands, which she held out to Paul in a gesture of welcome.

"Why, Max, what a pleasure. I see you so seldom." Her eyes flickered over and through Hanne. "What have you brought me this time?"

Paul stared coldly. "I beg your pardon. You seem to have me mixed up with someone else. I don't think we've ever met. But never mind, I have brought you a lovely young lady to dress. Can you show her a few outfits?"

"Max!" The woman's eyes flickered for a moment, then she recovered her poise. "Forgive me. I must admit all American officers do look the same to me—so very handsome. Of course, I should have realized you couldn't possibly be Max Grant."

Her smile was mocking. "Such a good customer, Captain Grant, and such a dear friend. But of course, you and I have never met. Now, what kind of clothes did you have in mind?"

Her eyes slid up, down, and around Hanne like measuring tapes, but her conversation was directed exclusively at Paul. "I have some new silks, straight from Paris, and some English tweeds. Marvelous quality. Shoes are a problem at the moment. The man who works for me is an artist, but good leather is hard to get. My good friend, Max Grant, sometimes finds some for me."

"I suppose I could try to get you some leather," Paul said blandly. "Now, what Honey needs is a couple of dresses, simple, classic, you know the sort of thing."

The saleswoman gave a thin smile. "*Jeune fille bien élevée*," she said, and Hanne thought her French accent was ostentatiously correct.

"*Mädchen aus guter Stube*," she said, to make it clear that she understood, and added defiantly, "That's me, all right. I'm only eighteen and excruciatingly well brought up."

Paul doubled up with laughter and the saleswoman unbent a little. "Charming," she said lightly. "Quite charming. It will be a pleasure to dress such a delightful young lady."

Paul got up and walked toward the door.

"You're not going to leave me here, are you?" Hanne protested. "I don't know what to buy, and I have no money."

"Frau Gerhardt will help you pick out what you need," he said with a reassuring nod. "Fix yourself up with a decent wardrobe. I'll be back to settle up and help you carry your stuff home."

Hanne followed the saleswoman into the back room, feeling thoughtful. So it was Frau Gerhardt. He did know her. So why all that business of pretending not to? And why had he been using another name? It made no sense at all.

But she forgot everything during the next hour in the delight of selecting her new clothes. The showroom of the shop might be bare, but the workroom in the back was a treasure trove. An elderly seamstress and a shy, awkward girl undressed her and slipped a short silky garment over her head.

"Eventually you will need a bra," Frau Gerhardt said, looking her over with a professional eye. "But not for a year or so, I think. These camiknicks are very useful. You had better take a dozen—say, six in pink, and two each in white, ecru, and black. The pink is really a flesh tone and can go under almost everything."

"But a dozen?" Hanne was overwhelmed.

"I advise it," Frau Gerhardt said firmly, and indicating several bolts of fabric the young girl had lined up, "Now which of these appeals to you? Personally, I would like to see you in the nile green."

"The red," Hanne said quickly, feeling the need to assert herself.

Frau Gerhardt trembled a little. "The red?" she said in a shocked voice. "It should not even have been brought out for you. It's quite unsuitable. Our friend would never forgive me if I let you buy something so wrong for you. Then you don't care for the nile green?"

"I dislike it," Hanne said promptly. "Green makes me seasick."

The saleswoman sighed and capitulated. "Very well. How about the blue?"

Hanne was beginning to enjoy herself. "Blue is all right," she said generously "but only if it has some red in it."

Frau Gerhardt took a deep breath. "I see. You are a young lady who knows exactly what she wants. Very well, perhaps I have just what you're looking for." There was a grudging respect in her tone. "Ilse, bring the plaid taffeta."

A bolt of silk was unrolled in front of Hanne and it almost took her breath away, it was so beautiful. It contained every shade of blue ever found in sea or sky, barred with stripes of glowing carmine, forming jeweled blocks of purple, from amethyst to deep violet. Every fold shimmered with a different burst of color.

"I never dreamt...." Hanne murmured, stroking the lovely cloth. "It's perfect."

Frau Gerhardt preened herself. "I knew it. It will indeed be perfect. A ball gown with a bouffant skirt, nipped-in waist, and no back at all." Her fingers draped the fabric over and around Hanne, pushing her toward the mirror. "You see what I mean? High in front, with a shirt collar, and then cut away from the collarbone to the waist."

"Will it stay put?"

"If we make it for you, believe me, it will stay put."

Hanne permitted herself to be measured. Having won a small victory in the matter of color, she found she had lost the war in every other regard.

"This will be our palette!" The elegant woman drew in the air with her hands, while Ilse, the apprentice, struggled with boxes. "Dark blue, red, and white. When we need an extra color—violet very brilliant, in very small quantities."

The elderly seamstress folded the plaid silk with elaborate care. Hanne hated to see it go. It was magic. Meanwhile Ilse had spread out a selection of garments on the shining-clean workroom table. There were several navy skirts, boxes of blouses, scarves, and a bundle of knitted jackets, all navy blue, but many different textures.

Frau Gerhardt seemed to feed on the excitement of planning the wardrobe. Her eyes glowed feverishly. Hanne, who had been a little frightened of her, now accepted her as a partner in this enterprise—the making of the new Hanne, a beautiful, well-dressed Hanne.

Even in the simplest of shirtwaist dresses—plain cotton, belted with a strip of leather—she could see the difference. So that's why Paul hadn't wanted her to wear the yellow silk dress. It was wrong for her. It was Mimi's style, a nice-enough dress but not for her. In the right clothes, she realized, she could look better than nice. She could look marvelous.

Ilse whispered to her behind Frau Gerhardt's back, "You're lucky. I wish I could get me an Ami. It must be nice to have a boyfriend."

For a moment Hanne thought she was using the French word for friend, but then she caught on: Ami—American. There was a wistful look in Ilse's eyes.

"Don't you have a German boyfriend?" she asked.

"Oh, no," Ilse said sadly. "Before the war I was too young, and then all the boys were at the front."

"They'll come home by and by," said Hanne. "There will be lots of boys again."

Ilse gave a sad sniff and moved away. Frau Gerhardt had come back into the room, this time accompanied by an elderly man who carried what looked like a toolbox.

Hanne's feet were first measured, then pressed into a box filled with wet plaster. These shoes, Frau Gerhardt assured her triumphantly, would fit like a second skin. Herr Scholte's shoes fitted so beautifully, people had sent their orders to him from all over Europe before the war.

Herr Scholte smiled and nodded. "I had a workshop with hundreds of lasts, Fräulein. There was an English lord who ordered his riding boots from me. And all the actresses came to me."

"Did you ever make shoes for Mimi Krall?" Hanne asked curiously.

"Oh, you have heard of her?" The shoemaker looked pleased. "One of my best customers. A delightful actress, they say, and very interesting feet, narrow but rather long. We usually made shoes with straps for her, to shorten the foot. You have seen her films?"

"No, but I met her," Hanne said. "She's very nice." Nice didn't seem the right word for poor, sad Mimi, but Herr Scholte was satisfied with it. He bowed over

Hanne's hand and clicked his heels before gathering up his paraphernalia and bowing himself out of the room.

"Such a Kavalier," Ilse said mockingly behind his back.

Frau Gerhardt turned on her sharply. "He's one of the last of them, the great craftsmen. You'd better treat him with respect, you silly girl."

Hanne had disliked Frau Gerhardt on sight, because of the likeness to her mother, but when she realized Frau Gerhardt's talent with clothes she had quickly come to respect her. At this moment, she almost loved her. She wasn't a bit like Mother after all. Mother would have laughed at funny old Herr Scholte. She shook off the thought. I'm not going to think about her ever again. Never again. It's going to be as if she never existed.

"Will you take home the things you've chosen?" Frau Gerhardt interrupted her thoughts. "Or do you want to wear some of them?"

"The pleated skirt, perhaps, with the striped poplin shirt."

Frau Gerhardt nodded. "An excellent choice. Your friend Max will approve." She did not seem to notice her slip, or perhaps it didn't matter anymore.

"Shall I pack up the rest?" Ilse asked, blank and colorless once again.

"No," Frau Gerhardt said sharply. "I shall do it myself. Make some coffee and bring it to the office."

Hanne helped put the lovely things into boxes, then followed Frau Gerhardt to a tiny cubicle off the empty showroom. It had a pleasant, cluttered look less like an office than a bedroom.

"Yes. I live here," Frau Gerhardt said with a smile. "The bed pops out of that closet. I used to sleep here when I was extra busy and didn't have time to go home. Now it *is* home."

"Bombed out?"

"Very thoroughly, my dear. The last time I went to look at my apartment, there were no floors and no roof, but my beautiful pink bathtub was hanging out of a window by a twisted pipe. It looked like a very modern piece of sculpture."

"You look so unflustered," Hanne said wonderingly. "It never occurred to me that you could have had any misfortune ever."

"A useful and necessary façade. Don't you ever need cover up some part of your life?"

Hanne blushed, and the question hung between them, unanswered, while Ilse brought in two tiny cups of thin china filled with strong, black coffee.

"Never mind," Frau Gerhardt said softly. "I have no right to ask, and Max would not like me to pry. Wherever did he find you?"

"He rescued me," Hanne said simply. "Why do you call him Max?"

Frau Gerhardt's eyes flickered. "He is a young man who likes change. Sometimes his name is Max Grant. It's as good a name as any, isn't it? We have been friends; we do business. There was a time when we were more than friends." She smiled ruefully. "Perhaps he reminded me of some other young man, long ago. It was just a bit of foolishness on my part. When you get to my age, these things don't last. One doesn't expect them to."

Hanne was shocked. "You were in love with him?"

Frau Gerhardt gently shook her head. "Too big a word for such a small episode. Anyway, it meant nothing to him, I'm sure. So, he rescued you, and now you love him?"

"Why, yes."

Frau Gerhardt looked at her intently. "I have no right, but—take care. Don't... Never mind, pay no attention to me. I'm being absurd."

"I don't understand," said Hanne.

Frau Gerhardt leaned back and closed her eyes. She looked older and somehow softer.

"One feels responsible," she murmured, as if to herself. "So terribly young! And you are Jewish, aren't you? Yes, I know. Blond hair and all, you remind me of a woman I was apprenticed to, long ago."

She seemed to lose herself in her memories. "She made marvelous clothes, such elegance of line, of fabric. She taught me everything, a wonderful woman. Martha Loewenthal. Did you ever hear of her? Her atelier was the best. She died in time, thank God. But one keeps thinking of all the others. One feels somehow responsible."

"You are not responsible," said Hanne. "I'm sure you never hurt anyone."

Frau Gerhardt shivered and seemed to make an effort to regain her normal manner. "The coffee is good, isn't it?" she said. "I don't know what I would do without coffee. I'm afraid it's an addiction. Now you must try on shoes. We must find something to tide you over until the custom-made ones are ready. Herr Scholte can't be rushed."

She smiled pleasantly. It was as if an old wound had closed up, leaving no visible scar.

Hanne was swirling in front of the mirror when Paul walked in. He whistled appreciatively.

"I've run up a tremendous bill, I'm afraid," she admitted. "I seem to have bought twelve of everything."

"You shock me," said Paul, making a face. "Being extravagant is all right, but to talk about it is vulgar."

She looked at him uncertainly. "Are you angry?"

He swung her off her feet. "How can anyone be angry with a girl who looks like you. Say, have you grown?"

"No, I'm wearing high-heeled shoes. Herr Scholte will make me lots of new ones to measure. These were the only ones in stock that fit me."

"Very nice. Now you're going to need nylons. I'll get them for you."

Frau Gerhardt handed Paul an envelope that probably contained a staggering bill, but Hanne was determined not to be accused of vulgarity again. She turned her back and started collecting her boxes.

"The first fitting next week, my dear," said Frau Gerhardt, writing in a notebook. "I will call Max and arrange the time."

Paul's good humor vanished abruptly. "I thought we'd cleared that up. I don't know you, and I prefer not to be addressed by that name. Perhaps you'd rather I took my business elsewhere."

Frau Gerhardt stared at him with the slightest of raised eyebrows. It was a look of such cold dislike that Hanne shivered, It was out of all proportion to his silly rudeness. But then his rudeness was out of proportion to the trivial offense of calling him by the wrong name. And why did he have to keep up the pretense of not knowing her?

She was relieved to get out of the shop. The air was cleaner outside and easier to breathe.

❧ *Chapter 5*

The first few days in Paul's house were wildly exciting. Everything was wonderful. There was an electric vacuum cleaner and a toaster and the electric stove.

She couldn't get over her delight. No carrying in of coal buckets and carrying out of ashes. Coffee first thing in the morning, without ever worrying about having to bank the fire the night before. It was a dream come true.

She would put on old shirts of Paul's to protect her new clothes, and spend blissful hours cleaning everything in sight and trying out recipes. Paul provided her with an American cookbook written by a lady from Boston, who seemed to use a lot of something called molasses. Paul was unable to get it for her, but he assured her that he wasn't crazy about it anyway. He did bring her most of the things she put on her grocery list, and seemed willing to eat her cooking.

He was so pleasant to live with, pleased with everything she did. At least he never criticized. And he loved her. He didn't use the words, but she was sure that he did. Of course he did. He told her she was beautiful, and he made love to her every night—and a lot of mornings, too. It was fun being loved by Paul.

Of course he loved her. Why else would he be so nice to her and give her so many presents?

After a while she found that there was nothing left that needed cleaning. She baked bread, but Paul didn't care for it. It was a bit on the heavy side, she had to admit.

Then she tried pastries. They looked beautiful, all glossy and decorated with swirls of whipped cream. Paul ate them without noticing. In all fairness she knew men didn't usually care about tiny decorated cakes. The princess would have adored them. But Hanne had no guests to impress with her new skills. It was discouraging.

Keeping house for someone who didn't seem to care what the house looked like began to bore her. She missed the princess, who did notice. She missed the glasses of hot, black tea, sweetened with raspberry jam, and the conversations. There was a phone, but she was not allowed to use it. It was an illegal phone,

Paul explained, which didn't make much sense to Hanne. How could a phone be illegal?

Anyway, the princess had no phone, nor did anyone else she knew.

Colonel Hosterly had a phone, of course. Hanne found his number in the book and used it just once, carefully choosing a time when all the men were at work. She had no desire to talk to the colonel. The one she was after was Ingelore, his girlfriend. She had carefully worked out an excuse. A broken earring had turned up after the party and she planned to ask Ingelore if it happened to be hers. It was a skimpy excuse, but Hanne hoped it would serve. She was lonely and the girl looked friendly.

Ingelore seemed pleased to hear Hanne's voice. Perhaps she was lonely, too. Hanne was invited over for afternoon coffee.

It was fun. Hanne had almost forgotten how much fun it was to be with a girl her own age. They drank coffee, ate Hanne's petit fours, and talked about food and clothes, and finally about men.

"Americans are all right," said Ingelore thoughtfully. "Robert—that's the colonel—he's very good to me."

"Are you in love with him?" asked Hanne.

Ingelore considered this. "I suppose so—in a way. He's nice. Of course, he drinks too much and he's a lot older than the boys I used to go with—but nice."

"Did you..." Hanne had trouble framing her question. "Did you do it with them, too?"

Ingelore laughed. "Of course! Not all of them, just the ones I liked. Didn't you?"

Hanne numbly shook her head. "I was brought up by nuns," she said.

"You poor thing."

"They were very kind," Hanne said.

Ingelore held her cup with both hands and slowly swirled her coffee. "I suppose nuns are all right," she said thoughtfully. "But you couldn't have had much fun. Old people have different ideas. I don't think my mother wanted me to go with our boys either, but it was almost a duty, wasn't it? I mean, they were fighting for us." She laughed. "Of course now she's all for it. She's crazy about Robert."

Hanne was startled. "She knows about Colonel Hosterly?"

"Of course! We go to visit her once a week. She lives in Birchenfeld now. Our flat in town was bombed out, so she moved in with a friend. They've got an old summer cottage. Robert managed to get a stove for them, and he gives them food and cigarettes. You should see those two old girls fuss over him. They get all twittery and girlish."

Hanne found this faintly worrisome. It all seemed so practical and prosaic.

"But he's married," she said at last. "What happens when his wife gets here—or when he goes back to America?"

Ingelore shrugged. "When he goes, he goes," she said cheerfully. "By that time our boys will be coming back."

Paul, it turned out, did not want her talking to Ingelore. He flew into a rage when she mentioned the afternoon coffee. Hanne could see no real reason for him to object.

"Because she's a cheap little slut. That's why. I don't want you picking up her vulgarities."

"But she's not vulgar. She has very nice manners."

"She's your typical petite bourgeoise. Berlin's full of them. If there's one thing you don't need, it's a Berlin accent mixed with Hosterly's nasal drawl. For God's sake, hang on to your accent. At least you sound like a lady."

"But I've got no one else to talk to."

"No!" It was flat and final.

Hanne felt trapped. Paul didn't seem to want her to talk to anyone.

She tried to do some sewing. She had learned to do beautiful needlework at the convent and was rather proud of her skill. Paul brought her a little army-style sewing kit, and she resewed all his shirt buttons on the theory that ready-made things never had buttons sewn on right. Then she found a few loose threads in the seam of a jacket lining. Everything else was depressingly perfect.

She went for short walks. Paul had set limits: no farther than two blocks in any direction. And even then she was not to strike up conversations. Picking up people in the street was vulgar.

If he had come home and talked to her, it would have been nicer, but after the first week he got used to having her around and stopped talking to her. Sometimes he made love to her without saying a single word. She felt he didn't even see her.

She began to read voraciously. After starting with some books she found on German mercantile law, which were dreadfully boring as well as difficult, she happened upon a bunch of history books, which were much more fun. Better yet, there was even some Shakespeare in English.

Finally, hidden behind a row of false book backs, she found the ultimate treasure trove—a pile of French novels. Her French, pure of pronunciation and grammatically correct, had not prepared her for anything like these novels. They were an eye opener.

Paul was amused. "Oh, Lord, you've found our Gerda's secret stash of erotica," he said, shaking his head, "I don't suppose it'll hurt you. If you understand it, it's too late to protect you, and if you don't—no harm done. I always wondered about her and the Nazi boyfriend. Now we know what they did when they drew those curtains."

"It's very interesting," Hanne said seriously. "All about love."

"Love? Is that what you call it?" He mocked her.

"All right—sex. But I need to learn more about it," she defended herself. "Nobody ever told me about these things. I don't even know some of the words."

"Look 'em up in the dictionary," he said, bored. "Just don't use them in public."

"What public? I haven't seen a soul in days. Paul, I'm lonely."

He gave her a cold look. "Don't start that, for Christ's sake. You wanted to come and stay here, right? Now all of a sudden you expect me to keep you entertained."

"It's not that," she tried to explain. "But you're gone all day, and you don't want me to go visit Ingelore or to meet some of the other people who live around here. And I promised the princess I'd visit her...."

"When I have time," he said irritably, "I'll take you to see her."

"If you gave me some money, I could take the bus or the Stadtbahn."

"I won't have you using public transportation." His voice was curt.

Hanne exploded. "You won't let me do this and you won't let me do that. What am I supposed to be, anyway? I seem to belong to you. But you don't belong to me, do you? I guess I'm just a girl you picked up off the street and set up as your mistress—"

She got no further. He had turned on her in a black rage and smashed his flat hand across her face. She staggered back and fell across the couch. She felt blankly amazed. This wasn't real. It hadn't happened. Paul couldn't do that to her.

She touched her mouth and saw blood on her fingers. Paul was staring at her with a look of pure horror on his face.

"Oh my God," he said "Oh God, oh God, Honey, are you all right?"

She touched her face gingerly, and nodded.

"You're bleeding," he said, tears in his eyes. He knelt down beside her and started wiping the blood off her face with his handkerchief. His touch was gentle and loving. Hanne felt confused. He was not angry with her now. She had yelled at him, and she knew—she had been told at least—that men got angry sometimes and hit people. But he wasn't angry and he behaved as if the whole thing had been some sort of accident.

Perhaps she had imagined it? Could she have fallen and hurt herself? No, the look in his face and his hand coming at her were not her imagination.

She let him wash her face, which he did tenderly. He made her rinse out her mouth and looked inside with a flashlight.

"We're in luck," he said with a sigh of relief. "You cut the inside of your lip on your teeth, that's all. Teeth intact. Just keep rinsing with salt water and it'll be all right."

"But what happened?" she finally dared to ask.

His eyes seemed to become opaque. He turned away from her. She did not bring it up again. Nothing had happened. She hadn't yelled at him. He hadn't hit her.

He didn't make love to her that night. His manner was gentle, polite, and slightly distant. But the next day he brought home a peace offering, obviously the largest peace offering he had been able to find.

Hanne dissolved into laughter at the sight of him struggling with a huge tub containing a flowering lilac tree. It was a gorgeous little tree, and it took both of them to lug it into the house. It sat in the middle of the living room and looked ridiculous.

"I saw it in front of the Blue Goose—you know, the German nightclub on Joachimstaler Strasse, in the English sector—and I thought you'd like it. You do like it, don't you?"

"I love it." She flung her arms around him. "I love you. You're crazy and I love you."

"We haven't been to the opera lately," he said over dinner.

"Not lately?" she squeaked. "I've never been to an opera in my whole life."

He grinned at her. "I've suspected all along that you're a philistine. No culture at all. High time you were educated. As it so happens I have two tickets for the Staatsoper tomorrow. Care to go?"

"Can I wear the long dress?"

He laughed. The plaid silk dress, finally ready after several fittings, hung in the closet and she was dying to wear it. "Can you imagine yourself sitting in an open jeep in that dress? No, Honey, you'll have to save that for the next time, As soon as I get a decent car, I'll take a whole box to show you off."

"All right, then I'll wear the short silk dress with the little white dots embroidered on it," she decided happily. "And the new navy shoes. The heels are so high, I'm almost as tall as you when I put them on."

"Don't you want to know which opera we're going to hear?"

She blushed.

He pulled her down on his lap and nuzzled her neck. "It's Eugene Onegin, you uncultured girl, and a great Russian tenor has been imported specifically for the occasion. Of course he gets killed in the second act, so everybody who is anybody will walk out at that point. Who needs to sit through the third act just to hear the German baritone?"

"But if we leave after the second act," Hanne objected, "how are we going to know how it ends?"

He laughed at her. "We know how it ends. It's a Russian opera. Everyone will suffer dreadfully. Is that worth staying for?"

"I suppose not." She cheered up a little. "We could make up a happy ending for ourselves, couldn't we? What is it all about?"

"Suffering and more suffering," he assured her cheerfully. "Onegin is a cold-hearted young man, so the girl who loves him suffers. He flirts with his best friend's girl, so the friend suffers. Then he kills his best friend in a duel, so the friend's girlfriend suffers. I'm damned if I can figure out how you can slap a happy ending on that."

She chewed on a strand of hair, considering the problem seriously.

"The two girls gang up on him and shoot him," she decided. "Then they run away from the police and become famous acrobats."

"Why acrobats?"

Hanne wasn't sure. She rather liked the idea of acrobats, though she had never seen any.

"It's a fine new ending," Paul agreed. "And if Tschaikovsky had had your help, he would have written much better operas."

Being with Paul at the opera was even more wonderful than dancing with him. Hanne was quite willing to overlook the pushy crowds and the smell of many unwashed bodies, compounded by the specific fragrance of her neighbor, a Russian officer who was munching on a raw onion. The Russian was amiable enough, even to the point of offering her a bite, but at close range the smell was overwhelming. Paul leaned across her and started a conversation in Russian. Much to her relief, he asked her to switch places, so that he and the Russian colonel could talk more easily. It was a big improvement for Hanne, who now sat between Paul on her left and a French soldier on her right.

She began to try out her French on him, but he made it plain that he had come to hear the music, not to talk. She, decided that people who said all Frenchmen were flirtatious were as wrong as the ones who insisted that all Russians were rapists and all Englishmen were cold fish.

The moment the music started she forgot all about the people in the hall. It was better than any record she had ever heard, and it was right there, all around her. It was bliss.

Then the curtain went up and she got lost in the story. It was wonderful—all about Madame Larina and her daughters, Tatyana, so romantic and soulful, and Olga, pretty and cute. And the set—had people ever really lived like that, all that elegance, that space?

She was prepared to dislike Onegin, and the actor made it easy, being so large, awkward, and conceited. But his friend, Lensky—ah, what a man!

She was not alone in her rapture. The audience as a whole bent forward toward him, loving him. The Russian tenor, specially imported for the production was short and compact. Graceful where the other was stiff, blond against Onegin's darkness, he offered the perfect contrast. He represented warmth and goodness against Onegin's arrogance—and his voice was glorious.

In the next scene, Tatyana's maunderings about her love were rather boring. The set was lovely of course, as were the filmy white wrappers the girls wore. But Hanne had to admit that Tatyana would not make a good acrobat. She was played by a German woman of imposing proportions, and by no stretch of the imagination could you see her balancing on a wire.

The silly mooning and sighing and letter writing was over at last, and the story finally got back to the two young men. Lensky was in love with Olga, the cute one. Onegin was being stuffy about the letter from Tatyana, which was really not hard to understand. Why should he be interested in an overweight lady old enough to be his mother? So at the party that night—oh, those dresses!—he flirted with Olga. Big deal, Hanne thought. Olga was the sort of girl people would always flirt with, and very nice, too. Sort of a Mimi type, only younger.

At the end of the party there was a wonderful dance. The corps de ballet, in pale blue dresses and flower wreaths in their hair, whirled in a circle. In her mind's eye, Hanne was whirling among them.

"What happens next?"

Paul was delighted with her excitement, and explained patiently that the two men would duel, Onegin would kill Lensky, and they would leave.

"Oh, all right, I can see that there's not much left if you kill off Lensky."

The Frenchman on her right interrupted irritably in heavily accented English. "The third act, young woman, is exquisitely beautiful, musically speaking. If you choose to walk out, you miss some great music." He glared.

Paul leaned back, smiling blandly. Hanne turned a questioning look to him. "Do you think we should stay?"

"Musically speaking," Paul drawled, "we will most likely miss another fine set of a ballroom and another round of prancing from the corps de ballet. And of course, musically speaking, a German basso no one's ever heard of will be making a fool of himself as Prince Gremin."

The Frenchman flushed and pressed his lips together. Hanne felt rather sorry for him. Paul could be very rude when he felt like it.

"Then you don't want to stay for the third act?"

Paul raised his eyebrows in mild surprise. "Of course not. Whatever for? We're going on to the Blue Goose afterward to meet Colonel Arpov." He indicated the officer on his left, who had finished the onion and was smoking a cigarette that smelled almost as bad.

There was a general exodus during the second intermission. Only the most determined opera lovers were left behind. As she climbed into the jeep, Hanne was still submerged in the magic.

"I did love the dance at the end of the first act," she said dreamily. "The girls in those high-waisted dresses with wreaths of flowers, and the black ribbons around their necks—do you think that life ever was like that? So beautiful?"

Paul shrugged. The opera was over and he was already somewhat bored with it.

"I've got another happy ending for it," Hanne announced happily. "Onegin reforms and marries Olga. She's sort of a silly soul, isn't she, and doesn't deserve anyone better. Lensky would have gotten very bored with her."

"Forget it," Paul advised. "Let's stick with the murder and the acrobats. Now on to the Blue Goose."

"The place where you got my lilac tree?"

"Right. You'll like the colonel. He's really a very nice fellow."

Hanne's heart sank. "Do we have to meet him? I can't talk to him and he smells awful."

"The onion will have worn off by now. And anyway, I'm the one who's going to talk to him. I think we can make some sort of deal."

"What kind of deal?" She could see her lovely evening going down the drain, but felt helpless to prevent it.

"He's interested in watches and I have a hunch he has access to vodka and caviar—well, vodka for sure. We can do each other a lot of good."

"I don't understand," Hanne said sadly. "Are you dealing in the black market?"

Paul sent her a warning glance. "Keep out of my affairs, okay? Just smile at the colonel and enjoy the floor show. They have a terrific pianist. You probably know her already from Lydia Ivanovna's—Renée Cartier."

"Yes, the enormous one. She scares me a bit."

"She's tame enough. The thing is to get her to sit down, Luckily she does sit to play the piano, and she plays damn well."

"I wish we could go home."

He merely shrugged, and Hanne let it drop.

Joachimstaler Strasse was drab and the Blue Goose was poorly lit and shabby. Hanne had expected something more like the Femina, but this was a German nightclub. Everyone brought their own bottle and paid the waiter to serve it. There was no food, and unluckily for Hanne, no soft drinks.

Refusing the wine Paul had brought along, she sipped water and watched the entertainment without much joy. Miss Cartier was a White Russian girl, raised in Paris, whose playing was much admired. But Hanne's head was still filled with the glorious opera, and she simply didn't want to hear anything else, especially not Miss Cartier's crashing dissonances.

After a while the pianist came and sat with them. The conversation was all in Russian. Hanne felt sleepy.

Colonel Arpov wanted to dance with her, and she dutifully allowed him to push her around the floor. The onion had not worn off, but he seemed determined to be pleasant, smiling an enormous smile that displayed a gleaming steel tooth.

"He really admires you," Paul assured her on the way home. "He hates to see young girls drinking—a bit of a puritan, I suspect, at least where other people's morals are concerned. Your drinking water makes you a real lady—very *kulturna.*"

❧ *Chapter 6*

As the swelling on Hanne's lip went down, Paul seemed to forget all about her complaints of loneliness and boredom. She saw less and less of him. Her carefully cooked dinners would dry up in the wonderful electric oven, and when he finally came in at ten or eleven at night, he would be surprised that she hadn't eaten.

"Good heavens, Honey, don't hang around my neck like an albatross. Find something to amuse yourself."

"You said you'd help me get a job."

"I will, I will. These things take time."

"Can I go visit the princess?"

"I'll take you when I have time."

"But what am I supposed to do all day long? You never come home. Where do you go every night?"

He looked at her coldly. "If you must know, I've been spending some time with Renée."

"With her? But why?"

He ignored her.

"Are you having an affair with her?"

Paul shrugged. "Always melodramatic, aren't you? Yes, I'm having an affair with her."

She glared at him miserably. "She's six inches taller than you, and weighs a ton. And she's old—a lot older than you. Why did you fall in love with her?"

"Don't be a bore, Honey. Who said anything about being in love? Renée is a big woman, but she's very attractive. And she's amusing—a witty, civilized, grownup woman who doesn't go on and on about love."

Hanne turned her back on him. There was nothing else left to say.

"Look, if it bothers you that much, I'll stop seeing her. Okay?" Paul made the offer in a careless voice, as if offering to take out the garbage.

Hanne swung around angrily. "I don't understand you. If it bothers me? Did you really think it wouldn't? And what about Renée? How about her feelings?"

"Her feelings are no more involved than mine," Paul assured her, looking mildly surprised. "You've really been reading too many novels."

Hanne fought down her rage and forced herself to speak in what she hoped was a reasonable manner. "I have nothing to do but read—and think."

"Well, it's getting nice and warm out," Paul suggested carelessly. "You like plants, don't you? Make a garden. And while you're at it, get rid of that lilac tree. It's a mess. Dead flowers over everything. I think it's had it."

The next day, dressed in Paul's fatigues, Hanne attacked the front yard. In a small toolshed behind the kitchen she found a spade, rusty but serviceable. It felt good to be outside, in the promising air of an early spring day. It felt good to be doing something. Her misery and confusion about Paul's unfaithfulness seemed somehow less important. Digging up the hard-packed soil became the only important thing in the world.

Several hours later, soaked in sweat and discouraged, she had little to show for her work. A patch no bigger than the kitchen sink had been loosened. The soil around the house was stamped down and hard as iron. Getting desperate, she jumped on the top rim of the shovel with her full weight, only to hear an ominous crack. The next moment she found herself flat on her back. The handle had snapped off and the blade was rolling down toward the street.

Grimly, she picked herself up and examined the broken handle. The break was lengthways. Perhaps she could glue it together. She collected the bottom half and fitted the two parts together experimentally.

"It's not going to work, Miss," a voice interrupted.

Hanne looked up, startled. A sandy-haired GI was sitting in a jeep parked at the curb, watching her sympathetically.

"You understand English? Look—you can't fit it back together. It'd be a waste of effort. Honest."

"But what can I do? I did so want to dig all this up."

The GI swung his long legs over the edge of the jeep and ambled over. "I've been watching you these past ten minutes, and I was wondering what you were up to. This is terrible clay you have here. It's just like cement." The way he said it, it sounded like "seamint."

It took Hanne a while to figure out what he meant. Then she nodded. "Yes, just like cement," she agreed. "But I did so want to make a garden."

The young man brightened. "It's the right time of year for it, all thawed out. And a garden sure would look nice. What did you want to plant?"

"Oh, roses, I suppose," Hanne said grandly. "Or maybe some fresh vegetables."

He took off his cap and scratched his head thoughtfully. "Have you ever had a garden?"

She blushed and searched his warm brown eyes. "Well, no."

He looked doubtful, then smiled. "You've grown stuff indoors, maybe?"

"Well, when I was young—younger, anyway—I was in an orphanage. We used to make dish gardens."

He nodded. "Yeah—we did that in first grade. We had Mrs. Clark. She was big on dish gardens. All the mothers hated her because we'd come home with mud all over our good school pants. But it sure was fun."

She nodded, liking this lanky, comfortable young man who was so easy to talk to.

"Making a real garden isn't exactly like that, though," he went on, squatting down on his heels and settling in. "You see, the first thing you need is proper soil. This soil is no good."

He opened a penknife and poked it into the ground. "Just look at it, miss. If you were a young plant, would you want to poke your delicate little roots down into that? No way. What you need is some decent soil, and a new shovel."

"Perhaps I'd better give up on my garden," she said sadly. "Maybe it wasn't such a good idea."

"I think it was a fine idea," he said. "Fine and dandy. Will you be home tomorrow?"

Hanne nodded half-heartedly. Paul had never actually told her not to make friends with GIs who happened to stop by, but she had a hunch that he would like it even less than the forbidden afternoon coffee with Colonel Hosterly's Ingelore. But to hell with Paul. "I'll be home," she said. "My name's Hanne, just like that—HAH-ner—and I hate it when people pronounce it English to sound like a chicken."

He grinned and bobbed his head. "My name's funny, too—Rip Tyler. You wouldn't believe some of the names we have in our family. I have an aunt called Dicey Bundy."

Hanne looked puzzled, then started to giggle.

"Her daddy couldn't have known she'd marry George Bundy, or he wouldn't have done that to her. Or maybe he would. He was that ornery. My grandpa, you know, my mother's daddy. Ornery as a mule. All the Carter men are like that."

He grinned. "Me, I take after my dad's side, of course. We Tylers are known for our pleasant tempers."

Hanne didn't quite know what to make of all this. But it was lovely having someone to talk with. "Will you show me how to make a garden?" she asked hopefully.

He nodded, and put his cap back over his short-clipped hair. "Tomorrow's my day off. So I'll come by around ten, if it's all right by you. I'll try and find some compost or something for your patch there."

Nodding amiably, he loped off without another word.

Paul came home a little earlier that evening, but he was silent and absentminded. Hanne had a funny feeling that he was waiting for her to ask questions, so he could then say something nasty. She served his dinner without a word and went to bed immediately after washing the dishes.

If he wants to talk to me, she told herself, he knows I'm here. Let him come to me. I won't run after him.

He came up several hours later and made love to her, but in a distant sort of way, as if trying to do her a favor. Hanne felt lonelier than on the nights when he had not come home at all.

He had left before she woke up the next morning. He hadn't even made himself a cup of coffee. For some reason this depressed her. It was as if he had stopped living in the house.

But the sun was shining, and she felt happier when she remembered her funny GI, Rip Tyler, and his promise to help her plant her garden. She dressed in her prettiest cotton dress, felt silly, and changed into the least attractive one, a brown and white striped nurse's uniform Paul had given her for working around the house in. It had a lot of stains that wouldn't come out anymore in the wash, and it seemed the right thing for gardening.

She made up carefully, putting on a thick layer of pancake makeup and lashings of lipstick and mascara, looked in the mirror, and hastily washed it all off.

I'm acting crazy, she decided. Like a woman waiting for a lover, not like me at all, waiting for a friend to help me plant a garden.

Determined to behave sensibly, she mopped the kitchen, and finally decided to do something nice for Paul, to get rid of the lilac tree for him. She didn't quite see why getting rid of it had suddenly become her problem, but she did want to do something to please him.

It was every bit as heavy now as it had been when they had carried it in together. Humping it along inch by inch, she managed to maneuver it toward the front door. Her hair was hanging around her face in strands and she was soaked in sweat.

Straightening up and rubbing the small of her back, she found herself looking up into Rip's face. He looked back and forth from her to the tree, and shook his head.

"I'm not going to make a guess," he said. "You tell me what you're doing."

"I'm just trying to put this tree outside," Hanne explained, putting her weight against it and budging it another few inches. "It was lovely a couple of days ago, but now it's shedding."

"Well, a tree doesn't belong in a house," Rip said peacefully. "Figures, doesn't it? If you'll just step aside, I'll heft it for you. Now, if you don't mind my saying so, that's a mighty fine tub you have there." He deposited the planter in front of the steps and started pulling the tree out of it.

"What are you doing?" Hanne demanded nervously. "I've got to get rid of that tree. It's messy."

"Only because it's in the wrong place. Now, if we were to plant it somewhere, it could grow into something nice. I'll take it with me and find a place for it."

"Do you always rescue trees?" Hanne stared in amazement, as he tenderly wrapped the bare roots in sacking and hoisted it into the back of his jeep.

"Only when I get the chance," Rip admitted. "But now we have that tub. I've been thinking it'd be nice if we had some sort of container to plant your garden in."

While she watched, almost breathless with delight and excitement, he produced a large sack from the depths of the jeep and started filling the tub with rich, black soil that smelled unmistakably of horse.

"You wouldn't believe how hard it is to get good manure in this town," Rip said, looking down at his offering with pride and pleasure. "But I found a stable where they tend racehorses—prettiest horses I ever did see. Well, it took quite some dickering, but it's ours now."

Hanne squatted down beside the tub and ran her hands through the soil. Rip nodded sociably.

"I can see you've got the right feeling for growing things." He folded his long legs and hunkered down beside her. "Some people just think of a garden as a mess of pretty flowers and giant tomatoes, but this is where it starts. Good soil."

"It's lovely," Hanne said. "It feels so—so alive."

He nodded. "That's it. You've said it. Now, what did you want to plant?"

Hanne sat back on her heels, her hands buried in the crumbly black soil. "Pretty flowers and giant tomatoes," she admitted. "How do I start?"

Rip took off his cap and scratched his head. It seemed to be his favorite gesture. "You've never grown anything at all?"

"Well, only the dish garden. That came up pretty nice."

Rip nodded. "Yeah, I remember you telling me. Just like Mrs. Clark's. Did I tell you about our topographical map? Mrs. Clark was crazy about that map. It started off as a map of our county, but since every first-grade class worked on it, it became more and more fanciful. The thing took up half the classroom and was supposed to teach us geography."

Hanne nodded seriously. "We learned horticulture through the dish garden."

"Mrs. Clark would have loved you for that. Well, think of this here tub as a big outdoor dish. Meanwhile, I'll bring you some seeds next week. You'll have to start them under a lamp—if you really aim to grow that giant tomato, that is."

"Will you show me how?"

"I'd like that." He grinned at her hopefully. "Are you always home on Saturdays?"

"Always." She looked at him curiously, wondering what he thought of her, the way she was living. He seemed to think it the most natural thing in the world that she should be living inside the army area. He didn't seem to be prying, either. A comfortable man.

He now ambled toward the jeep, paused, and turned back to her. "I don't suppose you'd have time to come and help me plant the tree, Miss Hanne?"

"You got my name right," she said, absurdly pleased.

"'Twarn't nothin'," he said smugly. "I practiced."

"I'd love to come along," Hanne said eagerly. "Only I have to be back in time to cook dinner. About three would be good."

"Can do. You want to put on a coat? It gets chilly the moment you step in the shade."

Hanne ran inside and slipped one of Paul's wool shirts over the wilted cotton dress. She wouldn't have let Paul see her looking like this, but Rip didn't seem to be the kind of man who cared. And anyway, what was correct wear for tree planting? Frau Gerhardt might have been able to advise her.

Driving with Rip Tyler was quite a different experience from being on the road with Paul. For one thing, he talked. There were no bursts of brilliant wit or temperament—he just talked easily, slowly, gave her time to ask questions, and listened to her as if he wanted her to talk, too. It wasn't very exciting, but it was ever so nice.

"You're not going to get into trouble with the folks you work for, are you?" he asked as they drove slowly north toward the bomb-scarred center of the town. "Do they treat you right?"

So that was it. He thought she worked for some army family. Hanne was surprised. Did she look like a maid?

Well, why not? Rip had only seen her in Paul's old fatigues and this wrecked cotton dress. If it didn't bother him, it certainly was all right by her.

"My employer's okay," she said primly. "You see, the house is so small. It's easy to take care of."

It wasn't really lying. After all, she did do all the housework. Paul was delighted not to have Fräulein Stulp underfoot anymore. Thinking of herself as the housekeeper helped her to feel more at ease with Rip.

"My mom worked as a hired girl when she was twelve." To Hanne's surprise, Rip sounded rather proud. Most Europeans would have been embarrassed to admit that they came from a working-class family.

"She was so small, she had to stand on a stool to get at the sink," Rip rambled on. "She's still on the small side. I take after Dad in size. All the Tylers are beanpoles. You should see my brothers. Well, the way it was set up, Mom was supposed to live in with these folks and take care of their baby, do the dishes, and maybe go over the floors with a dustmop now and again, and they were to drop her off at school every day. Turns out they expected her to cook and wash and take care of four little kids, and there was no time for school at all."

"What happened?"

"Well, the teacher noticed she wasn't coming to school, so she went to see my grandfather about it. That's my grandfather Carter. He's a mean man. Now, he married a second time, the durndest woman you ever did see. Was no one could get along with her. And of course he's ornery as a mule—always was. That's why my mom had gone off as hired girl in the first place. Couldn't stand it no more."

"But what happened?"

"I'm telling you. The teacher found out where Mom was working, and she got into that old jalopy of hers and drove right up to the place. It was way out of the way, other side of the mountain. She saw the truck wasn't there and no one outside, so she just walked in and looked around careful like. She said, 'You doing all this work by yourself, Betty Carter?' and Mom said, 'Yes, that's about it.' So the teacher said, 'Pack your bag, You're coming along with me.' 'What about the kids?' Mom said. 'We're taking them along,' said the teacher. So they did."

"Well?"

"You mean what happened to the kids? I guess the parents got them back by and by. Mom never explained that part of it."

"No. I mean what happened to your mom after that?"

Rip grinned. "She stayed with the schoolteacher, but not as a hired girl. Sort of got adopted. Years later, when she was getting married to my dad, Grandpa Carter wanted to get into the act and make like a father. But Mom wasn't having any. That little old-maid schoolteacher walked her down the aisle and gave her away."

Hanne sniffed a little. "That's sweet."

"I don't know about sweet," Rip said seriously. "But it just goes to show—the things that can happen when you hire yourself out. You gotta be careful."

The Tiergarten was a shabby-looking park in the center of town. It was difficult to imagine what it had looked like with trees and bushes growing.

"Chopped everything down for firewood," Rip explained. "Can't blame them, but it *is* a mess, isn't it?"

"It looks sad," Hanne said, looking at the wilderness of tree stumps.

"Well, we're going to do our bit to get it back to normal," Rip assured her, producing a folded shovel from the clutter of tools in the back of the jeep. "Now, help me pick a good spot."

"What is a good spot?" It all looked pretty desolate to her.

They considered this together, and were soon joined by a German policeman who seemed to consider it his duty to object at first but was subsequently drawn into the project. Slowly, they were joined by a woman pushing a baby carriage piled with bundles, a one-legged man holding a small child by the hand, two old ladies clutching onto each other for support, and a schoolboy in short leather pants. All became involved. Rip had every opinion translated by Hanne and listened with respectful interest to every point of view. Finally, the perfect spot was decided upon. The little lilac tree was placed into a fine, large hole, and some of the precious horse manure was added to the soil. The schoolboy offered to fetch a bucket of water, and everyone looked very pleased about the whole thing. Rip shook hands all around and gave everyone two cigarettes, even the boy. There was much bowing, smiling, and nodding, and soon they were alone again.

"Do you think it was right to give cigarettes to that little boy?" Hanne was mildly bothered.

"I don't suppose the old ladies smoke either. They'll just trade them off for coffee or a bit of candy."

Hanne knew all about cigarettes being used as money, but the idea of giving them away like this was new to her. Paul didn't hand out cigarettes. He was rather stingy with them, though he was so generous with other things.

"Is our tree going to grow big and strong?" It was terribly important to her that their little tree survive.

Rip scratched his head. "It's not going to stay a tree. I don't know why it was ever pruned back to look like one. It's all right to cut a plant back to keep it healthy, but lilac wants to be a bush. Turn it into something else, and it gets stressed. That's probably why it got to be so puny—'though keeping it indoors didn't help any."

Until Rip mentioned it, Hanne had known but not registered that there was something odd about the tree. So much of life in Berlin had a surreal cast. "So now it has a chance to grow into a big, strong bush." It was terribly important to Hanne that the lilac branch out and flower naturally again.

"It just might." He caught the wistful look on her face and corrected himself. "Sure it'll make it. We've liberated it. It'll grow. Maybe we should come back now and again and see to it. Would you like that?"

"Yes, please." Hanne felt oddly happy.

"Next Saturday, then. How soon can you get off?"

She did a bit of planning. "I can be ready by ten."

"Tell you what. I'll pick you up at ten and we can have a picnic, if the weather holds. We can have lunch right here by the tree, and there'll still be enough time to get your seeds started."

Rip was so easy to talk to, on the way back, Hanne found herself telling him about the orphanage, and especially Sister Celestine.

"That's not a German name."

She nodded. "She isn't a German nun. She's French. The order sent her in exchange for a German teacher. So we got to learn French."

"Fancy." He whistled admiringly. "You speak real good English, too."

"The Ursulines are very good teachers," Hanne said with some pride. "And Sister Celestine was the best."

"You really liked her, didn't you?"

"I loved her." She felt again the warmth that flowed from the rather dumpy figure of the French nun, the energetic way she dealt with small problems and her sensitive restraint when faced with big ones. If only all the nuns had been like her.

"You been back to see her?"

"No." She could hardly explain to him that she had taken Sister Celestine's purse. And it hadn't even been her own money. Nuns had no money of their own. It belonged to the community and was probably earmarked for school supplies. Compared with the things she had done since—living with Paul and all that—it wasn't a terrible sin. But it made leaving the convent quite final.

"I'm never going back," she said.

Rip was quiet for a moment. "I went back to see Mrs. Clark on my last leave. Would you believe someone had ruined my part of the county map? I'd taken a lot of trouble with that. It was our side of the mountain, and I'd marked out Uncle Charlie's old place as pretty as can be. Used green modeling clay for the top meadow. And some kid had mushed it down and put a creek across the middle. Now Uncle Charlie's place doesn't have that creek. I was real mad."

It was strange how Rip could say one thing and you could plainly hear him saying something else altogether. "You think I should go back?"

He smiled. "I've always found it best to finish things. You're not finished with those nuns yet, are you?"

"Finished," she said, and her voice sounded rather thin in her own ears. "All in the past."

"Well, that's all right, then," Rip said. "I just thought— But you know best. Don't fret about it."

He rattled on amiably about a number of ordinary things—the kinds of flowers compact enough to grow in the tub and a miniature tomato they might be able to get. Gradually she relaxed.

"Well, what do you know?" he said, seeing a jeep parked in front of the house. "Your boss is home early, or is his wife driving?"

Hanne jumped out hurriedly. "I'll have to hurry. Goodbye and thanks."

"Next Saturday at ten?"

"Yes—and thank you."

He grinned. "Where I come from, the boys say thank you, and the young ladies say you're welcome."

"You're welcome," Hanne flung over her shoulder and ran into the house.

❧ *Chapter 7*

Paul was lounging on the couch looking irritable.

"Where have you been? I've been waiting for hours."

"I wasn't expecting you. I went to plant the lilac tree. It was dying."

"Well, at least you got rid of it. Why didn't you toss out the tub at the same time?" He sounded slightly more pleasant.

Hanne hastily made him a martini, just the way he had shown her, and handed it to him as a peace offering. "I'm keeping the tub to grow flowers in."

"Okay, that'll be nice." Paul took a sip. "Good martini you make. Want one for yourself?"

She shook her head and sat down opposite. For the first time he noticed her clothes. "For God's sake, get cleaned up. And kindly ask me before you take my shirts. What have you got all over yourself?"

"Horse manure," she said, squinting down at her dirt-encrusted legs.

"Not funny," said Paul, eyeing her with distaste. "How often do I have to clean you up? Take a bath and put on that high-necked wool dress. We're going to church tonight."

"Oh, no." Hanne shrank away. "I'm not going to church—not ever again."

"You'll like this one," he assured her. "Russian Orthodox, not Catholic, and it's the Easter service."

"Easter? It's not Easter today."

"Russian Easter. Hop to it and get clean. It's a lovely church service and there'll be one hell of a party afterward."

When they got there the church was dark and crowded. Hanne felt rather than saw the crowds pressing around them. The chanting was monotonous and almost unbearably sad. Yet it was not a hopeless kind of sadness. There was a sense of expectation.

Paul settled down beside her with a sigh of contentment. After having hustled her into the church, he seemed happy just to sit and wait.

Nothing happened for a long time, and she was beginning to feel uneasy. She always felt bad in church. All the terrors were waiting there for her: the shame of being Jewish, the guilt for being so bad and worthless. But there was no terror in this church. It was quite different. She looked at the faces around her. They were all turned toward the altar with intense longing. Something wonderful was coming, and they were happy to be there, together in the dark, waiting for it. She felt it too, a hopefulness.

Suddenly she remembered the good part of church, the marvelous quiet she had felt when the nuns sang. Plainchant it was called, and it was as clean and unadorned as the nuns' lives. So it hadn't been all pain and ugliness. Perhaps it was safe to look back after all.

As her eyes became accustomed to the darkness, she was able to examine the faces around her individually.

One woman especially caught her attention, her old, tired face turned up rapt, with an air of excitement and passion. Hanne looked at Paul, but he was staring steadily at the darkened altar, ignoring everything else. Then he, too, leaned forward, almost hungrily.

The chanting had taken on a more urgent tone, and he grabbed her hand, holding it tightly. "Now," he said, as if releasing a breath he had held back for hours.

At first Hanne could see nothing at all, but she became aware of a swell of happiness, and a filtering of light throughout the church. It really was getting brighter.

Paul pressed a candle into her hand and made her hold it up. The man in front of her turned with a joyful smile to light her candle, murmuring something that sounded happy, to which Paul replied in Russian. Responding to his gesture, she turned and lit a candle behind her. The same phrases were exchanged.

Gradually the whole church was alive with dancing candlelight, and the two phrases repeated over and over formed a happy humming like a swarm of bees.

"What are they saying?"

Paul held her hand tightly. His face looked calm and happy. "Christ is risen," he whispered. "And the answer is 'Truly risen.' Now we are all glad together. Can you feel it?"

"Yes," she said. The happiness was inside her and all around her. She stopped trying to understand it and let herself be swept away by the lovely emotion.

The altar was now brilliantly lit and the organ started thundering out a glorious, joyful hymn. A procession paced regally down the center aisle, consisting of four bearded priests—two carrying banners, one bearing an enormous candelabrum, and the last, an old man with the longest, whitest beard she had ever seen, holding up an icon. They passed close enough to touch, close enough to see their faces. They looked almost drunk with joy.

The congregation followed the priests outside and broke into excited chatter. Hanne was grabbed and kissed repeatedly, by men, by women, all complete strangers, all exuberantly joyful. It was like a carnival.

"Now to the princess's flat," said Paul, grabbing her elbow. "I promised you a wild party, didn't I?"

She looked at him, amazed. The ecstasy was wiped off his face. He was very much his own man again. She hated to leave the celebrating crowd. There was such a feeling of shared delight. It was like belonging to a big, loving family. Hanne clung to the comforting warmth of being included in the magic.

But Paul had already lost interest. He wanted only to move on. She allowed herself to be guided through the crowd of celebrants to the car. It hadn't really struck her before that they weren't driving the jeep tonight. She commented on this now, and Paul looked pleased.

"I wondered why you hadn't said anything. Nice, isn't it?"

"Is it yours?"

He laughed and tweaked her ear. "No more than the jeep was. Let's say it's been assigned to me, and in the nick of time. Look in the back."

The back was piled high with boxes. "Couldn't have left that in an open jeep, could I?"

"Presents for the princess?'

He laughed oddly. "Why, yes, of course."

However, when they got to the apartment house, he took out only one box and gave her two small bags to carry.

"How about the rest?" she asked. "I could take more if you want to load me up."

"You've got enough to carry," he said. "We'll get the rest later."

The door opened to reveal the biggest, wildest party she had ever seen, even at the princess's flat. Some of the furniture had been taken out of the salon and the dining room—piled in the bedrooms, she found out later— and the dining table had been extended to its full length. Two dozen people could have sat down, but no one was sitting. The table, with its heavy damask cloth, was loaded with food and drink, and the guests milled about eating and talking, and doing a great deal of kissing.

Hanne kissed the princess with real pleasure. The dear old soul was dressed amazingly in what appeared to be a brocade tent, and almost bursting with pride and joy.

"It's a dream come true," she whispered in her harsh voice, looking around the room. "The midnight feast, just as I remember it from my childhood. Isn't it beautiful?"

"Was it always like this?"

The old woman smiled. "Was anything ever quite as wonderful as we remember it? How about you? Don't you remember things more splendid than they possibly could have been?"

Hanne shook her head. "I wish I had memories like that, but mine are mostly bad. There are so few good ones—I hope those at least are real. Otherwise I'd have nothing."

"But that's wonderful," the princess assured her. "That means all the best things are still ahead of you." The princess kissed her again, touching her soft old face to Hanne's. "I love you, child," she murmured. "Have Paul bring you here more often."

As she milled about, Hanne noticed that many of the guests were familiar, Mimi and Petya and their crowd. Not Renée, thank God, but surprisingly the Russian colonel, and with him a tall, thin man with a narrow, handsome face who attached himself to Hanne in a rather determined way. She could not get rid of him.

"You must learn to drink vodka properly," he instructed her, offering her a tiny glass of the ice-cold liquid together with a slice of black bread with a piece of fish upon it.

She made no move to accept either. For one thing she liked neither the man nor the refreshments he offered, and she certainly had no intention of getting drunk just to be polite.

"This is a Russian party," he said with a smile. "You must take a bite of bread and herring, and then you swallow the vodka. Try it—it's good."

"Your German is excellent," Hanne commented, ignoring the food he was offering her.

He shrugged and followed his own advice, bolting first bread, then vodka in two gulps. "Ahhh," he said. "That's excellent. You really should try it. It's real vodka, you know. My friend Colonel Arpov brought it."

"How kind of him." Hanne wondered how to rid herself of this persistent new admirer. She didn't really like him, and she wanted to talk to Mimi, who was sitting disconsolately in a corner, apparently in the process of getting drunk as fast as possible. Her eyes were roving about with a hopeless air of looking for something or someone. In spite of her fixed smile, she looked sad.

Catching Hanne's eye, she got up and started threading her way toward their side of the room. She was a little unsteady, but not too obviously drunk yet.

"Dear, dear Honey," she said, catching on to Hanne's arm to steady herself. "You look absolutely marvelous. Doesn't she, Major Kuprin? I can see you think so, too." She took the glass the major handed her and sipped it with an affectation of girlish reluctance. Hanne felt pity for her, as well as a strong urge to slap her.

"The major told me you should gulp it—not sip it." Would that man never go away? Mimi was simpering at him.

"Russians gulp," the major corrected her. "Germans sip. And beautiful young ladies pass it up altogether. Such a sad waste."

Mimi made a face at this. Not being included among the young and beautiful was obviously an affront to her vanity. It really was a bit rude of the major, especially since Mimi was not looking her best tonight. Her skin was puffy and blotched-looking, and her makeup too thick and badly put on. The slinky silk dress was too tight. It showed off a lot of depressing little folds and bulges.

Mimi finished her drink and at once reached for another one, which the major handed her with a rather sardonic smile. Hanne decided she really disliked him. His eyes were too close together. He belonged to the new Russia, not the one of the candle-lit church. The loveliness of the Easter service was already slipping sway from her.

There was no indication that Paul was planning to extricate her. He was huddled in a corner with the Russian colonel, talking ten to the dozen and looking pleased and excited. She was definitely on her own.

"Mimi, I must go fix my hair," she said desperately. "Will you show me where I can do it?"

"But you know the flat." Mimi was either being deliberately unhelpful or she hated to get too far from the drinks.

"Everything is changed around tonight. Please come and keep me company." Firmly gripping Mimi's hand in her left, she took a full glass in her right and, using it like a carrot, drew her companion along with her. The major noted her stratagem, and his sardonic laughter followed them out of the room.

"Aren't you having fun?" Mimi said, sipping her drink in a darkened bedroom, stuffed with furniture and coats. "You should be having a good time. Major

Kuprin really likes you—the way he looks at you. And you do look nice tonight, very well turned out. You'd be wise not to discourage the major. It's good for Paul to see he's not the only one."

"But I don't like him, Mimi. Who is he, anyway, and why is he here?"

Mimi looked vague. "Oh, you know these Russians—so sentimental. He and Colonel Arpov spend a lot of time here lately. They say it reminds them of Russia. I suppose they're homesick."

"I'd say Major Kuprin is the least sentimental man I've ever met," Hanne said firmly. "I don't know about the colonel, but that young man is after something."

"After you, maybe? Fishing for compliments, aren't you?" Mimi's voice was not quite friendly. "Look. I want to go back to the party. Haven't you finished fussing with your hair?"

Frustrated, Hanne made as long a business of running a comb through her hair as she could, then took a few more minutes to straighten the seams of her stockings. Mimi watched enviously.

"Are those nylons? Petya said he would get me some, but he never did. All my silk stockings are gone, worn to shreds. And they say nylon is much better."

"They're very nice," Hanne agreed. "I'll get you some if you like."

Mimi's mood immediately became more friendly. "That's sweet of you, just sweet. I always said to Petya: Honey is a real friend. I'd like the black mesh ones, if you can get hold of those for me. They're very sexy, aren't they?"

"I'll certainly try. I haven't seen any black mesh nylons myself," Hanne said wearily. "Just keep them away from heat. They melt if you put them on a radiator to dry."

"Fancy that. I had a maid who always ironed my stockings." Mimi's expression was wistful. "Did I ever tell you that I had a maid?"

Hanne sighed. "That must have been very nice."

Mimi's chin was thrust out defiantly. "She took care of all my things. I had so many clothes. One wall of my bedroom was all wardrobes, built in, like they have in America. And for every outfit, there were matching shoes and gloves and handbags and hats. I was very thin then." The edges of her mouth drooped.

"Well, you are very pretty now, and lots of people prefer women with curves," Hanne said, again fighting the pity and irritation. "Petya likes you the way you are now, doesn't he?"

"He's Russian. They don't go for thin women." Mimi didn't sound too cheered. "But then again—look at you and the major. He certainly doesn't seem to mind all those bones sticking out."

"Just being polite." Hanne disclaimed the doubtful compliment.

Mimi gave a sad little gulp of a laugh. "You've changed," she said, struggling to her feet and weaving toward the door. "You were a little mouse, a dear little country mouse, so pure and good, and now you are—What exactly are you now, Honey?"

"I am the same," Hanne said. "The clothes are different. That's all."

"Ah, the clothes." Mimi turned, momentarily diverted. "Paul certainly has tricked you out nicely. He's a clever boy. You're lucky. Just see you hang on to him. You're pretty enough, in an unripe sort of way, but you'll find that's not enough."

The exchange left a bad taste in Hanne's mouth. She felt unclean. It was as if Mimi, with her foolishness and bad temper, had touched her love for Paul and left a stain on it. Obviously, as far as Mimi was concerned, she was just a kept woman. Love, real love, did not exist in Mimi's world. You made the best of your looks and then you peddled them for a salary or a wedding ring, or for clothes and jewelry. It was all quite straightforward and practical, and there seemed to be a lot of people who were satisfied with it. But it had nothing to do with the feeling she had for Paul.

The major was waiting for her, this time with a plate of food. It looked wonderful and she found she was hungry, so she accepted this offering. He seemed delighted.

"I'm glad to see you're human after all, Miss Honey. I was beginning to fear that you would turn out to be an ingeniously constructed robot. You know—like Coppelia. Just a lovely doll, not a human girl."

After the humiliating conversation with Mimi, he didn't seem quite as bad as she'd thought. The compliments were soothing, and his eyes were really quite nice, not so very close together after all. She smiled her best smile at him, and he reacted much as men usually did. He moved closer to her, and brushed his mouth against her ear, as if accidentally. She giggled.

"I have offended you?"

"No, it felt nice. And anyway it's the sort of thing people do at this kind of party, isn't it?" He really was rather attractive.

Taking this as encouragement, he took her hand and carried it to his mouth, touching his lips to each finger in turn. It seemed playful rather than seductive, and his eyes were very watchful. She withdrew her hand and moved a step away from him.

"Who is Coppelia? Is she in an opera?"

"No, a ballet. Would you like to see it? The German ballet isn't much, but the Bolshoi is coming to the Staatsoper soon. I can find out if they are doing *Coppelia*."

"How lovely." Hanne forgot all about discouraging the major and stepped closer to him again. "Would you let us know?"

"Us?" He raised an eyebrow. "Does that mean I have to include your friend Paul in the invitation? I don't suppose I could persuade you to come by yourself?"

She shook her head emphatically.

He sighed a rather theatrical sigh. "Well then, I will settle for half a loaf, which they say is better than none. Perhaps we should tell him that we plan an evening at the ballet."

"I'm sure he'll be pleased," Hanne said, but it sounded doubtful even to her own ears. The major laughed at her. He seemed to find her hilariously amusing, no matter what she said.

She looked around for Paul, but he was not in sight; neither was Colonel Arpov. Still tailed by the major, Hanne made her way across the room to the princess, who had at last given in and collapsed into her upholstered chair. Her smile was brilliant, but she looked tired.

"I hope no one can tell that I've taken off my shoes," she confided cheerfully. "I seem to remember that shoes fitted better when I was young—or maybe my feet were more easy to please. Are you having a good time, Honey? You mustn't let the major monopolize you."

"I am a selfish man, Excellency," the major said, bending over her hand. "Forgive me this once."

The princess gave a delighted laugh. "You are so thoroughly Russian. I think I would forgive you almost anything. But you will have to make your excuses to Honey's other admirers. It's really not polite to monopolize the prettiest girl at a party."

Paul joined them at this point, throwing his arm possessively around Hanne's shoulders and glaring at the Russian. After having ignored her all evening, Hanne told herself resentfully, he now seemed annoyed to find her talking to someone else. It wasn't fair.

Even the princess came in for some of his bad temper.

"You're very fanciful tonight, Excellency. So Honey's supposed to be the prize of the evening? I'd say the room's full of pretty women." His voice was sharp with sarcasm. "And of course you're the prettiest young thing of them all, Lydia Ivanovna." He gave a bark of laughter that made the absurd compliment sound downright insulting.

The princess frowned fleetingly but recovered fast. "Really!" she murmured, then turned away.

That was beastly, Hanne thought, feeling surprised and upset. He hurt her. And she's such an old darling, and so kind to us. She hated the way he was holding her, too. His fingers dug into her shoulder. It was not an affectionate grip.

The major was watching attentively, and Hanne thought he was looking at them curiously, like a scientist staring down at a slide of interesting microbes. "Miss Honey has been kind enough to express an interest in Russian ballet, and I hope to get tickets for *Coppelia* when the Bolshoi comes to Berlin. I trust you will join us, Paul Denisovitch?"

Paul gave a small, stiff bow. "With great pleasure. Although I was hoping to see *Petrushka*. It's my favorite. I hope they'll be doing that, too."

The major smiled into Hanne's eyes. "Why can't we see both ballets? Dolls for you, Miss Honey, and puppets for your friend."

There was no mistaking the angry tightening of Paul's grip. Hanne almost cried out, but managed to control herself and turn her gasp into an expression of polite pleasure. As soon as the major turned away, she wriggled out of the painful hold.

"What's the matter with you?" she whispered angrily. "First the princess and now me. What's wrong with you tonight?"

She thought Paul went white round the nostrils, but he said nothing. He did kiss the princess's hand and thanked her rather nicely for the party.

Her tired smile was forgiving. "Ah, my poor Paul Denisovitch. I know how it is with you. I know."

"It was a lovely evening," Hanne said, kissing both painted cheeks. "The Easter service was so beautiful."

The princess was smiling again, but her eyes were moist. "Someday I will tell you—but you must come and visit soon. I'll tell you about Easter when I was a little girl. The blessing of the eggs and the *kulitch*—so beautiful."

"I'll bring her next week," Paul promised. It sounded like a peace offering.

Then turning to Hanne with narrowed eyes, he added, "Next Saturday, okay?"

❧ *Chapter 8*

The back of the car was empty. All of the boxes seemed to have been unloaded at some point during the evening. Paul made no comment on that. In fact, he remained silent and sunk in thought all the way home. Hanne felt vaguely guilty. Obviously she had done something to upset Paul. But what?

Not until they were in bed did he really look at her, and then it was to apologize in a roundabout way, with-out quite explaining what he was talking about.

"I didn't mean to hurt you, Honey, you know that, don't you?" he said gently, between kisses. "I never, ever want to hurt you—never."

"But you did," she said sadly. "And you hurt the princess. Why?"

He held her gently, tenderly, and his voice came out soft and muffled by her hair. "Forgive me."

"Why?"

He let her go and faced her with tears in his eyes.

"You are so hard, Honey. I never realized how hard you are."

She felt hurt and confused. Paul was the one who went around hurting people and then he said she was hard. It made no sense.

"Well, I'm not going to cry, if that's what you mean," she said, moving away from him. "You made me cry once, and I told you then. No one is going to make me cry ever again."

He got out of bed and stood by the window with his back to her. Every line of it looked stiff and unhappy. She had to hold on to herself not to run and try to comfort him. But how could she, without seeming to be telling him that it was all right to hurt people? And it wasn't. Not even for him.

Finally he turned with a decisive gesture. "All right," he said crisply, without any trace of emotion, "I'll tell you." He seemed to have forgotten his tears and his anger as well. His tone was all practical business. "I think I've underestimated you, Honey," he explained calmly. "You can be of more use to me if you know what I'm trying to do. Now, about tonight...."

Hanne felt chilled, but she sat up in bed and eyed him attentively.

"You probably didn't realize that I run a little business, or did you? Well, how did you think we could afford to live as we do? On my salary alone? No. I pick up supplies and distribute them. Lots of people do it. I just do it more intelligently. You understand, don't you?"

"You're a black marketeer?" Hanne felt cold and sick.

Paul glared at her. "If you want to be crude—yes. And may I point out to you that you eat black market food and wear black market clothes? Don't be such a ninny. Everybody deals. The money isn't worth the paper it's printed on. What do you expect people to do?"

"I don't understand," she said in a small, scared voice.

"Look, Honey," he said patiently. "It's like this: Let's say you have an apple tree, and want to sell the apples. Now, would you sell them to a shop that gives you worthless paper money, or would you trade them to me for something you can use—say, a sack of potatoes?"

"But that's just barter," she said, astonished. "There's nothing wrong with that."

"Of course it isn't wrong," he said, slapping his hands together. "But the people who print the money don't like it, see? Puts them right out of business. That's what you call black market—a bartering system. Now do you understand?"

She nodded doubtfully.

Paul looked satisfied and went on in a stronger voice. "I've been dealing with the Germans, the English, and the French, but 'til we lucked out with Colonel Arpov I had no contacts with the Russian army at all. So that was a real windfall, and he's very interested. We had arranged a delivery tonight, and then that blasted major came along."

"So that's why you don't like him?" Hanne said brightly.

Paul groaned and made a gesture of pulling out his hair. "Heaven grant me patience," he said dramatically, then, with a sudden change of mood, grinned at her. "All right, my lovely idiot-child, we'll start with lesson number one. The colonel and I had business to conduct. Right? The major was in our way. Now, good luck smiled on this deserving soul. The major fell for you in a big way, and you, my clever little love, kept him out of our hair. Business concluded."

"Then why were you so angry?"

He sighed. "All right. Lesson number two. The major is no special friend of Colonel Arpov's. He was there to keep an eye on him. Oh, for goodness sake, don't look so shocked. Your admirer is an agent, a spy."

Hanne nodded calmly. "Yes, I can believe that."

Paul looked pleased. "Good. Now you see my problem. How would an honest man behave if his girl was being monopolized by someone else all evening? Would he say, 'How nice of you to keep out of my way?' No! He would get hopping mad and be as rude and obnoxious as possible. Right?"

Hanne frowned. "I suppose so. But that still leaves a question, doesn't it? Why did the major follow me around instead of doing his job, watching the colonel?"

"Good girl," Paul said approvingly. "You are thinking straight now. There is, of course, always the possibility that he fell for you in such a big way that he forgot everything but your lovely eyes. Nice if it were so, but I doubt it."

"So do I," Hanne said glumly.

He laughed at her. "I wouldn't blame him if he did. You looked like a million dollars tonight. Poor old Mimi was green with envy, the silly little bitch. But our major is too well trained to indulge himself like that. He was hoping to get at me through you. Well, we're going to fool him, beat him at his own game."

She drew the covers around her and shivered. "I'm not clever enough to play games like that. Please leave me out of it, Paul."

"You're in it now," he said cheerfully, all his bad temper mysteriously evaporated. "And you are smarter than you realize, smarter than I realized. Honeychild, you and I are going places together. We can work as a team."

She couldn't stop shivering.

"You want to help me, don't you? All this scrubbing and cooking you've been doing—who needs it? We can get any old bimbo to take care of the house. You're special. You're going to be my good right hand."

She leaned her head against his chest and felt his heart hammering with excitement. His arms felt warm and strong around her.

"My good right hand," he repeated. "My clever, lovely little love."

Fräulein Stulp returned, stringy and sour-tempered as ever, and looked around critically, as if to check on Hanne's housekeeping. Her sharp eyes noted and disapproved of every little change Hanne had made. With an air of outraged proprietorship, she removed a vase from the coffee table and placed it on the mantelpiece, twitched the heavy drapes back and folded them neatly into the cords that acted as tiebacks, then gasped with indignation when she saw that the sheer curtains that had hung behind them had been taken down.

"The place needs a great deal of straightening up," she said with a sniff.

Hanne started to explain and apologize, but Paul cut her off.

"Miss Honey has arranged the house the way she likes it. And the way she likes it is the way it's going to stay. So you can just damn well put everything back the way you found it."

The German woman looked venomous, but started toward the kitchen without a word. Hanne felt the pain behind her anger.

"Let her do it her way," she begged. "Please, let her. It doesn't mean anything to me, and it does to her."

"She forgets that she's a servant," Paul said irritably. "You can't let her walk all over you. But all right, we'll let her have it her way—up to a point."

That point was reached when the housekeeper came to the tub of soil and began to muscle it down the path toward the garbage can. Hanne flew after her in a passion.

"No, that stays. That's my garden."

A surprised smile lit up the dour face. "A garden? You're going to grow something in that?"

"Yes, flowers and maybe tomatoes." For the first time since she had met her, there was a crack in the German woman's armor.

"Did you ever have a garden here?" Hanne asked.

"Not here. You can see, there's no real soil. But my friend was born on a farm. In summer we would go to his parents' place and I worked in the garden." Her eyes were dreamy. "I liked to pick beans. You know how they train them up on three sticks that are tied together at the top? You stand underneath and it's like being in a green tent. Beautiful."

"I've never had a garden," Hanne said, pleased at having broken through the woman's defenses. "Perhaps you can tell me how to do it right. But look here, I have a friend who's going to bring me seeds. He's coming on Saturday—only I won't be here."

"Send him a message."

Hanne blushed. "I don't know how to find him. He's a GI. His name's Rip Tyler, but I don't know how to get hold of him."

"And Mr. Karinof can't help?" The German woman's smile was a little sly. "I see. Well, I can be here when he comes. Leave me a letter for him. And he can always contact you through me."

Hanne thanked her, uncomfortably aware that a new interpretation had been placed on her friendship with Rip. Still, she decided there was no harm in letting the poor old thing fantasize a bit. She seemed to have so little fun in her life. Let her have one small scandal, even if it was an imaginary one. After all, it didn't hurt anyone to let Fräulein Stulp think Hanne was having an affair with another man.

Saturday, as promised, Paul dropped her off at the princess's, helped her carry several boxes upstairs, and left after a few minutes' polite conversation.

It was odd being in the shabby, overstuffed flat again. Every sign of the party had vanished, except the stale scent of spilled wine and tobacco. The princess was dressed in her usual tent-shaped dress, only this was the spring version, pink and yellow flowers on gray silk. Instead of the felt slippers, she had bandages on her feet.

"The party was too much for my poor toes," she said pointing to the wrappings. "Five hours in hard leather pumps was a dreadful mistake. But it was worth it, wasn't it?"

"It was a lovely party." Hanne took off her coat and untied the silk scarf she wore over her head. "Now that I'm here, what can I do to make myself useful? Shall I do a bit of dusting? Would you like me to brush the carpet again? Or do you have some laundry that I can do?"

"Good heavens, no, you're here as a visitor, not to do work."

"But I like to do things. You never made me feel like a servant when I was staying here, just a family member doing her share." She looked around at the piled-up clutter with affection. "Please say you want me to do something useful."

"Very well, then, make tea. Then we can sit and talk. When you were staying here we did not talk enough. I realized that after you left."

"You're going to tell me about Easter when you were a little girl," Hanne reminded her. "You promised. All about blessing the eggs and *kulitch*. What's *kulitch*?"

"We had it here last week. You can't have Easter without it. It's the round bread with the white icing on top."

"Oh, the cake."

"Cake—or bread—depending on how much butter and fruit you can spare. But that doesn't matter, not one bit. It is a symbol—like the *paskha*, the cream-cheese affair that goes with it. Once, when I was small, we went to the house of the priest for the midnight feast. He was a poor man with too many children. Perhaps it is better not to let priests marry—or one should pay them more. But his wife was charming, and they all looked so happy. The *kulitch* was very plain—not a single raisin—but beautiful, decorated all over the top with bits of colored sugar, it glittered like a church window.

"It was such a small house for so many people, and they insisted we sit down on their stove. There were embroidered cushions for us to sit on, and the walls were covered with embroidered tablecloths and towels, yards and yards of linen covered with tiny, bright stitchery. Not a scrap of the wooden wall showed through. They must have emptied out all their chests to make it look so festive. And the priest's wife—all stiff and splendid in twenty petticoats, at least—stood with her hands pressed together and smiled and smiled...."

"That must have been a wonderful Easter," said Hanne.

"Ah, that was the best," said the princess with a sigh. "I remember others later on—with richer *kulitch*, with champagne and caviar, in finer rooms. But I think that was the very best."

"How old were you?"

"Four—or maybe five. Small anyway. My mother seemed huge, wide as well as tall. It was just before Alexey, Petya's father, was born. That is the only way I can recall time. I have these pictures in my mind. I just count the people in the picture. That Easter there were my parents, my mother's maid, my brother's tutor, us children, and our governess—all crowded into that bright little room. And such a sense of joy."

"How many brothers did you have?" Hanne asked.

"Just two," said the princess, "Ilarion and Alexey, and one sister, Sonya. Now they're all gone. Pour me some tea, dear." She was suddenly serious.

Sitting opposite the princess, sipping her strong, black tea out of the glass in the filigree silver holder, Hanne was struck by the intent, gloomy expression on the old woman's face. Of course, she told herself, that was the Russian temperament for you—deep, dark drama. But it made her uneasy all the same. She didn't get the same feeling as when the princess was making one of her fine, enjoyable, emotional scenes. The worry seemed to be real.

"Do tell me more about all the different Easter celebrations in your childhood," Hanna prompted gently. "I've finally figured out why I enjoy those stories so much. You see, I didn't have a real childhood. This way I can live yours secondhand."

"It was a good time for us children." The old woman sighed. "Now I know that it was not a good one for others. You know, Honey, we felt in our family that we were so progressive because we didn't ill-treat our servants. We treated them well, like friends. And we took an interest in the peasants, like going to visit the priest. It was meant as a big favor, and strange as it seems now, the priest seemed to think so, too. We almost thought of ourselves as revolutionaries. But we knew nothing of the misery all around us, nothing at all. And then when the Revolution came, my poor parents couldn't understand what was happening."

Hanne nodded. "Like my grandmother. She always said the Nazis weren't so bad. They were only mean to the nasty Jews, and we weren't even real Jews—we were Germans."

The princess gave a bitter laugh. "Poor woman."

Hanne nodded. "We were really Jews, German or not, and in the end they took her away."

"But they didn't get you." There was satisfaction in the princess's voice.

"Not me, I was hidden by the nuns."

"The dear, good women. Does Paul know about all this?"

Hanne made a helpless gesture. "I don't think he wants to know. I've tried to tell him about myself, but he thinks I'm making up stories. Sometimes I think he likes to pretend I popped out of the water on a shell full grown, like the girl in the painting."

"The Botticelli Venus?" The princess considered her thoughtfully, her head cocked to one side. "Yes you do look a bit like her, but with more blood in you—you know, earthier."

"Earthier? Oh, yes, I am earthy." Hanne laughed and launched into a happy description of her gardening venture describing the planting of the tree, the horse manure, and the promise of flower seeds.

The princess listened with a smile. "And Paul knows about this?"

"Well, no," Hanne admitted. "It's not that I've tried to keep it from him, but he's given me no opportunity to tell him about it. So he doesn't know yet."

"He offered to bring you here on a Saturday, didn't he? Your friend Rip is only free on Saturdays. A coincidence?"

Hanne shivered. "Why would he be so roundabout? He could have said something, couldn't he? Then I could have explained. Rip is just a friend. It's not a flirtation or anything like that. He can't be jealous of Rip."

The princess continued reminiscing about her childhood, and it was not until the tea things were washed and put away that she got back into her serious mood. "I find this so hard," she said.

"What?" Hanne's mood was light and happy by now, caught up in the princess's golden memories, embellished by distance and imagination.

The old woman frowned. "I must speak to you of Paul. And it is hard because I care for him."

"But so do I," Hanne said eagerly. "I do so love him."

"I was afraid of that, and it is not good."

Hanne drew away, hurt. "Why? I'm not good enough? Because I'm Jewish and have no money?"

"You foolish child, what does that matter? No, it is not good for you. What do you know about him?"

All the steam went out of Hanne. "I know I love him," she said softly. "I know he is a wonderful man, and he is kind. He took me in when I was cold and hungry, and he took care of me. He's good and kind and clever. Isn't that enough?"

"Is he always kind?"

Hanne thought of the tempers and the slap across her face, the long, cold silences when Paul withdrew into his own world. She tried not to think about his hitting her. After all, it had happened just that once, and he had cried afterward.

"He is kind," she said firmly.

"He has never beaten you?" The princess's eyes bored into hers. Hanne shook her head. You couldn't describe a single slap, immediately regretted, as a beating.

The old woman sagged back, looking uneasy but somehow relieved. "I needed to know, Honey. Forgive me for prying. Perhaps I am wrong. Perhaps he is different. But if ever he raises his hand to you, don't wait for the second blow. Come to me at once. I will protect you."

It was said with such force that Hanne had to smile at the idea of the old woman standing between her and some imagined danger. She took the soft old hands, distorted with arthritis, and held them between hers.

"If I'm in trouble, I will come to you. Thank you for caring about me."

The princess looked dissatisfied. "It's not enough," she finally said. "You can be better prepared to fend for yourself if you know about Paul's parents. I knew his mother quite well, and his grandmother was a dear friend."

"I didn't know that." Hanne leaned forward eagerly. "I had no idea. Did you know Paul when he was a little boy?"

The princess shook her head. "No, they moved to Vienna before he was born. But I was at his parents' wedding. Petya's father, Alexey, my younger brother, held the crown over the groom's head. It was a beautiful ceremony. Paul's mother wore a veil of old lace, all handmade. It was worth a fortune even then. She looked beautiful. Paul is much like her."

Hanne listened enchanted. "Tell me more about the wedding."

"I get so easily distracted," the old woman said mournfully. "Always I start and then what I have to say gets away from me. It is so hard. It hurts so much."

Hanne waited, watching her friend struggle with herself.

"Bad blood," she said harshly. "Paul's father was not the man for an innocent, soft girl. He destroyed her, as he destroyed other women, too. In the end she killed herself, but who could blame her? Her life was misery."

"How do you know?" Hanne couldn't look away from the tortured face of the old princess.

"She wrote to me. I was her godmother, you know. That means a lot among Russians. And my friend, her own mother, was dead by then. She had no one else to turn to. She wrote long letters. I wrote again and again, begging her to leave this man and come to me. But she was too weak. I should have gone and fetched her away. I failed her."

"But she could have come, if she had wanted to." Hanne tried to imagine a woman submitting to ill treatment without defending herself or trying to get away. It made her strangely angry, not only with the man but with the victim, too.

"But she loved him," the princess said ironically. "She so loved him. She absolutely believed that she deserved to be beaten. She took it as a proof of his love, that he cared enough to try and correct her behavior."

"No." Hanne said angrily, and it came out like a battle cry. "No—no—no."

The princess sat back, satisfied. "Good. You will not fall into that trap. You are now armed. I have done what I could."

"But whatever makes you think Paul would behave the same way?" Hanne felt quite indignant. "He's not a bit like that."

"Perhaps not." The princess smiled faintly. "But remember, Honey, we learn about love from our parents. He learned, when he was very small, too small to make judgments, that women are weak and despicable, and that it is right for men to hit them. If he wants to feel like a man, he may need to be brutal. If he is gentle, he may feel weak and helpless, like a woman. I care for him, but I wish you didn't love him."

"But I do love him, and he is good."

The princess nodded. "Then I'm content," she said. "Perhaps I worry for nothing. I am sure he does care for you—look how jealous he was of that handsome Major Kuprin That's a good sign, they say."

❧ *Chapter 9*

"And what did you talk about all day?" Paul seemed to be a splendid mood, had been talking exuberantly all the way home. He appeared utterly relaxed, and the question caught Hanne by surprise.

"About Russian Easter and the Revolution," she said, looking straight at him. "And about your parents."

There was a flicker in Paul's eyes and he turned away. After a while, he gave a small laugh. "She is a good old soul," he said lightly, "but she does love to gossip."

"She told me about the wedding, about Petya's father holding the crown and the handmade veil your mother wore. It must have been beautiful."

Paul looked relieved. If anything else had been discussed, he obviously did not want to know about it. He started talking very fast and loud about his mother's clothes, which he remembered as being very elegant and fashionable, and about the way she wore her hair.

"It was black and very thick and she braided it and wound it around her head like a crown. It was quite lovely and regal-looking, but the poor woman could not get a hat to fit on top of it, and hats were important in her world. She would drag me along from one milliner to another, but all those charming creations perched on top of that mass of hair like little bumps. So finally she had hats made with the crown cut away, and fitting over the head like the rim of a saucer. It was fine while she was standing up. When she sat down, of course, everyone could see all that hair bulging up behind the trimming."

"Why didn't she cut it short?" Hanne asked curiously. "Or at least a little bit shorter?"

"Cut her hair?" He gave an odd snort of laughter. "My father would never have permitted that. If she had cut off a single centimeter, he would have killed her."

Dinner was grim. Hanne poked unhappily at the watery stew on her plate. Fräulein Stulp might be a great legal brain and an energetic cleaning woman, but she certainly did not know how to cook.

Paul glared at the soggy mess as though it were a personal affront. "How did she manage that? Can you eat it? I'm damned if I will."

Hanne thought of the meals she had prepared so lovingly without his ever noticing how good they were. Apparently food caught his attention only when it was bad.

"Cooking doesn't seem to be her special talent. Let's throw it out, shall we? If there are any eggs left, I'll make an omelette."

Paul followed her into the kitchen and looked sulky while she prepared the omelette. He really wasn't being very charming tonight, she decided. Something was on his mind. She wondered if it had anything to do with the princess—or with Rip.

They ate in silence, Hanne waiting in vain for the compliment she felt she deserved for coming up with a meal at a moment's notice. She watched him eat, fascinated by the fastidious way he handled his fork and his habit of dabbing at the corner of his mouth with a napkin after every bite. One of the older nuns had done it, too, probably a prissy little habit left over from her childhood. It was odd to see a young man doing the same thing. She giggled.

"I'm glad you can laugh about it," he started in a huffy voice, then caught himself and laughed, too.

"Bad food isn't tragic," Hanne tried to explain. "No food at all—now that's tragic."

He nodded. "Oh, I've been hungry."

"I never would have guessed that." She leaned forward and tilted up her face to his. "Do you realize I know nothing about you? Tell me about when you were little."

He moved away a fraction. "So that you can then tell me about yourself? No thank you. I do believe you are a gifted liar and it's sure to be a delicious story, but no thanks. I'll let you keep the mystery."

Hanne drew back. "You know something," she said thoughtfully. "You can be awful—an absolute shit."

He exploded. "Where did you pick up that word? Don't you ever say that again. It's vulgar. It's something I don't want to hear from you—ever."

He looked so outraged, so stuffily indignant, that she had to laugh in his face.

"I'll tell you where I picked it up, Paul. From you. You say it all the time."
She gave him a wicked smile. "I learn such a lot of English from you. Soon I'll
speak perfect American." She followed through with a string of choice words,
uttered in her clearest schoolgirl diction. It seemed so comical to her that she felt
sure that Paul would start to laugh, too. But he listened with a tight, cold face
until she began to stammer and came to a stop.

"A charming display," he said coldly. "Do you expect me to applaud? Am
I supposed to find that charming? Let me explain something. A man can use
words that are rough and forceful, and still be a gentleman, especially if he only
uses these words in the presence of a female who does not happen to be a
lady."

Hanne stood up shakily and started stacking the plates, trying to close her
ears to the sound of his voice.

"You can always distinguish a lady," he continued pedantically, "in that she
is able to remain pure and poised under all circumstances. A lady would simply
not hear these words. As for actually using them... When you behave like a
foul-mouthed slut, you deprive yourself of the protection you seem to take for
granted."

Hanne felt something snap. She turned on him and looked him up and
down. "Very well, Paul," she said slowly, "I'll avoid the words that offend you,
the words I've learned from you. I'll phrase it another way, so as not to hurt your
delicate sensibilities. You are an arrogant, mean-spirited, hypocritical, bad-tem-
pered, egotistical snob. I hope you approve of the way I express myself. I believe
all these words are socially acceptable."

She felt better for having said it, but before she got to the kitchen door, Paul
had caught her by the shoulders and swung her around. The plates smashed to
the floor, and she hung in his grasp, too surprised to fight back. He slammed her
against the door frame, then stepped back, letting go of her. Hanne slid down
among the broken plates and stared up at him, sickened by the cold fury on his
face.

Suddenly his face crumpled. "Oh my God," he said, kneeling beside her. "Are
you all right?"

She nodded doubtfully. "I cut myself, but I don't think it's too bad."

He picked her up with immense care and carried her up the stairs. Hanne felt
muddled by the abrupt change in him. He was suddenly the soul of kindness.

"Let me wash it for you."

A gash ran across her left buttock, not very deep, but producing a spectacular amount of blood. Paul's hands were gentle and skillful as he disinfected and bandaged the cut.

"Honey, my little Honey," he said, stroking her hair. "My poor little love. Just lie there and rest. I'll get you some brandy."

She turned over carefully, propped herself up on her elbows, and shook her head.

"No, Paul," she said. "I don't want brandy, and I don't want to rest. I want to know why you behaved like that."

He knelt beside the bed and dropped his head in her lap, a childish, trusting gesture. "I've a rotten temper," he said sadly. "Now and then something happens—like today. And it gets away from me. You must forgive me, darling."

She resisted the urge to run her fingers through his hair. She wanted to hold him, comfort him. He so obviously needed love and comfort. But she held back.

"I can't forgive what I don't understand, Paul," she said quietly. "I love you. I want to understand. Help me."

"If you loved me—" he said, then broke off, confused. "I don't want you to love me."

"Well, you don't seem to have much choice about that." She smiled down at him, unable to maintain her indignation in the face of his absurdity. "That's the way it is. I love you. But I'm not going to let you hit me and just nod my head and say, It's all right, I forgive you, it's forgotten already. Because it's not all right, and I can't forget it."

He got off his knees and sat on the foot end of the bed, facing her.

"You're marvelous," he said in an astonished voice. "What happened to the urchin I rescued? When did you turn into a great lady?"

"So now I'm a lady?" Hanne couldn't resist the jibe.

"Always," he said humbly. "What can I say? There's no excuse for the way I acted. But I was upset. That damned GI of yours—the sergeant."

"I see," Hanne said in a small voice. "Rip was here."

"He didn't introduce himself. Just stood on the doorstep with a box of weeds and a silly grin. Can you imagine how I felt?"

"Oh," Hanne said. "Oh, dear. What did you tell him?"

"Nothing."

"And what did he do?"

"He left." Paul's tone was dry and unhappy. "My least favorite housekeeper, the incomparable Stulp, caught up with him on the sidewalk, and they had a lovely chat. He was smiling as he drove off. Can you imagine how that made me feel?"

Hanne threw herself into his arms, and clung to him, all good intentions gone.

"You felt like shit?" she inquired demurely, settling herself comfortably against him.

"Honey, my Honey," Paul groaned. "If you use those words, I'm going to hit you, and if I hit you I'll hate myself. What's going to happen to us? I'm afraid I'm falling in love with you, and you don't even like me."

❧ *Chapter 10*

Hanne had thought that being loved by Paul would make a great, wonderful change in her life. It didn't. Having admitted it, he never mentioned it again. She waited for some expressions of love, plans for their future together, but Paul was off by himself again.

He took her to a doctor to check on the cut, but made no further reference to the circumstances. The German doctor asked how it had happened, and Paul curtly explained that she had slipped and fallen on a broken plate.

"The cut is clean and will heal well," the doctor told her. "There'll be a scar, of course. I'll put a stitch in it, to keep that to a minimum. Next time, don't wait twenty-four hours before you come in."

There was a big change in her life, but it had nothing to do with love. It came the day after the visit to the doctor, when Paul walked in crowing triumphantly and waving an envelope at her. "I've done it, Honey. You're in."

She eyed the envelope curiously. "You've done what? I'm in where?"

He looked enormously pleased with himself. "Sit down," he ordered. "You are now a bona fide DP, a person with papers proving you to be a Nazi victim. That means you get a ration card, which is worth money, and it means you can be employed at OMGUS—the Office of Military Government, United States. How about that?"

Hanne's head was spinning. "That's wonderful. But are they going to hire me?"

He laughed and waved the envelope at her. "You're hired. Look, it's all in here. Identification, work pass, ration book, affidavits from Rabbi Kalb, from Miss Peterson of the Jewish Relief Committee, and from Colonel Hosterley, all attesting to your high moral character and correct political convictions."

Hanne shook her head, to clear out the cobwebs. Neither Rabbi Kalb's nor Miss Peterson's name meant anything to her, and her acquaintance with Colonel Hosterley was sketchy, to put it mildly. She put out her hand for the envelope and emptied it onto the coffee table. It was an impressive collection of documents. From the middle fell the work pass, and an unfamiliar face looked up at her. The face was round and snub-nosed, with squinty eyes.

"We'll have to replace that," Paul said nonchalantly, picking it up and slipping it into his breast pocket. "We need to get a passport photo of you. I know a place where they'll do it while we wait, and he'll fake the stamp, too."

"These papers are for someone called Lotte Kramer," Hanne said slowly. "Who is she, and why do I have to use her papers?"

"Lotte Kramer, whoever she is, sold these papers," Paul explained with an air of infinite patience. "It's quite possible that there never was such a person as Lotte Kramer, but that's your name now. It's no worse than Honey Goldsmith or Maria Weber, is it?"

"Why do I have to be Lotte whatever?" Hanne demanded mutinously. "I'd rather be me. Why couldn't we get papers in my own name?"

He turned up his eyes to heaven and made a gesture of prayer. "Because your private life, dear child, does not bear looking into. For one thing we would have to document your sufferings at the hands of the Nazis. Yes, I remember your story. It's a lovely story, but you'd actually have to prove it. Secondly, there is your moral character. Admittedly, Colonel Hosterley will sign any damn thing I push under his nose, but the rabbi and the Peterson woman would want to check you out. How those signatures got on this stuff I don't know, but there they are. Worth their weight in gold, which is about what I paid for them."

Hanne swallowed hard. "Okay," she said. "What next?"

"That's my girl." Paul eyed her with approval. "Next the OMGUS job. We're in luck there. You're starting Monday as file clerk in Supply. It doesn't need special security clearance, and the work is a cinch."

"I've never done any office work. Couldn't I get a job in the cafeteria? Even if they don't let me cook, I could clear tables and wash dishes."

Paul stared. "Are you out of your teeny little mind? What good would that do? You don't honestly think I went to all this trouble to have you scrub pots in the cafeteria? Supply, Honey, Supply—doesn't that ring a bell for you?"

She shook her head.

"Look," Paul said with a sigh, "never mind the whys and wherefores. Just go to work and do a good job. You don't need experience to do filing. You know the alphabet, don't you? If not—hell, look it up."

She was sure she would get arrested when she presented her doctored work papers at the gate of the office compound, but the guard merely glanced at the pass and waved her on. She walked a couple of steps, then went back.

"Where do I go?" she asked humbly. "I'm supposed to be at this office at nine o'clock."

The guard looked surprised. "First day? Didn't they interview you in Supply?"

"Well, no," Hanne improvised. "I got the job through Miss Peterson. She just said to report this morning."

The MP nodded. "Peterson? Yeah, the social worker, that explains it. Well, just go straight ahead to the second building on the right, Miss Kramer, and show your pass at the door. They'll see you to the right place."

"Thank you."

He seemed to have noticed nothing strange about her. She was glad now that Paul had made her wear ugly thick stockings and clumpy shoes. She hadn't wanted to. Paul hadn't even let her wear one of her pretty pleated skirts and cotton blouses. To her horror, he had come home with a dreadful, saggy brown tweed skirt and a dingy cardigan made of scratchy wool in a sickly mustard color.

Now she saw he had been right again. Dressed like this, with her hair scraped down from a middle part and braided into two lumps, one over each ear, she looked strangely anonymous. Maybe that's how a file clerk was supposed to look. Now all she had to do was find out what a file clerk was supposed to do.

File clerks, she found out, took big untidy piles of paper and put them into the right place. Once you figured out where the right places were, all it took was painstaking attention. It was just like tidying up or sorting laundry at the convent. Paul was right. She could do it.

Her immediate supervisor was a middle-aged German woman with saggy jowls and eyes hidden behind thick glasses. Her name was Ulla Printz, and she had been an executive secretary for the past thirty years.

This and much more was explained to her when they took their coffee break. Coffee breaks were a new and delightful experience to Hanne. A buzzer went off, and Miss Printz signaled her to stop working and sit down. A couple of minutes later, a girl came by with a tea cart, stacked with snacks. You could take anything you wanted and it was all for free. Hanne got a mug of coffee and a lovely sticky bun.

It was all done to increase efficiency, Miss Printz told her. They could sit and relax for fifteen minutes, until the buzzer went off again. An American efficiency expert had determined that twelve percent more work got done when the work-day was broken up like this.

It was Hanne's first chance to look around. The thing that struck her most was that everything was so big.

All around her were huge corridors, cavernous rooms with enormous windows, row upon row of shiny olive green filing cabinets, and the great lamps overhead, casting cold, clean light into every corner. So much lovely space, and now coffee and cake as well.

"I'm going to love working here," Hanne said between bites. "Does this happen every day?"

Miss Printz gave a sad smile. "Coffee morning and afternoon, and an excellent lunch for free, off the ration. Why else do you think I'd be working here?"

"Don't you like it?"

Miss Printz looked around furtively. "I like it well enough, Miss Kramer. But it's really not my kind of work. Before the occupation I was personal secretary to one of the top men at I. G. Farben—a very important man—in an office with twelve persons under me. This is quite a step down for someone with my background, you must see that."

Hanne was suitably impressed.

"To be fair," Miss Printz continued. "the Americans are very pleasant to work for. They have excellent manners. It's really very much like working in a German office. In fact, I find them so sympathetic, I sometimes wonder why they weren't on our side."

"Maybe because some of them are Jews?" Hanne suggested gravely.

Miss Printz gave her a quick look. "Of course, Miss Kramer. You are Jewish. Believe me I have never been anti-Semitic. Some of my best friends...."

"Of course," Hanne said demurely, stifling a giggle.

"Well, it's all in the past," Miss Printz went on briskly. "I'm delighted to have you here. We've been very understaffed, and you are catching on beautifully. Have you had much office experience?"

"None," Hanne admitted "I'm just out of school."

With horror she remembered that she was supposed to be Lotte Kramer, who was twenty-three years old. But all was well—Miss Printz nodded approvingly.

"I myself had four years of college before I became a wage earner. It pays off in the end to have a sound academic background. Did you take business courses?"

Hanne wondered wildly what she was supposed to have been doing during the war. The forged papers had given her no hint of what her background was supposed to be. Hidden away? Masquerading as Aryan? Whoever she was, the Jewish Miss Kramer would certainly not have been in a German business college.

"Unfortunately not," she explained trying to look very honest and open. "The circumstances you know. I had few choices. I concentrated on languages and history. I don't even type."

Miss Printz clucked her tongue sympathetically. "Never mind. I'm sure you will do well, and good organizational talent is worth more than typing." She sniffed. "Unless of course you want to be a typist all your life." She made it sound like a joke. "Typists," she explained, "stay typists, unless they have a great deal more to offer."

The employee cafeteria was for Germans only. Hanne had been worried about meeting someone she knew, but it was quite safe. Only German civilian employees ate here, and the food was nowhere near as good as the stuff Paul brought home.

She poked at the starchy lump on her plate and thought about Paul's rage over Fräulein Stulp's watery stew.

"Aren't you hungry?" An elderly man beside her eyed her plate wistfully. "You don't want to waste good food."

She turned to him and pushed her plate over, "Please, I've had enough. Do take it. Look, I haven't touched that part at all."

"It doesn't matter if you had," he said, producing a plastic bag from his pocket and carefully scraping the contents of the plate into it. "It goes into a soup."

She nodded with understanding. She had helped to make soups of that kind during the war.

"If you boil it for twenty minutes, it kills all germs," he explained seriously. "You can get plastic bags from the kitchen here or you can bring a tin can. Are you sure you can spare all this?"

"Oh, yes, really. I don't have a big appetite."

"The portions are very generous." He smiled sweetly, revealing broken teeth. "Thanks to your kindness, my wife and granddaughter will eat well tonight."

At five-thirty sharp, Miss Printz slipped into her mothball-scented fur coat, placed a pot-shaped hat squarely over her severe hairdo, and nodded good-bye.

"You lock the files by pushing in the button at the top. Be sure they're all locked before the cleaning women come in. You don't mind, do you? I have to catch a bus."

Knowing that Paul was waiting a block from the gate, Hanne hurriedly finished putting the rest of the papers away. There was no way to really finish a job like this. New piles of papers came in all the time. She put the unsorted stuff in an empty drawer and went around clicking all the locks.

Another MP was guarding the gate, and he only wanted to check her handbag to make sure she wasn't taking home something more than leftovers in a plastic bag. She wondered what he would have done if he'd found a pencil or a bunch of paper clips in her purse. There was nothing else to steal.

Paul was waiting in his new car. "Well, how did it go?" he asked.

She sat close to him and told him about Miss Printz and the very important man at I. G. Farben, how she had had twelve people under her, and the nice old man who took his lunch home to his family.

"Does this Printz woman watch you all the time?" Paul asked. "I mean, does she trust you?"

"Of course." Hanne preened. "I caught on right away. You were right. It's not difficult at all."

"So she leaves you alone?"

"Oh, yes. She even left me to tidy up at quitting time. She had to run for her bus, you know. I got to put everything away and pop in the little buttons to lock up."

Paul smiled and hugged her. "Excellent," he said.

❧ *Chapter 11*

Rip Tyler was a calm young man. He was not overconfident, but he knew himself to be quite capable of handling most things that came his way. When he did not get to see Hanne, he left a note for her with the German woman and waited.

Several days went by and the phone call he had hoped for did not happen. Unfazed, he went back and talked to the housekeeper again. No, she hadn't been able to give the note to Miss Hanne personally. Mr. Karinof had taken it away from her, but he had promised to give it to Miss Goldschmidt. Her sympathetic shrug left little to the imagination. His letter had ended up in the wastebasket.

Rip decided to find out where this Mr. Karinof worked. It wasn't easy to track him down. The man seemed to have a very flexible job.

He finally found him in the front office of the motor pool, in conversation with a rather uneasy looking private. He considered pulling rank and interrupting, but decided against it, leaning against the door instead to watch. Rip suspected that the boy took Paul for an officer; an easy mistake to make when dealing with uniformed civilians, and this man had a very sharp, authoritative manner. So this was the competition, not a type Rip particularly admired. Paul was very smooth, a city boy. It was hard to know what was going on behind the surface. Nothing very pleasant, judging by the looks of the squirming soldier. Karinoff's expression, however, remained bland and casual.

The GI finally made his escape, and Rip moved in.

Paul turned to him, his manner pleasant if cautious. "I don't know you, do I?"

"Have not had that pleasure," Rip admitted.

"You work here?"

"Sometimes. Mostly in maintenance. The name's Tyler."

Paul lost interest. "Nice meeting you, Sarge. Now I know where to come when my vehicle starts acting up."

Rip made no move to go. "I was sort of hoping you might help me contact a mutual friend, Miss Goldschmidt."

Paul's face closed up. Rip was fascinated by the change. The man was still smiling, more widely in fact, but his eyes had become opaque.

"Indeed?"

"Well you see." Rip's natural drawl became more pronounced. "This here young lady is interested in growing things, and I thought maybe I could help her make a garden."

"A kind thought."

Spoken that way, it was a straight insult, but Rip had his own way of meeting hostility. He simply pretended not to understand the other person's intent. It worked most of the time. "Not kind really," he protested modestly. "I like growing things myself. I'm a farm boy, so I come to it natural-like."

"That must make for a fascinating life," Paul sneered, and turned away.

Rip ambled around to face him smiling broadly. "So if you'd just let her know that I got the seeds she wants…"

Paul looked up and through him. "If this girl had any interest in gardening at one time, she has obviously forgotten about it. "

"But you'll mention it to her?"

"Certainly, if I happen to bump into her. Now will you kindly get out my way and stop wasting my time."

This unsatisfactory conversation left Rip thoughtful. Now he knew where he stood. He was just going to have to fight for her.

It would have been nice if the girl he loved had not been involved with someone else, but there was no reason why she had to stay involved. After all, he told himself reasonably, she hadn't known about him. So, why should she hang around and wait? Come to think about it, he hadn't known about her. It had just happened, and it felt right and good. He had a gut feeling about the whole thing. It just had to work out.

So while Paul became stiffer and colder by the minute, Rip found himself becoming more and more folksy, his hillbilly drawl a perfect caricature of his normal way of talking.

Paul was considerably shorter than the gangly soldier. On the other hand, he had the compact build of a prizefighter. Rip thought he could see what Hanne saw in the man. He didn't like the type himself, but he had seen women go crazy for these smooth, slick types. Still, he was not exactly lacking in style himself. The style was merely different. He thanked Paul for his time and slouched away. Paul gritted his teeth as he watched him go.

Paul said nothing to Hanne about this meeting. The thing meant nothing, he decided grimly, and she would not be seeing the GI again. He'd see to that.

Hanne made it easy for him. She was busy with her new job, and wildly excited about it. She was crowing.

"I've got a job, a real job. Isn't it marvelous? I can do it. Do you realize what that means, Paul? I can be independent."

"You don't want to be dependent on me?" He was surprised and hurt.

She thought about that. "No, I don't think so. I love it when you give me things, like all those beautiful clothes. But being dependent is so—so undignified."

"Undignified." He whooped with laughter. "I wish you could see your dignified self right now. Miss Kramer in her working garb. So help me, I could pass you in the street and say to myself, 'What a dog.'"

Hanne felt deflated. "You're the one who makes me wear this stuff. I know it's awful. You picked it out specially to make me look awful. These shoes are three sizes too long and so wide, I had to stuff them so they wouldn't fall off."

"I know, I know." But he was still laughing.

"Where do you get off making fun of me?" she demanded huffily. "I never had a job, and I'm doing well. Miss Printz is pleased with me. She said I'd get a raise in three months. And you know what I'm going do with the money? I'm going to buy myself decent working clothes."

"Don't you dare." He was still laughing. "You don't know how much trouble I had finding the ones you've got on. Have you any idea how difficult it is to make you look plain? This outfit is a triumph of stagecraft."

"But why? I like to look nice."

He kissed her and she stopped being mad at him.

"Take it all off and look nice for me," he suggested "And if you're not too tired, I'll take you to a nightclub afterward."

Hanne peeled out of her office clothes like a butterfly emerging from its cocoon, leaving them in heaps all over the bedroom floor.

"Shall I take a quick bath?" she asked, smiling at him. "Or what?"

"Definitely what," he assured her, starting to unbutton his shirt. "What first—bath later."

Afterward Paul lit a cigarette, as he always did, and Hanne soaked in the tub and thought about their lovemaking. She liked it, she decided. It was nice. He made her feel good. But it wasn't at all like the books described it. She wondered if the people who wrote those books really felt all the complicated sensations they described. Probably not. Trouble was that it was easy enough to describe the things people did together—though to be honest some of the things in the French novels sounded peculiar and not terribly comfortable—but feelings were harder to describe. It was probably easier to go on and on about wild ecstasy, moving mountains, roaring seas, and thunderous music, rather than tell simply and honestly what you were supposed to feel.

"Paul," she called out. "Come here a moment."

He stuck his head through the door. "Want your back scrubbed?"

"Yes, that, too. But mostly I want to ask you something."

"Ask away."

"You know the stuff they write about love—I guess I mean sex. Why is it so different from reality?"

"What have you been reading? Those French novels in yellow paper wrappers, you little monster of depravity? If you read the right books, you'd find reality enough."

"If you mean Krafft-Ebing, no thanks." She shook her head emphatically. "I saw that on the bookshelf and took a look at it. Ugh. I'll take my sex without pathology."

He tickled the back of her neck. "I was thinking of Shakespeare, you ignorant girl. He has a few things to say on the subject—not at all kinky. How's this: 'What is love? 'Tis not hereafter; Present mirth hath present laughter.' Meaning it's supposed to be fun. I'll go with that any day."

"I know the poem," Hanne said slowly. "But the next line is: 'What's to come is still unsure.'"

"Of course it's unsure. The man knew what he was speaking of. But if you know that, you know the best part, too." He twisted her wet hair around his hand. "'Trip no further, pretty sweeting; Journeys end in lovers meeting, Every wise man's son doth know.'"

"And where will our journey end?" she said dreamily, sliding down into the warm water. "We started with the lovers meeting. Where will we go from here?"

"We'll be very rich and fashionable. A penthouse in Manhattan, a ski lodge at St. Moritz, maybe a yacht, certainly a racing car."

She frowned at him. "There you go joking again. I was being serious."

His eyes were very bright. "And what made you think I was joking?"

As if to make up for the ugly clothes he had made her wear to work, he picked out her dress for the evening with special care. It was a periwinkle blue faille with a full skirt and long, tight sleeves ending in flared points that came down over the back of the hand. Three rows of matching velvet ribbon ran around the hem.

"Spectacular," he said, kissing her neck. "Much too good for the Blue Goose, really."

"The Blue Goose again? Aren't we going to the Femina?"

"Lord, no." He looked honestly surprised. "What gave you that idea? I've made all the contacts I need at the Femina. Why would we go there?"

Hanne found herself blushing, as if she had said something indecent. "I thought you were taking me out," she stammered. "I didn't realize this was only for business."

"It isn't. You know I like to take you out. But tonight we have a chance to combine pleasure and profit—at least I hope it will be profit."

"Can't we go somewhere else, just the two of us, and forget about the profit?"

He was still standing close to her, but she sensed a withdrawal, as if in his mind he had already walked away from her. "If the profit is good enough, Honey, you can get your ears pierced."

"Why would I want to do that?" She stopped herself just in time from clinging to him. The moment for closeness was gone.

Paul seemed quite unaware of the change between them. He was cheerful and talkative as he finished dressing.

"I was thinking of earrings. How do you feel about that? You have such pretty earlobes. Of course, you're a bit too young for diamonds, but pearls would be good, don't you think? Personally I like aquamarines, but perhaps amethysts would be better on you. I met a man the other day who has some quite good stones, but I'll have an expert check them out. I don't know enough about gemstones yet. What kind of jewelry do you like best?"

"I had a locket once," Hanne said slowly. "It was very old. The gold plating was rubbed off in places, and it was sort of dented. But it had a lovely dark blue stone in it, with little gold flecks."

"Lapis lazuli, probably. But I meant real jewelry, not sentimental pieces."

"It was real enough for me. I guess I am sentimental. Anyway, it got lost. I'd like to have something like that again, if you want to make me happy."

"Of course I do. But for something real, how about sapphires? You like blue, don't you?"

She felt trapped. The mere idea of sapphires made her feel weighed down. But Paul looked so pleased with the idea. All she could do was hope he'd forget about it.

"Isn't Renée playing at the Blue Goose?" she asked, more to change the subject than for any other reason.

Paul looked surprised. "Sure, but you needn't worry about that. It's over. She's got someone else already."

"You don't mind?"

He shrugged. "Why should I? It was amusing, but it didn't mean anything."

Before leaving he selected the bottles for the evening, and handed Hanne a small package.

"Put it in your handbag, will you? I hate to bulge out my pockets. Ruins the fit of the jacket."

"What is it?" she asked, weighing it in her hand before putting it into her big shoulder bag.

"A little something for Colonel Arpov. Just trying to do him a favor. Or you might call it a sample. There's one thing, though. I may need your help."

Hanne's heart sank. She put down the shoulder bag and pushed it toward him. "I just decided—I'm going to use the little clutch bag tonight. I'm afraid I won't be able to carry your package for you."

He picked up the bag and thrust it at her irritably. "Don't be tiresome, Honey. We're not smuggling military secrets, you know. This could be a sweet little deal—and no one gets hurt."

"And the help you need?"

"Maybe—I said maybe. Don't make a big thing out of it. If Major Kuprin is watchdogging again, you have to keep him amused. You can do that, can't you?"

"I don't like him at all," Hanne said, reluctantly picking up the big bag. "I don't like the way he looks at me."

Feeling he had won his point, Paul became very cheerful. "There's always a chance Arpov has been able to give him the slip. Worst comes to worst, you'll flirt with the man. You don't have to like him for that. Good grief, I'm not asking you to go to bed with him. Just keep him out of my way."

"I wish I didn't feel so cheap doing it," Hanne said sadly. "If I have to do these things, I wish I could be exciting and glamorous—like Mata Hari."

Paul took her into his arms and kissed her nose. "Mata Hari nothing," he said. "You *are* exciting and glamorous. I know you don't like all this, but if you give me a hand with it, I'll make it up to you someday. I promise."

Colonel Arpov was alone, and Hanne felt a weight lifted from her shoulders. Now she could relax and enjoy the evening. Paul had brought a bottle of Coca Cola for her, so that she had something to sip while the men did their serious drinking. Paul never seemed to get drunk, but the colonel got very red in the face after the second glass and started undoing the top buttons of his tunic.

Hanne hoped she would not have to dance with him again. But even if it happened, it was still a nice evening. Renée was not in sight, and a string quartet provided undemanding background music. She wondered what Paul and the colonel were talking about. Their heads were very close together.

At one point, Paul took her bag and extracted the package. Just as he seemed about to hand it to the colonel, he replaced it and ostentatiously pushed the bag over to her.

"I was wondering why it's so heavy," he said with a laugh. "Don't you leave anything at home?" Hanne's confusion made her stammer something silly about never knowing when you might need this or that, Then she turned her head and saw Major Kuprin behind her. He was looking at her handbag with great interest.

Hanne picked it up and slung it over her shoulder. It felt clumsy and much too big.

"What a delightful surprise." The major bowed over her hand. "My good friend Petya promised me that you would be here tonight."

"How clever of Petya," Hanne said grumpily. "I didn't know myself."

The major turned to Paul with a small nod. "May I ask this young lady to dance?"

Paul jumped up and grabbed Hanne's wrist, "Later maybe. This is my dance."

He maneuvered her to the opposite side of the room and started talking into her ear. It sounded odd, because he was trying not to move his lips.

"Hang on to the bag. Don't give him a chance to look into it. Do you understand?"

She nodded slightly.

"Okay. Now, I want you to go to the powder room without drawing attention to yourself. Make sure you're alone. I'll try to prevent Kuprin from following you.

You know that urn at the end of the corridor, between the doors to the men's and the ladies'? Just drop the package into that."

They circled the floor, Paul making a big show of holding her very close and talking amorous nonsense. As soon as they were out of sight of their table, she whispered anxiously, "How will you get it back?"

"No problem. Relax, Honey. Just remember, go on being very possessive of the handbag. As long as he thinks you're carrying it, he won't be watching the rest of us so closely."

She sat down and reached for her glass, glad to have something to drink. Her mouth was unpleasantly dry.

Petya and Mimi had joined the Russian officers, and all the bottles and glasses had been moved to a bigger table.

Hanne drank thirstily and started to splutter. Her Coke tasted awful. Mimi was giggling behind her hand.

"Don't you like it?" she asked innocently. "It's rum and Coca-Cola. The major mixed it for you. We all thought you'd like it. Only it isn't rum, is it, Major? It's arrack—so much better."

"You all know Honey doesn't drink," Paul exploded angrily. "That was a miserable trick to pull on her. Are you all right, Honey?"

She shivered. Was the major trying to get her drunk, or was this just a malicious joke of Mimi's? Whatever the reason, it had scared her and made her feel sick. But now she could use it for her own purposes.

"I feel awful," she announced, standing up shakily. "I think I'm going to be sick."

Mimi jumped up and grabbed her arm. "Come along, I'll take you to the toilet."

Hanne turned on her angrily, surprised at how easy it was. "You stay away from me, Mimi, you—you snake, you. Next time you try to poison me, take care. I'll kill you."

She ran out of the room, shivering with a mixture of panic and hysterical laughter. Behind her she could hear Mimi bleating defensively, while Paul was yelling at her and at the major.

The corridor was almost empty. A couple of French soldiers were leaning against the wall, heads close together. Some sort of deal seemed to be going on. Was Paul right? Was everyone in Berlin dealing in something? The restrooms were in the opposite direction, and she saw the container Paul had mentioned right away. It was a big brass urn, set on a low lacquer table. There was no lamp at that end of the corridor, and she felt confident that she could get rid of the package without the soldiers' noticing anything. It seemed the most natural thing to stop under a lamp, in front of the mirror, halfway between the soldiers and the washroom doors. She made a big business of examining her face, fished out a lipstick from her handbag, and palmed the package at the same time. Raising her head, she glanced into the mirror to check the corridor.

Major Kuprin was leaning in the doorway, watching her. She swallowed hard. His expression was bland and bored. He pulled out a cigarette case and made a great to-do of selecting and lighting one of the long, paper-tubed cigarettes.

Hanne dropped the package back into her bag, brought out a handkerchief, and dabbed her face with it. She didn't have to playact feeling sick. She felt sick. Now he must know she had whatever it was they all wanted. How else would you explain running out to the toilet and then standing about in the corridor?

Luck was on her side after all. The washroom door opened and a woman came out murmuring something apologetic about staying inside so long. Hanne nodded and went in, grateful to be able to lock the door behind her. The washroom was tiny, really just a commode, with a hand basin wedged into the corner opposite the door. There was no mirror. Good luck again. To anyone who knew the nightclub, it would make sense to use the mirror outside to fix one's face. If the men's room was the same, the major might make that assumption. So far so good, but how could she get rid of the package? The major was probably still standing guard outside.

She sat on the lid of the toilet and unwrapped the package. There was a great deal of paper, but at the very core of the wrapping was a metal box containing five small medicine bottles. The labels had numbers on them instead of lettering.

She had expected watches or jewelry, and the bottles scared her. She was tempted to flush them down the toilet, but the thought of Paul's rage stopped her.

The little box with the medicine bottles actually fitted inside her sleeve, hidden by the flaring cuff that came down over her hand. She emptied her makeup bag, a little pouch of quilted velvet, and slipped the box inside. That would deaden the sound of the drop. Then she tried out several ways of holding it until she felt sure she could let it slip by lifting her thumb, without moving the fingers. She reassembled the package, putting her lipstick inside, to fill the space of the pill bottles. It looked about the same as before.

The lack of a mirror bothered her. She would have liked to practice the maneuver she planned. As it was, she could only cross her fingers and hope it would look convincing.

Clutching the parcel in her right hand, with the box hidden inside her left sleeve, she stepped into the corridor. The major was watching her from the door to the bar.

Catching his eye, as if noticing him for the first time, Hanne fell back against the wall in a gesture of panic and brought up her right hand, with the parcel in it, as if to shield herself from him. Her left hand groped for something to steady herself with, connected with the rim of the urn, and let go the box.

The major's eyes were fixed on the package. There was a faint, pitying smile on his face. Hanne hurriedly stuffed the package back into her handbag and walked toward him, her head held high.

He barred her way, taking hold of her elbow, and steered her toward the street door. The French soldiers had left. Short of screaming for help, she didn't know what to do.

"I must talk to you," he said softly. "You probably won't believe me, but I really like you—not because you're such a pretty girl, but because I think you are at heart a decent human being."

"I'm not sure that's a compliment," she said, edging away from him.

He made no move to crowd her, merely stood between her and the way back to Paul.

"It wasn't meant as a compliment," he said dryly. "You're not really so stupid as to think every man wants to seduce you? You know exactly what my interest in you is, don't you? I think you do."

"I've no idea what you're talking about," Hanne said loftily. "Now, will you please step aside so I can get back to my friends."

He made no move to let her pass, only stared at her in a worried sort of way.

"I've got a feeling you don't even know what your friend's involved in," he burst out irritably. "I've no idea what fairy tales that young man tells you, but what you are doing is criminal."

"And what am I doing?" She opened her eyes very wide and looked up at him innocently.

"Let me have that package," he countered. "I promise you—you will not be prosecuted."

"Prosecuted for what?" she demanded indignantly. "This is too much, Major. I'm going back to the bar. Paul will be furious."

He made as if to hold her hack, but she took the package out of her purse and waved it mockingly in his face.

"Is this what you want? Well, that's just too bad, Major. I have no intention of giving it to you."

She thrust it back into the bag and marched past him, head held high. Paul's face was quite blank as she strode in, followed by the major.

"We were worrying about you," Mimi babbled inanely. "You were gone such a long time. You do feel better, don't you?"

"Much better," Hanne said. "No thanks to you."

"I meant no harm. Can't you take a little joke?"

"There are too many jokes going around tonight," Hanne said angrily. "I might enjoy it more if I weren't the butt of them all. Your friend Major Kuprin has just been threatening me, demanding that I turn my handbag over to him."

Paul's eyes flickered, but to a stranger his face would have appeared only mildly amused.

"I'm surprised at you, Major," he drawled. "Have you any idea what girls carry around in their bags these days? To the best of my knowledge, Honey has her most secret diary stashed in there, all three volumes of it. Not to mention a spare pair of nylons and a bag of peanuts. You never know when hunger may strike. And of course her toothbrush—in case the evening takes an interesting turn."

Hanne felt herself blushing, but the major merely shook his head seriously. "Miss Honey misunderstood me. I'm not interested in the contents of her hand-bag in general—only a large brown envelope tied with string. I must admit I'm very anxious to look at that."

Hanne pulled it out and smacked it down on the middle of the table. "This envelope?"

The major nodded.

Hanne started to laugh hysterically. They were all leaning forward, except for Colonel Arpov, who was owlishly drunk, and Paul, who looked bored and started getting up.

"Please stay, Mr. Karinof," the major demanded crisply. "Miss Honey will open the envelope. Don't you want to see what's in it?"

"I don't share your interest in Honey's possessions," Paul said coldly. "If you'll excuse me."

The major half rose to follow him, but Hanne made as if to slip the envelope back into her bag. His fingers came down on her wrist like steel clamps.

"If you please," he said in a flat, hard voice. Hanne let him take it, but placed her hand on his as he was about to open it.

"I haven't got the slightest idea what you expect to find, but I wish you wouldn't do that. It will be embarrassing for you and will make it hard for us to meet as friends in the future."

He paused for a moment. "I would regret that," he said softly. "Can you tell me what's inside?"

"Nothing of interest to you," she assured him gravely. "A little something I promised the princess. I was going to ask Petya to take it to her."

Petya looked nervous and angry. Mimi refilled her glass and looked up with glazed boredom. Colonel Arpov smiled foolishly and hiccuped.

"I will see to it that the princess gets her present," Major Kuprin said dryly, and started untying the string that held the envelope closed.

Hanne was aware that Petya had almost stopped breathing. He was staring with frozen horror at the major's hands.

Major Kuprin made quite a production of unwrapping the many layers of paper. At last he came to the center and the lipstick in its gold case rolled out.

He opened it and sniffed it, touched it to his finger, then replaced it carefully and rewrapped the package without comment.

"How pleased the princess will be," he said with a bleak smile. "American makeup is so much better than what is being sold in Germany now, isn't it?"

"Now don't you feel like a fool?" Hanne demanded. "I did try to tell you."

"Yes, I've been very foolish," the major said gently. "Please forgive me. I quite misunderstood the part you were playing in all this."

"Honey doesn't play parts." Mimi giggled foolishly. "I don't think she could act to save her life."

His eyes still fixed on Hanne, he said, "You underestimate our young friend. I'm afraid we've all underestimated her. She has just given a star performance as a red herring."

"You did it," Paul crowed, as soon as they were in the car. "You handled that like a pro. That was wonderful."

"Did you find the box?" Hanne felt tired and let down in the face of his excitement. She had been high as a kite while it was going on, but the feeling had evaporated in the face of Major Kuprin's contemptuous comment.

A red herring, a decoy, no more. Not Mata Hari, a glamorous adventuress—just a cheap little trickster.

Paul made her go back over every movement, commenting admiringly on her quick thinking.

"I'll get you a new makeup case," he promised, gently rubbing the back of her neck with his free hand. "Damn, but you are tense. Were you scared, little Honey? There was no danger, you know. The major was bluffing. He has no authority outside the Russian sector. But I admit he could have ruined the deal. Our friend Arpov would have run like a hare if we had been caught with the stuff."

"What is the stuff?" Honey asked. "It's drugs, isn't it?"

"Drugs," he mimicked her. "Dreadful, dangerous drugs. If you must know, it's penicillin, something new. Real fine stuff, knocks out infections like magic. Our medics have as much as they want and more. Everyone else needs it. Doesn't seem fair to keep it for ourselves does it?"

"But you're not giving it away. You're selling it."

"I'm selling it at a fair price," Paul explained patiently, "The thing is to get it out on the marketplace so everyone who needs it can buy it."

"You make everything sound too simple," she complained sadly. "The major said it was criminal."

Paul merely laughed. "He would. What a stick of a man. By those standards, he's the only honest man in Berlin."

She thought of the French soldiers and Rip giving cigarettes to old ladies so they could buy coffee. Everyone else seemed to be doing it, or helping others to do it.

"Do you think I'm a terrible prude?" she asked. "I want so much to do things right."

"Well, don't worry so much," he suggested. "I wouldn't ask you to do anything wrong, would I? I'm much too fond of you, even though you're such a horrible prude. Now, be honest—did you have fun?"

She nodded. It was hard to explain, but it had been fun, playing Mata Hari games and fooling everyone.

"Now I've got something else for you, not as much fun, but very useful. Will you help me?"

"What do you want me to do?"

"Tell me about the filing system again," he suggested. "The requisitions come to you after they have been approved, right? You pull out the stock sheet, attach the requisition, and that goes back to the order desk. Then what happens to the requisitions?"

"They go into the inactive file. I mean, they're finished with, aren't they? Once the replacements are ordered, they're not needed anymore."

"No one tears them up?"

"Oh, no. You see, every scrap of paper is saved as backup. It does make for a lot of paper. Miss Printz says we are going to get ten new file cabinets."

Paul chewed on his lower lip. "Sounds good. Now, I need some of those requisitions."

Hanne laughed with relief. "I can't get them for you, if that's what you have in mind. Don't you know they search us as we leave?"

"I don't expect you to smuggle them out, Honey. Good grief. All you have to do is not lock them up when you go. Leave them on top of the file or stuff them in a wastebasket. I'll let you know what to do with them."

She wriggled uncomfortably. "What if I get caught?"

"No way." He scoffed at her worries. "How can they catch you? If the papers aren't there, everyone will assume they've already been filed. Have you ever been asked to dig up any of that inactive stuff? Of course not. It's a cinch."

❧ *Chapter 12*

Fräulein Stulp couldn't tell Rip where Hanne was working. "Somewhere in the OMGUS offices, I think. But I don't see her these days. She's gone before I get here, and I leave before she comes home. Mr. Karinof does not like me to hang around, as he puts it."

"Can't you try and get a note to her?"

The German woman shrugged. The tall young American was rather sweet, but she couldn't risk her job to help him. Mr Karinof was not the kind of man who tolerated interference.

"Look, miss, I'm going to plant that big pot with some flowers I've been raising from seed. I think Miss Hanne will like that, and I can't imagine Mr. Karinof kicking up a stink about it. I mean—it's just a handful of flowers."

"That'll be nice," Fräulein Stulp agreed. "She said something about wanting to plant a garden in that tub. She was going to grow tomatoes, too."

"Couldn't get the proper seed. You'd need a special, small kind of tomato for growing in a pot like that. Some company back in the States has them, but I couldn't have got the seeds in time."

Paul was mildly irritated by the flowery offering, but Hanne was thrilled. Luckily, the tub had drain holes. She expressed her devotion to the plants by pouring gallons of water on them, morning and night.

She had felt bad about not having heard from Rip after standing him up for the picnic. But he couldn't still be mad at her or he wouldn't have brought the flowers.

There was something very nice about the way he had just come and planted them without expecting thanks. She wanted to tell him how happy he had made her.

She thought of sending him a note but had no idea where to send it. All she had was his name and rank. Sergeant Rip Tyler. It hardly seemed enough as an address.

Paul would have known how to find him, but she didn't want to bring up a subject that had made him so angry. There were some things one just couldn't discuss with Paul. Her harmless little friendship with Rip was one of them.

And Paul was very nice to her these days. Since she was sort of working with him, he didn't withdraw as much. They spent more time talking, though it was always about deals and new prospects—never anything personal anymore. He hadn't even made love to her in a week. But he paid her lots of compliments and brought her presents all the time. That was nice. She did appreciate it, but it was rather like being paid.

Something had changed between them. He was just as handsome and just as charming, and of course she was lucky. Mimi and Ingelore had told her how lucky she was, and by their reckoning she had everything a girl could ask for. But there were times when she found herself looking at Paul and he seemed like a stranger—and a stranger she didn't even like very much. She pushed that feeling away. It was scary.

And she did miss the comfortable companionship she had had with Rip. Not that she was in love with him, she assured herself nervously. Nonsense—of course not. How could she be in love with him when she belonged to Paul? But she did miss him. Finally she decided to ask the nice MP who was on duty when she checked in to work every morning. In the evening there were always different ones, but when she came to work, it was always the same guard who had been so kind to her that first day.

"How would you go about finding a GI?" she asked him one morning.

He pretended to think about it. "Well, Miss Kramer, first of all I'd go to a beauty shop and get my hair done, and then I guess I'd put on some lipstick—if that's what I wanted."

She blushed fiercely. It was so easy to forget that she still came to work disguised as an ugly duckling.

"Not just any GI. I met this nice boy, and he gave me some flowers. I'd like to send him a thank-you note, only I don't know where to send it."

The MP looked sympathetic. "You don't know what company or where he works?"

She shook her head. "Only his name."

"Well, that's something. Write it down for me, and I'll see what I can find out for you."

"I wrote him a note," Hanne explained, pulling it out of her pocket. "I do appreciate it—your taking the trouble."

"A pleasure," the guard assured her. "But you know, I meant it about the hair and the lipstick. You could be quite nice-looking if you took a bit of trouble with yourself, honest."

She almost kissed him, but held back. How could he know that his awkward compliment had given her a lovely warm glow. He probably wouldn't have been too happy about being kissed by poor, homely Miss Kramer. She wondered how he would have reacted to Hanne Goldschmidt in her strapless silk sheath, with her amethyst earrings and ankle-strap sandals showing off her pretty, nylon-clad legs.

The MP felt sorry for Miss Kramer. She was too young to have such a dull life. Personally, he liked his Fräuleins with a bit more class, but he was glad that she had managed to find an admirer. He started looking for Sergeant Rip Tyler and found him supervising repairs in the motor pool.

"Miss Kramer?" Rip said doubtfully. "Can't say that that rings a bell. Did she say when we were supposed to have met?"

"No, she didn't. I wonder if she made it up about you liking her. She's really plain. Nice, you know, but awful plain. She said you'd given her flowers, and she wanted to thank you."

Rip's ears started to tingle. "Did she now? That's mighty interesting. I'll take that note, if you don't mind. Maybe it'll come back to me."

"Now I don't want her feelings hurt," the MP said firmly. "She's a real nice little girl, even if she is a dog."

"Last time I hurt a girl was when I pushed my sister in the duck pond, and I got a walloping for that," Rip explained cheerfully. "Plumb broke me of the habit. I've been mild as milk ever since. Now, if I promise to treat this here plain jane very kindly, how do I find her?"

He was waiting for Hanne at lunchtime, when she was on her way to the cafeteria. He was propped up against the door frame, grinning hugely.

"Miss Kramer?" he inquired with lifted eyebrow. "My goodness, I hardly would have recognized you. You have changed since we last met."

She squinted down at herself. The shoes alone were enough to make her look silly. They were enormous, and the wrinkly cotton stockings drooping around her ankles didn't help.

"Hi, Rip," she said with a small wave. "Nice to see you."

"Nice to see you, Miss Kramer," he said politely. "Can we have lunch?"

Hanne turned nervously to Miss Printz, who was waiting behind her, impatiently tapping the tip of her shoe. "I don't know, Rip. I'm supposed to eat in the cafeteria."

Rip turned to Miss Printz with a deep bow. "You're the boss?" he asked engagingly. Encouraged by her curt nod, he continued. "Good. Would you give this gal the afternoon off? I'd really appreciate it."

Miss Printz looked troubled. "I don't know, sergeant. She gets paid for eight hours of work. I can't just send her off for a whole afternoon."

"And she gets paid for overtime?"

"Why, no."

"And does she put in overtime?"

Miss Printz looked nervous. Since Miss Kramer was so agreeable about locking up, she had gotten into the habit of leaving early enough to catch her bus in comfort. What it boiled down to was that Miss Kramer worked an extra half hour every day.

"Well, all right, just this once," she decided generously. "But we can't have this happening all the time, Miss Kramer. You must understand that."

"Of course," Hanne agreed demurely. "I do appreciate it."

She clumped along beside Rip in her big shoes, hardly daring to look up at him. She felt confused but happy.

He ushered her to his jeep with utmost courtesy, helping her into the front seat. She peeked into the back. It was as full of tools, sacking, and bundles as ever.

"Where are we going?" she asked when they were clear of the compound.

"Last thing I remember, we had a date for a picnic," Rip said. "I was looking forward to that, had them make up a box of real fine sandwiches for me at the mess hall. Of course, they got a bit stale, so I did finally replace them last week—or was it the week before? You in the mood for a picnic?"

"I'd love it. I do hope you didn't waste the first batch of sandwiches."

"What do you take me for—a spendthrift? Lord, no, I sold them on the black market."

"What did you get for them?" she asked laughingly. She found she could joke about the black market with Rip.

"Two butts, one pack of matches, and a Steinway piano."

"A sweet deal," she said admiringly. "Was it a full pack of matches?"

"Almost full—and the Steinway had nearly half the white keys left. Not the black ones, of course."

"Of course not. After all, the sandwiches were a little stale."

He grinned at her. "I feel happy all of a sudden. Just to have you next to me, even though you are not turned out the way I remember you. Your summer outfit, I suppose?"

"I was wearing old, washed-out fatigues the first time we met."

"True, and I'll never forget how nifty you looked in them. Why are you got up like this?"

"Well, you see—Oh, damn, I don't know. I thought it was the right way to dress for an office job."

"Well, it doesn't do much for you," Rip said, grinning. "Are those shoes a good fit?"

"No," she snapped. "They're stuffed with rags to make them stay on."

"Want to take them off?" he suggested. "And you could let your hair down while you're at it. Those pins must be poking holes into your poor scalp."

After a moment's hesitation, Hanne kicked off the shoes, slid out of the offending stockings, and unpinned her hair. The air brushing against her bare skin felt lovely. She was intensely happy. "Where shall we have our picnic?"

"Under our tree. Where else?"

"Will it be big enough to sit under? It was sort of small the way I remember it."

"We may have to scrunch down a bit," he agreed "But that's what I was promised—a picnic under the lilac tree."

"I'm sorry I wasn't able to come with you like we planned. Were you very mad?"

"In a towering rage. And of course I was stuck with the sandwiches. That was a bit upsetting. I did leave a letter for you."

"You did? I never got it."

"I guess your boss decided I shouldn't be seeing you. I gave it to the housekeeper, and she gave it to him."

"He never told me. That was a rotten thing to do."

Rip shrugged. "I don't know. I might have done the same. You know, good help is hard to find. I knew a man who tried to get a farmhand away from his best friend. Would visit when he knew the friend wasn't home, offered the man a better house, more money, even a couple of acres for his own. This farmhand was a wonder with sheep, just about talked to them. Of course, I'm not sure a sheep's worth listening to. What do you think?"

"I've never talked to a sheep."

"They're not clever. Definitely not clever. Dull even, but maybe I never knew how to draw them out properly. Maybe they sparkle in the right company."

She leaned back and closed her eyes. "You make me feel sparkly. I can't think why the sheep wouldn't sparkle for you."

"I treat you differently than I would a sheep. Maybe I should try picnics on them. I never thought of that. Hey, wake up. We're here."

Hanne sat up and looked around. The Tiergarten looked a little better in summer. There was grass around the tree stumps and a few flower beds had been planted. The little lilac tree hadn't grown any, but at least it looked alive.

"You good little tree," she said, throwing her arms around it, "I've missed you."

"My Aunt Dicey talks to plants," Rip offered. "She says it encourages them to grow."

"And do they grow for her?"

"She won a blue ribbon one year for a potato that looked like a pig. Otherwise she hasn't had much luck. Worst garden you ever saw. Weeds up to your shoulder."

Hanne sat down under the tree, bending a little to fit under the low branches. Rip lifted a box out of the back of the jeep and settled beside her.

"Maybe your aunt talks to the weeds, too," she offered helpfully.

He nodded. "That would explain it. Now, I hope you're hungry. This is a very special picnic lunch I rustled up for us."

She looked down at two packages, sealed in khaki waxed wrappings.

"What is it? It doesn't look like food."

He broke one open and handed it to her. "There are people who would agree with that. But they're wrong. It's U.S. Army issue K rations—finest kind. You haven't lived 'til you've dined on this stuff. Would you rather have breakfast or supper? I wasn't able to get a lunch. They seem to run out of lunch a lot. Must be because that's the one with Lobster Thermidor."

Hanne chose breakfast and started unpacking. "Well, here's a package of instant coffee, and sugar, and something that says orange juice, only you have to add water."

"I brought that," Rip said, proudly producing a thermos. "Of course, you'll have to drink hot orange juice, but that's better than cold coffee. It's one of those difficult choices, like which child to save when your boat's sinking. Did you find the chocolate yet?"

"Chocolate for breakfast?"

"You bet. That hard stuff is crackers. They'll break your teeth if you attack them too vigorously. And that can there—that's the main course, ham and eggs."

"Mixed together?"

"Right. You will also find two cigarettes, a small pack of matches, and some toilet paper."

"They think of everything, don't they?" Hanne marveled.

"Just about. Now you use that tongue depressor thing as a spreader or spoon, or whatever, if you don't like it, I'll change with you. I've got corned-beef hash, cookies and cocoa. And the chocolate, of course."

"This is a lovely lunch," Hanne said, "Maybe, it's being outside. Everything tastes so good."

"Picnics will do that," Rip agreed. "Have you ever had a toasted marshmallow?"

"No. Are they good?"

"They're awful. But you have to have them at a picnic. it's traditional. You put them on a stick and hold them into the campfire. First they expand and get fluffy. Then they start to drip all over the place, and finally they burn to a black gummy nubble."

"You eat them?"

"Have to. You can't give them to the dogs. Would make them sick."

Hanne stretched luxuriously and sipped her hot orange juice. "This is the first picnic I ever had. I love it, Rip. I never knew one could have so much fun."

"We must do it every week. I get Mondays off these days."

"But I can't just take off from work. Miss Printz said just this once."

"I'll handle Miss Printz," he boasted. "We'll buy her off. Do you think she'd like a Steinway piano with a fine assortment of white keys?"

"How could she resist it?"

"Speaking of resisting," Rip said suddenly, "please don't." He pulled her close and kissed her. It was an awkward kiss, because of the way they were sitting, but Hanne found herself kissing him back enthusiastically.

Rip sat back on his heels and said, "Wow." He looked pleased and surprised.

Hanne jumped up, embarrassed, and started picking up the debris from their picnic. "Look, Rip," she explained hastily, without looking at him, "this doesn't mean anything, nothing. I kiss people when I feel like it. I do it all the time. It's just like shaking hands."

"Friendlier," he said. "I'd much rather kiss you than shake hands with you. Can we do it again?"

"Some other time," she hedged. "Now I have to get back."

"We have all afternoon."

"Not really. There's stuff at the office I have to get done. Please take me back now."

"Sure," he agreed, then pointed at her bare feet. "I'd get back into my disguise if I were you. Remember, Miss Kramer has knobby legs and big feet."

She dressed behind the jeep, feeling foolish but happy. Her hair didn't seem to want to go back into the earphone arrangement. After a tussle with it, she let it go.

"Okay, this'll have to do," she decided. "Perhaps I can fix it at the office. It's difficult without a mirror."

"You look a mess," Rip said, shaking his head gravely. "Miss Kramer won't approve. I bet she wouldn't be caught dead looking like that."

"Then we won't consult her," Hanne said. "Now get me back or I won't come out with you on Monday afternoon."

Miss Printz was pleased with her. "Some girls would have taken advantage," she said, nodding confidentially. "It just shows how conscientious you are—coming back so soon."

Hanne tried to put up her hair, but Miss Printz stopped her. "Leave it alone. I don't usually approve of loose hair in an office, but it really looks better on you. You look quite pretty."

"Yes, it's an improvement, isn't it," Hanne agreed. "But don't you think it makes me look unbusinesslike?"

"Maybe a little." Miss Printz patted her own tidy head. "But the way you usually wear it is quite unbecoming. I meant to tell you before, but I didn't want to hurt your feelings. And that nice young sergeant of yours will enjoy seeing you with your hair down. I suppose you are going to see him this evening?"

Hanne gave a dramatic sigh. "That's the whole problem. The people I live with—they're very strict. They won't let me go out at night. So the only time I can be with him is when he has a day off—Mondays." She let the request hang in the air and looked hopeful.

Miss Printz sighed. "All day Monday?"

"Oh, no, I wouldn't expect that. If I could leave at noon, I'd be back by three o'clock. And I'll be glad to work 'til six every night to make up for it."

"That does sound reasonable," Miss Printz admitted. "The only thing is... You seem to be a very carefully brought-up girl. Do you know about men?"

Stifling a giggle, Hanne kept her face carefully serious. "I know how to behave, Miss Printz. How could you doubt it?"

"Forgive me," the older woman said. "But that is not quite what I meant. I would feel most unhappy if I made it possible for you to get into trouble. You will be careful, won't you? Men are different from us. Even the best of them are at the mercy of their impulses."

"I'll be careful," Hanne promised her. "And thank you for warning me." Unable to resist, Hanne added, "Do you think it's all right to let him kiss me?"

Miss Printz considered this gravely. "As long you are in a public place, it's quite safe."

❧ *Chapter 13*

Hanne was determined to tell Paul about the picnic and her plan to have lunch with Rip again. She tried to bring it up several times, but Paul never seemed to be listening, and when he was paying attention to her, it was to discuss business.

Sunday would be a good time to bring it up, she decided. Sundays were nice lazy days, breakfast in bed with hours of nothing stretching ahead. If Paul could ever be said to relax, that was the time.

That Sunday, however, he jumped out of bed and started getting dressed.

"Tennis," he explained. "I'm going to play a few games every morning, Haven't you noticed I'm putting on weight? You should have told me."

"How could I tell you? I don't see it. You look fine to me."

He turned on her accusingly. "Look at that flab. I've never been so out of shape in my life. But I'll get back fighting trim in no time. I'm going to work out every afternoon, and tennis in the mornings. That ought to do it."

"Maybe I could learn to play tennis, too?" Hanne suggested hopefully.

He shook his head impatiently. "No point in it. You don't need it. You're just lucky the way you can eat all you want and sit around all day and not put on an ounce."

"And what am I supposed to do while you're out getting fit? Can I at least go visit the princess? You don't even have to give me the fare. I get paid these days."

"Major Kuprin has that flat staked out. I don't want you going there. Look, you've been working all week. Relax, read a book, take a bath. Paint your toenails green. Have a nice quiet day."

"You'll be gone all day?" Hanne's disappointment was turning into indignation.

"Well, I have a meeting set up after the game. But I'll probably be back for dinner."

"Probably," she said coldly to his disappearing back. "You may come back for dinner, or maybe not. I'm not to go out. I am to have a nice quiet day and have dinner ready just in case you come home. Damn you, Paul Karinof. Damn your selfish soul."

The MP at the gate gave her a wolf whistle.

"Why, Miss Kramer, You took my advice. You look real nice."

Hanne giggled. She had discarded the ugly shoes and stockings, and was wearing flat, rather shabby sandals on her bare feet. The awful tweed skirt was still hanging from her hips, but the cardigan had been replaced with a plain white blouse. If Paul had been there to see her, he would have raised cain. But Paul was off playing tennis at the break of dawn. He hadn't even given a thought to how she was to get to work. She had had to thumb her way to the bus stop. But it was worth it. For the first time in months she felt free.

"Your hair looks pretty this way," the guard encouraged her "If you were to put on a bit of lipstick, you'd look like an American girl."

"Really?" she said. "Maybe I'll get myself some makeup."

"Get Sergeant Tyler to buy it for you in the PX. He seems to be a real nice fellow."

Hanne agreed demurely.

"You seeing him?" he asked kindly.

"We have a date this afternoon."

"Have fun," the guard said with a sigh. "I wish I could get the afternoon off, too. You don't often get weather like this in this part of the world."

Rip was waiting for her. His grin told her that he approved the changes in her appearance. "You know what we're going to do today?" he asked, starting the car. "When you get a heat wave like this, there's only one thing to do... go swimming."

"I don't have a swimsuit," she squeaked. "I wish I did. I'd love to go swimming."

"Who needs a swimsuit?"

She looked at him sideways. "I do. What are you going to wear?"

"My underwear. Look, I'm not suggesting that we walk about the beach in our long johns. We'll rent a boat and go out on the Wannsee. Then we undress and swim."

"The Wannsee—oh, Rip! I haven't been there since I was small."

"How small?"

She showed him with her hand. "When we were living on Brunnfelder Strasse—when my mother was still with us."

"How old were you when she died?"

Hanne swallowed hard. "Oh, she didn't die. She just went away. You see, she's not Jewish, so she didn't want to be married to my father anymore. After that we left Berlin and went to live with my grandmother Goldschmidt in Neustadt."

"Is that far from Berlin?"

He did not seem shocked, or horrified, or bored. And it felt good to talk about the things that had happened. Talking made them seem ordinary—not scary anymore.

"It's near Dresden, about an hour and a half by train. It was nice at first. I went to school 'til they found out I was Jewish."

"How did you get to be so smart if you didn't go to school?"

"That came later. I'm glad you noticed how smart I am. Do you know I can write polite letters in three languages? And I know all the European kings, complete with dates, all the way back to Charlemagne."

"Impressive," he agreed. "But can you play the parlor organ?"

She shook her head. "Well—no."

"Good. I hate it. My cousin Millie plays it, and every time you visit her place you have to sit in that stuffy front room and listen to her."

"Then why did you ask about it?"

"Just wanted to be safe. I wouldn't care to get involved with the kind of girl who plays the parlor organ. Tell me more about living with your grandma."

Hanne tried to picture her in her mind. "She was a very starchy old lady, and she didn't want me to be like my mother, because Mother was so vulgar. And she didn't like me to be like my father either, because he was so Jewish. I never could make that out, you know. I mean, he was her son and she was Jewish, too. But she seemed to feel that it was a recessive trait that had skipped her generation."

"Interesting idea—sort of like cropped ears." Hanne looked doubtful as Rip tried to explain. "You know, ears without earlobes. They keep coming back in our family. For years we have normal ears and then suddenly *pow*—a crop-eared baby."

"Does the family mind?"

"Some do. I think it's rather cute. The girls say it makes it hard to wear earrings—they keep falling off. So, there you were, a throwback. What happened next?"

"For a while I went to a Jewish school, but that closed. And then they arrested my father." Her throat closed up. She couldn't go on.

Rip's hand came down on hers and stayed there, warm and comforting. He asked no more questions, made no chitchat, just drove slowly, holding her hand in his.

"Would you rather I didn't talk about this?" Hanne asked in a small voice. "It's sort of dull and gloomy."

"Had the war started then?" It was really an answer of sorts.

"No, that was in '38. I was ten. It was just after my tenth birthday. That was the last good one. I had a cake with candles and presents—roller skates and an autograph album, and Grandmother gave me an old locket of hers with a blue stone on it. The next day the police came for him. They were quite polite. They said he would be back in a couple of hours." The old rage boiled in her. "They lied. The pigs. I never saw him again."

"Damn them," Rip said softly. "Damn their rotten souls."

Hanne leaned against his shoulder, limp and tired. Just remembering was hard work.

"After that it wasn't good anymore." She remembered the darkness clamping down. "Grandmother got very quiet and then she took me on the train to Gleiwitz, to the Webers. They were my mother's people and they didn't want me. But Grandmother just left me there. She kissed me good-bye. That's the only time she ever kissed me. She didn't approve of kissing, She thought it was unhygienic. It was so strange that I felt embarrassed, and afterward I wished that I'd kissed her back. I think I knew I'd never see her again."

"And these Webers, were they good to you?"

Hanne laughed, a dry little laugh, almost a sob. "They prayed over me. They told me that God loved me even though I was Jewish, because God could forgive anything, and that my mother had done the right thing running away. She was just following her conscience. Living with a Jew was so disgusting." The rage boiled again. "That's the word they used, 'disgusting.' And I remembered how nice he was to her and how much fun we had when we were living together. Like going to the Wannsee."

"Will you tell me the rest someday?"

She looked at him in surprise. "How did you know? How did you know I couldn't talk about it anymore?"

"Because you came back to the Wannsee, which is where we are going to rent a boat and swim in our skivvies—if you're willing. Look, babe, I want to know everything about you—in good time, when you're ready to tell me, But right now the sun's shining and you need to splash around in the water to work up an appetite for the lunch I packed."

"I don't think I can eat," she said weakly. "Talking about it has brought it all back. I feel sick."

"Tell me about one of the good days—like something about your father."

She thought about it and felt the warmth welling up inside her. "Every Sunday morning we took the Stadtbahn to the last stop and went for a walk in the woods, in the Grunewald. He knew the names of all the trees, and sometimes we brought home caterpillars. Once we even caught a little frog—a tree toad, really. But we let him go."

"My sister and I collected caterpillars," Rip offered. "We built a house for them, a fine house out of stone slabs. Only it collapsed and squashed them. So we had a funeral."

"Isn't it funny how children like to make funerals? I once found a dead bird in the street, and I cried and cried. Then we buried it in a shoe box and put a board on top that said what a good bird he'd been. And then I felt better."

Rip nodded. "It's a fitting finish. It rounds things off. If you can say the words, it gives you back control."

"Doing something—not just having it happen to you. Hanne mused. "I think I will be hungry after all."

They lay side by side in their little rented rowboat, soaking up the sun and drying their underwear. The lunch had fallen overboard, and they were chewing gum to stave off hunger.

"It was such a fine lunch, too," Rip said mournfully. "Tunafish salad and coleslaw. It's a shame I dropped it."

"The fish will eat it," Hanne said to comfort him. "It isn't wasted."

"Shall we come next week and try to catch the fish that ate it? Somewhere in this lake is an extra-fat fish, stuffed with coleslaw—a balanced meal all ready for us."

"Let's come here, but I'll bring the lunch."

"That's what I like about women. Give them half a chance and they feed you."

She pushed her elbow into his ribs. "I've been warned about men like you. Given half a chance, you give way to your baser impulses."

He looked cheered. "Are you nervous all alone with me in the middle of the lake?"

"Certainly not," she said. "There's something about you that makes me feel perfectly safe."

"I can't put my finger on it," he said, shaking his head. "I wouldn't swear to it. But I do think I've just been insulted."

In answer she kissed him.

"You kiss very well," he said thoughtfully. "Mind you, I'm not complaining, but it does suggest practice."

"Constant practice," she agreed. "Sister Celestine always said: 'Practice makes perfect.'"

He nodded and suddenly changed the subject.

"Will you tell me about your Sister Celestine next Monday? She sounds like a good one."

Rip got her back to the office in good time. They didn't talk much on the way home. Hanne leaned against his shoulder and felt very content.

She knew something had changed—something important, but she was not ready to put it all together yet. She needed time—time to think, time to rearrange her life.

Miss Printz was just leaving when she walked in, her office dress neatly covered by a short linen jacket and a straw version of her flower-pot hat skewered in place. She gave Hanne a friendly nod.

Left alone, Hanne started to arrange the files according to Paul's instructions. She had been vaguely aware that more and more requisitions were being rerouted to his operation. There had been a definite upswing in this activity since the beginning of July. Mostly she had been doing it without thinking, but this afternoon she took time out to read through the papers and was frightened. It wasn't just a few little bottles of penicillin or even a dozen cases of bourbon. This was big stuff: X-ray equipment, carloads of food and of medicines of all kinds. This wasn't just an amusing little black-market operation, like dealing in a few packs of cigarettes. This was theft on a grand scale. Her knees started to shake. She sat down.

I'm a thief, she told herself bleakly. Not Mata Hari risking her life for love, not even a clever girl playing tricks—just a cheap sneak thief, taking advantage of the decent people who trust me.

Shivering slightly, she gathered up the papers she had sorted out and stuffed them into an empty file drawer any which way. She snapped the lock and felt better. That was that. Tomorrow she would put them away properly.

She'd just have to explain to Paul that she was through helping him. She couldn't do it anymore.

One of the guards commented on her working later than usual and warned her that her bus had left. So her comings and goings were noted. It wouldn't have been long before they'd have caught her if she'd gone on with it. It was just as well she was quitting the game now, she told herself.

She waited forty minutes for the next bus and then decided to walk home. For six months now she had walked very little. Mostly, Paul drove her wherever she went. She found that walking cleared her head.

Her feet got sore in the flat sandals, so she took them off and walked barefoot. The feel of the gritty pavement under her feet provided a good sense of reality. It gave her a different slant on the life she had been living, a soft life, luxurious and unreal, and not at all what she wanted for herself.

❧ *Chapter 14*

Paul was not home—out exercising to make himself fit and beautiful, no doubt. She thought of his well-shaped hands with their manicured nails, the smooth chest, and beautiful flat stomach. He was still one of the handsomest men she had ever seen. However, she found she could think about him without emotion. That wonderful love of hers that had changed her life and made it so beautiful had been gradually fading away for months until it was quite dead.

She mourned the loss. It had been so bright and lovely. Nothing like it could happen the second time. She would never be that young again. Right now, she felt dried-up inside, cold and alone and very, very old.

Paul had been her whole life. Without him, there wasn't much. As she set about preparing supper for Paul, more from force of habit than anything else, she thought about her future. She had loved cooking for him. She wouldn't be doing it anymore.

The refrigerator was almost empty. Normally, she would have been making a shopping list to make sure there would be enough butter and eggs and fresh fruit and vegetables. She put some potatoes on to boil, and fried the last onion with the last strip of bacon.

At least she wasn't leaving a mess behind. Miss Stulp, or Paul's next girl-friend, would have no trouble carrying on with the housekeeping. Of course, Paul would have no trouble replacing her. His life was full of women. He had always made that plain to her.

Her own life, she admitted to herself, was going to be empty. She thought she could live with that. Her only real friend was the princess. Ingelore might have become a friend, if Paul had allowed it. Now it was too late. She would not be seeing her again.

Hanne shied away from the thought of Rip. She liked him a lot, as a friend, and he seemed to like her—not just as a friend. He was so nice, the nicest man she knew. Maybe someday she would get to know him better. Perhaps, in time, if she ever got back to being young, they would fall in love and have fun together again.

But the princess was her friend, right now, when she needed a friend most. With her, she could be sure of a welcome and of being allowed to stay.

Packing was easy. She took a small suitcase and put in it her housedresses, some underwear, her hairbrush and toothbrushes, and a cake of soap. Perhaps Paul would let her buy some of the simpler clothes from him later. She had no use for the elegant things. Many of them, like the wonderful plaid evening gown, had never been worn.

She counted her money. There was enough to get her to Charlottenburg and to pay the princess for her keep, since she wouldn't be home enough to do much housework.

She considered going right away and leaving Paul a note, but she pushed that thought aside. She owed him an explanation. He had been good to her in his way, and she had loved him. It wasn't his fault that she had stopped loving him. He hadn't changed. She had.

He was looking pleased with himself, when he finally walked in.

"Boy, have I got a surprise for you," he said exuberantly.

"There's something I've got to tell you," said Hanne.

"I know, I know." He threw himself down on the couch and grinned up at her, "You're going to tell me that you screwed up tonight. My boy went to pick up the papers and found everything locked up tight as a drum. He was pissed, I can tell you. But everyone's entitled to one goof. Just remember next time that you don't have the keys, and be extra careful about locking up before everything's set."

Hanne stood opposite him and pressed her spine against the bookcase. "There won't be a next time."

"Of course not," he agreed cheerfully. "That's what I said. We won't mention it again. Hey, what's that damn awful smell?"

Hanne ran to the kitchen, turned off the heat under the burning skillet, and tipped the ruined meal into the garbage can. It hardly seemed to matter. When Paul had finished hearing her out, he wouldn't want to eat anyway. He'd most likely slam out of the house in a temper.

He had followed her into the kitchen and was leaning in the door frame, watching her with a grin.

"You're getting to be almost as great a cook as Stulp. Never mind, we'll go out and get something. You've been working too hard. Listen, you have no idea whom I've met."

"Sorry about the dinner," said Hanne.

"To hell with the dinner. Listen! I met this terrific woman. Actually, I met her months ago, and there was something about her."

Hanne didn't want to hear about his new woman. It made it easier for her to leave, but she didn't want to have to listen to the whole story.

"I'm very happy for you," she said stiffly.

Paul groaned. "You're not listening. This woman reminded me of you. Older, different accent, not as cute as yours, but there was this resemblance—tantalizing. The guy who works with her didn't introduce us, but I knew right away that she was the brains of that outfit. You've met Captain Polk, haven't you? He's a bit dim. I always wondered how he'd managed to parlay that lousy motor pool into such a sweet setup. The man's all wind and bluster. Well, this woman's built up the whole thing. She's terrific."

Hanne was barely listening. She filled the sink with cold water and put the burned pan in to soak. How silly, she thought. I won't be washing it anyway. I won't be here.

"Stop messing around with that stuff and pay attention." Paul sounded excited. "I'd forgotten all about her, and then today I had to stop off at Polk's billet— and there she was, obviously at home, in a very handsome outfit, sort of a house pajama affair, raw silk. I've got to get you something like that. It'd look great on you. Polk did his damnedest not to introduce us. He knows when he's on to a good thing, and he has no intention of sharing. You could see the poor boob struggling with the problem. Meanwhile, she just passed the drinks and smiled. . . and then it hit me."

"What hit you?" Hanne was now convinced that she would have to listen to the whole dreary story of his new conquest before she could have her say.

"I looked at that face and said to myself, no one but Honey has that mouth and those eyes. And then she introduced herself. Honey! I met Claudia Goldschmidt today!"

Hanne felt sick. There had been a time—a lifetime ago—when she had been small and still had parents. She had once had a mother by that name. The name no longer held any meaning for her. Hanne had wiped it out.

"No," she said in a flat voice. "Not Goldschmidt."

Paul was too ecstatic to catch the utter rejection in her tone.

"Yes, Goldschmidt!" He was almost crowing. "I've found your mother for you, Honey!"

"She has no right to the name," said Hanne. "It's Claudia Weber. The woman changed it back to Weber when she left us."

"Yeah, I suppose so." Paul brushed this aside. "She said something about that. You were just kid, and you wouldn't have understood what was happening. Things were pretty hairy."

"I knew what was happening," Hanne said coldly. "I got thrown out of school. My father was taken away, and then my grandmother. Believe me, I noticed."

"Damn it all, she's your mother." Paul was beginning to get irritated. "You can't blame her for those things! Christ, have you any idea what it was like to be married to a Jew at that time? She told me all about it. She had a rotten time."

Hanne could hardly breathe. All the old rage against her mother boiled up and found its focus on him.

"Stop glaring like that." Paul sounded comfortably superior. "You're not a kid anymore. I know you'll he crazy about her when you see her again. She's a great lady."

"I'm not going to see her again." Hanne was struggling against a nightmarish sense of unreality. "I have no intention of ever being in the same room with that woman."

Paul stuck his hands into his pockets and hunched his shoulders "Knock it off, Honey. It's been a long day. I'm in no mood for your dramatics. Damn it, I thought you'd be pleased. Most people would be tickled pink to find their mother again after such a long time."

Hanne just stood quite still, staring at him. He shrugged.

"What the hell, you don't have to be crazy about her. But you will have to be polite. She will be coming here from time to time."

Hanne took a deep breath. "That's all right, Paul. I won't be meeting her here. I'm moving out. I was trying to tell you."

He gave a short bark of laughter. "What the hell do you mean, 'moving out?'"

"I tried to tell you."

"Just because you don't like your mother?" His voice was heavy with sarcasm. "And when exactly did this great idea come to you?"

"I'm sorry, Paul."

He turned away with a shrug. "Lay off, will you? I'm too tired to play games. You have the damnedest timing. This is really your day, isn't it? First the snafu with the files, then the grandstand performance about Claudia... and now this. I hope you're not coming down with something. Get some sleep, kid."

"I'm leaving you," said Hanne. "I'm leaving now. Try to understand. I've changed. I can't live with you anymore. I'm not helping you steal supplies anymore, and I'm not going to sleep with you, not even for one night."

"And what brought this on?" Paul's voice was suddenly hard and nasty.

"It's been coming on a long time. I'm sorry. I know it sounds awful, but I can't help it."

"You bitch," said Paul.

Hanne turned away. She felt very tired all of a sudden. It was useless. He wouldn't, couldn't, understand. She might just as well have left a note. It had been a wasted effort.

"You miserable, ungrateful, useless little bitch." Paul came to a stop only long enough to snatch a convulsive breath and launch into a new attack. "You know what you are? You're nothing! You're less than nothing! And you dare to set yourself up to judge a woman like Claudia. You smug little kike. If your father was anything like you, I can see why she ditched him. He must have been a royal pain in the arse."

"I can't talk to you when you're like this," Hanne said wearily.

"You don't have to talk. You listen."

She picked up her handbag and tried to get past him. She didn't even see his fist coming at her. The floor rose up, and then she was dragged upright and hit again and again, until she was back on the floor. That was when he started kicking her.

When Hanne heard the car drive away, she dragged herself to her feet and made her way to the door. It was hard to walk. She could see a little out of her right eye, and her legs were all right, but her right arm hurt badly, and the left one dangled uselessly.

She went a few steps and sat down on the ground. It was nice and cool. She wanted to stretch out and rest, but she knew dimly that she had to get away before Paul came back. This time had been different. There had been no apologies, no comforting afterward. He had tried to kill her and he might be coming back to finish the job. She pulled herself up by sheer force of will and staggered on.

Ingelore opened the door and cried out, bringing Colonel Hosterley running.

"*Ach mein Gott. Die Arme. Die braucht einen Artzt.*"

"Stop driveling and get her inside. We have to call a doctor," the colonel said, quickly finishing his drink after one hasty look at Hanne's face. "Put her on the couch. Christ, what a mess."

"Send an ambulance," he bellowed into the phone. "No, not an army one, it's for a German girl. Looks like she was beaten up pretty bad.... Oh, hell—a stickup, I suppose.... Yeah, get her a bed in a German hospital. Do what you can."

He leaned over Hanne. "The police are sending an ambulance for you. Do you understand?"

She tried to nod, but it hurt too much. Ingelore started to dab at her face with a wet cloth, but gave up with an exclamation of horror when she saw the extent of the damage.

The elderly doctor who came to examine her was less gentle, but he got her onto a stretcher and into the ambulance with a minimum of fuss.

"We tried to get a bed for you locally, but they're all full up," he grumbled once they were on their way. "That damn occupation has taken over all our best hospitals. We were lucky to get a bed for you at the Charité. It's quite a ride—all the way to the Russian sector—but I'll give you a shot of morphine to tide you over, and the nuns will take good care of you."

"The nuns," she said with a ghost of a smile. "Always back to the nuns to be taken care of."

"The police will want to question you," he warned her. "They'll want you to identify the attackers. I'll do my best to keep them away from you, at least 'til you're stitched up and have gotten that arm set. What do they hope to get from you, anyway? They'll never catch the thugs. It's like this after every war. I remember in '18 when toughs roamed the streets terrorizing decent people. Always the same."

The morphine did its work and she dozed, aware of the movement of the ambulance, aware of the pain, but detached. The fear was gone and the rage. It was like being on a cloud. The doctor's grumbling voice was part of the dream.

The morphine didn't help while they were setting her arm and sewing up the gashes in her face.

"I think we can save the eye," she heard someone say, and she wondered what difference it made. She was going to die anyway.

Then another shot brought more dreams; one lovely dream of being tucked in by Sister Celestine, who was saying, "Stop pulling at that dressing, or we'll have to tie down your hands." But it wasn't Sister Celestine after all. It was a bossy nun with a long face, much more like Sister Angelika. After a time, there was real sleep without dreams, and then she woke up all the way and found that she was tied up like a package, strapped down and barely able to turn her head.

One eye was bandaged, but the other one was working quite well. She could make out the rows of beds opposite and the pleated linen screens on either side of her bed. The smell was vaguely familiar—carbolic soap and floor polish, the convent smell.

A nun rustled past, her sleeves pinned back, carrying a tray. Behind her came a man in a long white coat, and several others in short white jackets.

A nun materialized on her blind side and started smoothing the covers.

"Grand rounds," she whispered. "Be a good girl and don't say a thing 'til they're gone. Let them think you're still out, otherwise someone will bring in the police, and we'd like you to rest up a bit before they bother you."

Hanne closed her eye obediently, and listened to the flock of doctors as they made their way toward her.

"Nothing very interesting here," she heard someone say. "Clean fracture, no complications. It'll be an interesting job for the plastic surgeons later on, but right now it's nothing special."

This struck her as exquisitely funny, and when the nurse came back to her, she was surprised to find Hanne laughing.

"Not interesting," she tried to explain. "I'm not going to die. I'm not even interesting."

"I'm going to untie you now," the nurse said briskly, ignoring what she thought was hysteria. "We had to do it because you kept clawing at the bandage over your eye."

"Will I be able to see?"

"Oh, yes!" The nun was all cheerful encouragement. "The images will be a bit fuzzy at first, but in time you will see quite well."

"And what will I look like? They said something about needing a plastic surgeon."

"We mustn't be vain now, must we? Looks aren't everything. You're bound to have a bit of scarring, especially if you keep poking at that dressing. Now that you're awake, I'm going to take away the screens and have them bring you a cup of soup."

"But I'm not hungry."

The nun looked offended. "If you want to get well, you'll eat what's served you and not make a fuss. We don't tolerate temperament around here."

Yes, it was just like being back at the orphanage.

?❧ *Chapter 15*

She gave the police a vague description of her attackers. Two men, one tall and heavy, the other sort of medium. No, she had not seen their faces. It had been too dark. Did they have guns? She wasn't sure. They hit her because she didn't want to give them her purse. Yes, she had been foolish and would not go around by herself at night in the future.

The next visitor was from administration. They were happy to inform her that OMGUS was paying her entire hospital bill under their employee benefit package. She did not have to worry about that.

However, a bothersome little technicality had come up. The address provided by the personnel department did not exist. A clerical error no doubt, but to make it even more confusing the American officer who had called the ambulance knew her by a different name.

Just a nickname, Hanne was going to say, then changed her mind. No more lies.

"I don't have a work permit in my own name. The papers I've been using were bought on the black market. My real name's Hanne Goldschmidt."

The woman from the front office looked shocked and went away, and the screens went up around her bed again. The police came back, not the comfortable, fatherly policeman who had talked to her before but a narrow-eyed, older man, who reminded her somehow of Major Kuprin.

"You will please make a statement." the policeman said in a measured way.

Hanne shook her head mutely.

"I don't think you understand," he said with a twitch of irritation. "You have committed a felony in applying for work with forged papers. This so-called accident of yours is now open to a completely new interpretation. Was someone blackmailing you?"

She turned her head and stared down the ward.

"You're not doing yourself a favor," the policeman snapped. "It will soon be out of my hands and the Americans will take over the case. Don't expect too much understanding from them."

"You mean I'd be better off trusting to the kind hearts of the German police?" she asked sweetly. "They were so very understanding when they carted my father off to a concentration camp."

"Aha—Jewish," he said, looking satisfied, "In that case there's no more to be said. I'm sure they'll go easy on you."

"Were you a Nazi?" she asked him curiously.

He smiled without amusement. "I'd hardly have this job if I had been, but that doesn't mean I like Jews. To be frank, I don't, I just liked the National Socialists even less. Rabble."

He stalked off, his narrow back stiff with ancient arrogance. Hanne almost thought she could hear spurs jingling as he walked.

There were no more visitors until the day when the bandage came off the left side of her face. The eye worked better than she had dared to hope, barely fuzzy at all.

She got out of bed on wobbly legs and cautiously made her way to the window at the end of the ward. The light did hurt a bit, but it was wonderful to look at something other than a row of beds. There was a neat square of grass outside with a newly planted tree in the middle, carefully staked out with supporting wires. It looked like a healthy little tree, but the leaves were beginning to turn brown. So, the summer was almost over. She had been here longer than she realized.

Hanne went to the bathroom and had her first look in a mirror. It was strange. Except for the fading bruises, sickly yellow-green, she didn't look too bad. There was a puckered seam running across the left side of her face, from her ear, across the corner of her eye, and up to her shaved head. The ear looked peculiar—as if it had been put on crooked.

Her eyebrows had been shaved off, too, and that didn't help any. She wasn't exactly ugly, just very odd-looking.

She went back to her bed to find the princess sitting there, waiting for her.

The old woman stared at her accusingly. "You promised you would come to me. You promised."

"You'll never believe me, Excellency, but I was on my way when this happened to me."

The princess pursed her lips and looked critically at Hanne's new face. "I understand your not wanting to discuss it with the police, but you don't have to lie to me. I know who did it, and I shall never forgive him—never."

Hanne smiled at her old friend. "If they don't lock me up, can I come and stay with you?"

The princess clapped her fat little hands. "But that's why I'm here. I've come to take you home. They're discharging you today. Of course, you'll have to come back when they're ready to take off the cast, but meanwhile you'll stay with me."

"And the police?"

The princess pulled a face. "I had to sign a paper stating that you would not leave town, and that—how did they put it?—that I would make you available to them. Just a formality, I'm sure."

"But how did you know I was here?"

The princess smiled radiantly. "That nice Major Kuprin made all the arrangements. Isn't it a blessing to have true friends?"

Neither Petya nor Mimi was in sight when they got to the flat. The princess had somehow managed to get a taxi—probably the only one in Berlin. The stairs seemed steeper, making Hanne unpleasantly aware of how weak she still was, and they still smelled of drains and cabbage.

All she wanted was to go back to bed. The princess hadn't thought that far ahead, but was quite unconcerned. "You will sleep in my bed until you feel better. At my age one can sleep anywhere. You'd never believe me, Honey, but I sit up most nights in my chair and doze off in little snatches. Who needs a bed?"

"Have you seen Paul, Excellency?" The question finally had to be asked.

"You mean lately? No. I don't care to see him. He has moved beyond the pale of decent society. Not even the thought of his dear mother can make me overlook what he has done to you. Drink your tea, Honey. Is it sweet enough? Petya still sees him on business, but Paul is no longer welcome here."

"You know about me, don't you, that I helped him and that I'm likely to end up in jail? Am I going to make trouble for you?"

"Trouble? For me?" The princess gestured magnificently. "What can they do to me? I've lost everything. They can take no more. What we must do is plan for you. Your life is all ahead of you. This unpleasantness is nothing. It will blow over. These little complications can be taken care of. What we need now is a new set of papers, and then we must smuggle you out of Berlin."

Hanne collapsed in a muddled welter of laughter and tears. "No, Lydia Ivanovna, no more forged papers. No, I'm not hysterical—well, only a little bit hysterical. But I absolutely will not run away anymore. As soon as this silly cast comes off and I can get around on my own two feet, I'm going to the American authorities and make a statement. I'll try not to involve Paul. I'll just refuse to name names, even though I suppose they know by now that I was living with him. I'll just say someone else was involved. I'll make them think there's another person. And I can say I bought the forged papers from a German who said they were stolen."

The princess looked worried. "Honey, my child, already you are constructing new lies. It is better to accept the fact that we all have to tell lies now and again and make them work for us. I admit it's very nice and comfortable to tell the truth, but that won't work unless you're able to tell the whole truth. You can't do that, can you?"

Hanne sagged. "No. I can't involve Paul. I owe him that much."

"You owe him nothing," the princess said angrily. "But there are others involved. Poor Petya, that nice Colonel Arpov, and so many others. I think you'd better run away and start fresh in another place. You will be beautiful again. You will meet another man."

The eyebrow with the scar grew in crooked, and the ear remained off kilter, but she didn't mind her looks too much. By the end of September the hair had grown back, covering a lot of the damage. It looked rather funny, like a velvety fur cap with ragged edges.

She practiced doing things with one hand and was rather proud of herself. She could actually do most of the housework, even laundry, though it was a bit awkward. The princess was properly admiring and grateful for her company. No one else came to the flat these days, not counting an old man who brought groceries. It was almost eerie, considering the constant flow of visitors that had always passed through before.

There was no more talk of getting out of Berlin. There was no talk of the future at all. Both of them were tiptoeing around the subject. Hanne rehearsed various confessions in her head, trying to come up with something that was true and yet involved nobody else. She did not think about Rip at all. She dared not think about him. He belonged to another life, another reality.

The cast seemed to become lighter, though whether it was because her muscles were stronger or because it actually weighed less as it dried was hard to say. Hanne amused herself by drawing on it, butterflies, rabbits, and a recurring motif—a small flowering tree.

She answered the doorbell one morning and found herself face-to-face with Major Kuprin and another man. She stepped back without a word. So that was that. They had finally come for her.

The major walked past her and knocked on the door of the salon.

"Lydia Ivanovna, I've brought the doctor for Miss Honey's arm, and I was hoping you would offer me a glass of tea, and perhaps a little conversation."

Hanne was thunderstruck, but allowed herself to be taken to the kitchen, where the doctor went about cutting off the cast.

"It was the major's idea," he began. "He felt the trip to the hospital might be too much for you. I really would have preferred to take a few more X rays, but Dr. Pankau doesn't expect any further problems. A little atrophy, of course, but with exercise you will soon have those muscles back."

"You came all the way from the Charité?"

"I'm on the staff, though I was not originally involved with your case. Dr. Pankau really did a fine job on you, just splendid. You've been very lucky." He looked pleased with himself.

"What now?"

He stared. "My dear young lady, we are not in China. I understand that if you save a life there, you are forever responsible for that person. A dreadful idea." He laughed, "Here we just patch you up and then you're on your own."

She nodded. "Of course."

"Well, then," he went on heartily. "The exercises. This is what I want you to do. Start gently, no more than three of each twice a day. In a couple of weeks you should be up to fifty. Don't coddle yourself."

He looked with distaste at the mess he had made on the floor gave a stiff little bow, and left her. Hanne got out the broom and started sweeping up.

"Do you need help, Miss Honey?" The Major stood in the doorway, not particularly threatening. "I was sent for tea, but I think we need to get rid of all that plaster before we can do anything else."

"I can manage," she said stiffly.

He sat down and watched her sweep. His eyes were almost kind. "Do you remember the last conversation we had, Miss Honey? Yes, I see you do. I tried then to make you understand that I wanted to be your friend. I still do."

"It's too late," she said sadly. "I messed everything up. You did try to warn me. I appreciate that."

"You can still get out," he said softly. "I promised you immunity then. It's a bit harder now. You're in so much deeper than you were, aren't you? But if you come clean—as our American friends will have it—I can still promise you the same deal."

"You seem to know it all. Why don't you just arrest everyone and be done with it?"

"It's not that simple, Miss Honey. I don't have all the facts I need to go ahead. And it's awkward, because the people involved are of so many different nationalities. Everyone will try to protect their own and make the others look bad. My job is to extricate Colonel Arpov. He's a war hero and very popular back home. We can't have him involved in a black-market scandal. And the Americans will try to look out for their people. If we can pin it on your Mr. Karinof, everyone will be pleased. He's an outsider. No one will mind if he gets stuck with the blame. And let's face it—he's guilty as hell."

"So am I and you know it."

He shrugged. "Oh, that sleight of hand with the lipstick—very charming, but hardly criminal."

"That's not what I meant."

His eyes narrowed. "Yes, you were the little mole in the OMGUS supply department, weren't you? I didn't want to believe it at first. You know what gave you away? Locking up that particular pile of requisitions in an empty file. It was a rather interesting assortment, considering all the supplies that had been going astray lately. And only you could have put them there. If those papers hadn't been found, no one would have started looking for all the others that were supposed to have been filed. Ironic, isn't it?"

"So, arrest me and send me back to the Americans."

He sighed and shook his head. "We're not on such friendly terms as all that. Right now we've got you. Your American friends still don't know you got whisked out of the Charité. You are the ace up our sleeve. We don't really want to let this mess go public. That's why I can offer you a deal."

Hanne felt very cold. Every time you thought you had a friend, it turned out to be just another angle, another deal. And yet she trusted the major—to a certain point.

"If I don't make the statement, what then?"

"But you will," he said wearily. "Maybe not today or tomorrow. But when you have had time to think over your situation, I think you'll decide to be sensible. I know that dear old woman thinks she can get papers for you and spirit you away. Don't you believe it. Any forged papers you buy will come from us. And wherever you run, we will be waiting for you when you get there."

"You're trying to scare me," she said through stiff lips.

"I'm giving you a fair picture. If it scares you, and it should, maybe it's time for you to get out of this game. It isn't really your game, is it? I never thought it was."

"I will make a statement," Hanne offered desperately. "I'll tell you exactly what I did and how I did it. Only I won't involve anyone else."

"No good to me," the major said gently. "No one will believe you acted on your own. Who came and picked up the papers you left out so conveniently? Who doctored them so they could be used? Who actually picked up the stuff, and who handled the distribution? Can you answer any of these questions? No. But your friend Paul can, and he will once we've got him."

Hanne struggled against the feeling of a trap closing around her. "It'll do you no good," she said. "Paul will just give you the names of all the people you are trying to protect."

"True," the major agreed calmly, "but those aren't the names that will show up on the final report. We will have a few German nationals, maybe some low-ranking army personnel, nobody who knows enough to point a finger, and we can let those off with a slap on the wrist. Once this operation is shut down, it can be passed off as a minor incident. But it must be shut down before it causes a scandal, All we need is Paul Karinof."

"I can't do it."

"You must. Think about it. Being in love is very charming, but being free to come and go is better. Believe me, freedom is more important than love."

He looked at her with sad, wise eyes. Hanne shook her head.

"You've got it all wrong," she said softly. "Take away love, and you're left with nothing."

❧ *Chapter 16*

Rip knew something was very wrong when Hanne was not waiting for him for their picnic on the lake. The German woman she had been working with rushed past with wide, scared eyes, refusing to stop and talk. He asked a few questions and got crooked answers. No one had seen Miss Kramer. No, she did not seem to be working at OMGUS anymore.

He drove to the house in Zehlendorf several times, but no one was ever home, not even the housekeeper. All the houses had a shut-off, secret look, as if eyes were watching from behind drawn drapes. Once a dark-haired German girl came to the door of the house across the street. She smiled tentatively and looked as if she wanted to talk to him, but then she ducked out of sight without a word after all.

Finally he tried the MP who had brought him the note. He was luckier there.

"I'm sorry about that mess. It's got to be hushed up. Seems this little gal's been stealing—on quite a scale, too. I never would have believed it. And then she got herself beaten up—pretty bad, they say. They had to put her into a hospital. I heard she was a proper mess."

"Do you know where they took her?"

"That big Catholic hospital in the Russian sector—the Charité. She must still be there. The moment she gets out, I imagine she'll be prosecuted. Seems a shame, doesn't it? She's just a kid. Probably got into bad company."

"Yeah," Rip said grimly. "Real bad company."

At the hospital he drew a blank again. True, the girl had been there, but she had been discharged. Dr. Pankau had taken care of her. To see Dr. Pankau you had to have an appointment. It would be several weeks before he could be fitted in, and all the arguments in the world got him nowhere. The doctor was a busy man and the American soldier would wait his turn like everyone else.

Rip made an appointment, waited his turn, and finally got to see Dr. Pankau three weeks later. The man was curiously reluctant to discuss the case. The girl was no longer a patient, and it was a closed case. It was now a matter for the police. He was not free to give out information to unauthorized personnel. After a stiff bow, Rip was dismissed.

He was back at the hospital the following week, trying to get something out of the nurses. They smiled and shook their heads. They were all so busy. So many patients, never enough time.

Finally he sat down on one of the shiny wooden benches that lined the hallways. He felt beaten. Here was another dead end. For once he had no idea how to go on with his search.

A smiling young nun approached him.

"Are you the young man who is looking for Miss Kramer?"

He nodded hopefully.

"I hope you can understand me. My English is not very good. But I took care of her when she was on our ward—a very brave girl."

He swallowed hard. "Have you any idea where she went when she left?"

The nun looked him over doubtfully. "You mean well by her, no? I think I can trust you. Then I will tell you. She left in a taxi. I helped her get in. They gave the address to the driver—a Charlottenburg address. I happen to remember because I grew up on the Kaiser Allee, just around the corner. Burghof Strasse Number 9. She was with a fat Russian lady, very old."

"Could you write that down for me?"

She printed it on the back of an envelope. "I hope it will help you find her. You will be kind to her, no? Not make fun of how she looks."

"Lady, believe me, I don't care what she looks like. I've got to find her, that's all."

"Good luck," she said, tucking her hands into her sleeves and lowering her head. "I wish you well."

There were ten apartments in Number 9, but only one Russian name—Tschernsky. So that had to be it.

He ran up the steps three at a time, and pounded on the door, found the bell, rang, and went back to pounding. There was a scurrying noise and the door was opened a crack. Across a bolt chain, Hanne's dear face peered out at him for a brief moment. Then the chain was scraped back, the door flew open, and she flung herself into his arms.

"Rip, oh, Rip. How did you find me?"

"It was a heap of trouble," he said, holding her gingerly, because she seemed so fragile. "You should have sent me word. You sure do get around, don't you?"

"Who is it?" A scratchy voice came from the depth of the apartment. "Have we got a visitor, Honey?"

"A very special one," Hanne called back. "Come along. You must meet the princess."

"I never did meet a real princess before."

"Oh, she's not as real as all that. But such a darling. Come on."

He followed her down the hallway into the stuffy room, in which an enormously fat woman seemed to be squatting like a spider in a net. She examined him through a lorgnette.

"Come closer, young man. Introduce yourself."

"Rip Tyler, ma'am—Princess. I'm very pleased to meet you."

"And where are you from?"

"Pocahontas County, West Virginia, ma'am. I don't know if that means anything to you."

"I can't say it does. I met a man from Philadelphia once."

"A very nice town."

"So he said. But people always praise their own hometowns, don't they? Your hometown is no doubt bigger and finer than any other."

"Hardly. Our biggest town is Marlinton, about thirty miles from my folks' place. It's on the small side. Pretty little town. Main Street runs through the middle, with a couple of blocks on either side. As long as the floods don't wash out the bridge, which they do just about every spring, it's a nice-enough place, but personally I prefer the mountains."

The princess seemed puzzled by this but nodded graciously. The young man had passed the first test. He wasn't awkward and shy, and he didn't boast, as so many Americans were supposed to do.

"Do join us for a glass of tea," she suggested with a hospitable wave of her hand.

Rip sat down gingerly on a shaky chair and watched Hanne with his heart in his eyes as she drew water from the dented samovar and mixed it with the tea from the small pot on top. It was quite a production.

The princess watched him with hooded eyes. So that was it. This unassuming young man had managed to take Honey away from Paul. It made her want to laugh.

But was he good enough for her? It was so hard to tell with Americans. They were said to be kind to women and children but to have a tendency to tell lies about their background. Maybe they didn't have background, not as it was understood in Europe.

She examined him owlishly. He really looked quite nice, except for his nails, which were encrusted with grime—a workman's hands. She couldn't help but compare those hands with Paul's elegant, well-groomed ones. But Paul's beautiful hands had hurt Honey. So much for good grooming.

Quite unaware of the judgment being made on him, Rip sat and looked at Hanne. He was quite content just to be in the same room with her, to watch her handle the teapot with one hand. She didn't seem to be using the left one much. It looked puny and limp. Her hair was short like rabbit fur, and her left ear was on wrong. He wanted very much to kiss her again, and hold her. But for the moment it was good just to have her there in the room.

"It is my understanding that you are interested in my young friend." The princess interrupted his pleasant thoughts.

"Are you asking me my intentions?" Rip asked delightedly. "No one ever did before. That must mean I'm finally being taken seriously."

"Intentions—yes, that's the right word. I had an English governess, but that was so long ago, you understand. I am a little rusty."

"My intentions are quite honorable."

The princess made a sound that Rip would have described as a satisfied grunt in a less exalted lady.

"Honey, go and wait in the kitchen," she ordered crisply. "This young man and I have private matters to discuss."

Hanne gave him a comical look and went.

"Now, Sergeant Tyler, what have you got to offer?"

Rip was dumbfounded. The conversation had taken a turn he wasn't prepared for. "I wasn't planning to bid for her, ma'am. I just aim to ask her to marry me."

"Understood. What will you live on? What is your family? Do you have any property to settle on her?"

Rip settled back with a grin. "Oh, I see. We're going to dicker. I like that. My family's been farming on Back Mountain for five generations. They're well thought of— barring my Uncle Clarence, who made bad whiskey and was fool enough to get caught."

"We all have our black sheep," the princess assured him graciously.

"My brother'll get the homeplace, of course, being the oldest, but I plan to buy out my cousin Walt. He has a nice little place, just forty acres but real pretty, and he's going to give me a good price on it. He's settled in Akron and doesn't farm it anymore."

"You will be able to support a family on such a small farm?" she asked shrewdly. "It must be very rich soil."

"No, ma'am. It's all scrub and rocks. Best you can do is raise sheep on it— maybe a few head of beef cattle— but I don't expect to live by farming. I have a job waiting for me, in the forest service."

"A woodcutter?" She sounded horrified.

"Not exactly, though I expect to cut a tree now and again. I did get me a degree in forestry before I was drafted. You don't get rich in the forest service, but you don't starve either."

"You went to a university." The princess sounded enormously pleased. "I am quite satisfied. You may now go to Honey. You will find her in the kitchen, third door on the left."

He found her sitting on the table, dangling her legs and rubbing the left arm. There was a dreamy, peaceful look on her scarred face.

"I've just got permission to propose," he told her; "Your princess is a funny old duck, and she sure aims to look out for you."

"Is she trying to make you marry me?"

"I'm not putting up a big fight."

Hanne twisted her hands in her lap. "You think I'm a nice girl, don't you?"

He grinned. "I know you are."

"Well, there are a lot of things you don't know about me." She was watching him carefully, but it was hard to make anything of his expression.

"I should imagine so," he agreed pleasantly. "But I'm willing to learn."

She took a deep breath. "To start with, Paul never was my employer. He was my lover."

He nodded. "I did get that idea. He was quite careful to make it plain to me."

Hanne felt as if she'd been punched in the stomach, but there was no change in Rip's face. "How long have you known?"

"I guess from the beginning. You don't look like someone's hired girl. No way."

She felt a jolt of anger. "Then you were lying to me."

"I suppose I was." He scratched his head. "I reckon I'm not always as truthful as I ought to be. But I figured it would be more comfortable for both of us if I took that stand." His face suddenly broke into a happy smile. "It's like going hunting. You don't wave your gun and holler, 'Come out, you little old rabbit! I'm goin' to shoot you.'"

She gave him a sidelong glance under her lashes. "You were hunting me?"

"You bet," he agreed cheerfully. "From the moment I saw you. I said to myself: 'Rip Tyler, if you let that one get away from you, you're a bigger fool even than they say you are....'"

"And if you happened to catch me, what then?"

"Well... you're too skinny to make a good meal. I guess I'd take you home and keep you."

"As a pet?"

"Hell, no. I'd expect you to work. Have you any idea what's expected from a farm wife? My mom keeps house like any woman, but in addition she cares for the chickens and the vegetable garden, runs the tractor and can fix it as well as Dad can. And she keeps all the accounts, down to the last penny."

Hanne stared. "You really want to marry me?"

"My daddy always told me to marry a girl while she's young and doesn't know any better," he said with a completely straight face. "You see, once they get smart, they won't be trapped into it so easy."

"Oh, Rip, you fool," she said. It came out like a sigh.

"That's what they say," he agreed cheerfully. "Well, now that you've been proposed to, what about it? I'm dumb and a terrible liar, as you well know, but I have my good points. I'm hard-working, reliable, I have a good digestion, and I'm faithful."

She leaned forward and kissed his cheek. He pushed her away gently. "That's the most insulting kiss I ever did get, Hanne. Are you refusing me?"

"If you really knew me, Rip, you wouldn't want me. I hardly know myself."

"We could get to know you together," he suggested gently. "Sort of something to do on long winter nights."

"You make it sound so cozy. Can you imagine finding out some cold winter night that I'm not faithful at all?"

He stared at her solemnly. "You plan to mess around?"

She had to laugh at his owlish look. "No, you fool, of course not. But how can I tell you what I'm going to do? You know that I've been living with Paul. If I'm willing to leave him and take up with someone else, how can you be sure I won't do the same to you? Then what would you do?"

"I'd get you back," he said calmly.

"But you'd be angry," she goaded him.

"Yes."

"You'd want to kill me."

"Could be."

"You'd beat me up."

He looked startled. "What good would that do? I said I'd get you back, and I would—somehow. Anyway, what makes you so sure you'd be unfaithful? You might have so much fun being married to me, you wouldn't want to. You probably wouldn't have time, anyway. I'd keep you busy, cooking and cleaning and mucking out the chickens, having a baby every year. And I'm a wonderful lover."

His face was blandly serious. Against her will, Hanne burst out laughing. "How did you find that out? Is that what the girls tell you?"

"Well, no," he admitted. "I figured it out myself. You see...."

"No, don't," she said hastily. "Don't explain. I'm willing to take it on trust."

"I'd like you to find out for yourself," he said with a wonderfully silly grin. "But you'll have to marry me first. I'm hard to get."

"Oh, Rip."

"You don't have to make up your mind right this minute," he assured her. "I'll hang around for a while. I won't be a nuisance unless you say no. In that case, look out, I'll make a real pest of myself. You'll do much better to marry me. It'll save you a heap of aggravation."

"I wish I could marry you. I wish I'd met you sooner. Now I can't."

"Mrs. Clark in first grade always told us, 'Never say "can't." Just keep trying.'"

She leaned against him, helpless with laughter. "All right. I'll keep trying to marry you. Does that make sense?"

"It'll have to do for the time being. I do realize that we have some practical problems, but I'm good at stuff like that—jigsaw puzzles and working out disagreements about line fences. Just leave it to me."

❧ *Chapter 17*

Rip's elation had been a little dampened by the time he arrived at Miss Peterson's office. Getting married to a girl who was officially missing and quite likely wanted for fraud was more complicated than he had anticipated. Nor was Miss Peterson particularly encouraging at first.

The social worker was a crisp, efficient woman whose piled-up desk was proof that she had no time to waste on lovelorn sergeants. She barely smiled at him when he introduced himself, and by the time he had finished his request; her face was downright frosty.

"You seriously expect me to go to bat for a girl who forged my name to obtain a job fraudulently—a job she used to commit large-scale theft?"

"She did not forge your name. The person who masterminded the whole thing got the papers for her. She just went along with it because she was all mixed up. She had no idea what she was getting into. When she realized what it was all about, she walked out, and that's how the whole scam came to light. That's also probably why she got beaten up, but I have no proof of that."

"You seem to have proof of nothing. After the embarrassment this situation has caused me, do you really expect me to take your word for anything? And what has it got to do with me? The girl isn't even Jewish. There must be some other agency that would try to help you."

"She's half Jewish—and I've been everywhere else."

Miss Peterson sighed. "I should have my head examined. I'm not sure anything can be done in a case like this. There's not one scrap of paper to support your story."

She looked at this stubborn, hopeful man, so determined in the face of the impossible, and her heart melted. She sighed. "Look, get the ammunition, and I'll see what I can do."

Rip started breathing again.

"What do you need?"

Miss Peterson pulled out a clean new folder and wrote "GOLDSCHMIDT,

HANNE" on the tab. She clipped a sheet to the inside and pushed it across the desk. "There you are. That's what I need."

Rip's heart sank again as he went down the list: birth certificate, school reports, marriage certificate of parents, membership in temple, affidavits from rabbi, from teachers, from family doctor, from friends of the family, and from employers.

"You need all that?"

"The more you can get me, the better. Now, obviously some of these papers will have been destroyed. That's where the affidavits come in. Find people who will swear before a notary that she is who you claim. Get me some extenuating circumstances for what she did. If she suffered during the war, I might be able to convince the powers that be that she was in emotional turmoil. They might buy that."

"You're on my side, aren't you?"

She shrugged almost angrily. "Not yours—hers. Everybody is eager to embrace the poor victims, to somehow make it up to them. But you know something? The weak and helpless and innocent are mostly dead. And a lot of those who survived did it by learning some techniques that would make your hair curl. They started out quite law-abiding, and then they learned the hard way that the law was immoral. So its going to take a while for them to become socialized again. See what you can do—but, for goodness sake, no more forgeries. One more setup like that, and I'm out of a job."

His next stop was the Catholic chaplain.

"You're not one of mine, are you, sergeant?" he asked Rip kindly.

"No, sir, its about a German girl I want to marry."

"A Catholic girl? There will have be a prenuptial—"

Rip interrupted. "She's not Catholic."

"Then I really don't see how I can help you."

"It's like this. . ." He launched into the story, skipping some minor details, while the chaplain showed increasing signs of restiveness.

"I still don't see—"

"I need to find the convent, and I must get to talk to this Sister Celestine. She's the key to the whole thing. If I find her, and she decides to back me up, I bet the Weber family will help, too. How does one get in touch with a nun? And will they let me in, even if I do find the convent?"

"Where did you say this town's located?"

"In the Russian zone, an hour and a half from Dresden by train."

The chaplain shook his head. "Fast or slow train? Oh, never mind. Let's look at a map. There can't be that many towns called Gleiwitz."

With the help of the map and a prewar registry of educational facilities, they finally found the orphanage.

The chaplain looked pleased for the first time. "Ursulines? Yes, they would be. Look, I can't make any promises, but I will try and find out who runs the place for you. You'll have to arrange your travel pass yourself, and your transportation. I might be able to get you letters of introduction to the local priest and the mother superior of the convent. And I'll try to get compassionate leave for you. I do hope you realize that this may turn out to be a fool's errand."

"Well, sir," Rip said with a tired grin, "I've always been reckoned a bit of a fool."

By the end of the week, things no longer looked quite as hopeless. He packed two K rations in gift wrap and had the girl at the PX tie them up for him with a red-and-gold-striped ribbon. There was a bottle of brandy for the princess. He was ready to go courting.

Number 9 was as grimy as before but pleasantly familiar now. He ran up the stairs and made a *rat-tat-tat* on the door, No response. He rang the bell and assumed perfect posture. When there was no answer, he sat down on the steps and waited. An hour later, he tried again, and this time there was a shuffling sound in the hall, not at all the sound of Hanne running to open up for him.

The door opened cautiously and the princess peered out. "So, it's you," she said. "I don't often come to the door these days. It's usually someone I don't want to see, anyway. But, please, come in, come in. Just lock the door behind you and put on the chain."

She shuffled back to her armchair, and he followed her. "Where's Hanne?" he asked, concerned.

"You don't know? No one notified you? Oh, you poor young man."

"What happened?"

"The police came for her, the day after you were here. I think they must have been watching her all the time—like spiders waiting to jump."

"They arrested her?" He dropped his presents on a chair and strode toward the old woman. "How could you let them?"

She glared at him angrily. "And where were you when they took her away? Where were all her friends—all the people who said they cared for her? Where was Paul? Where was Major Kuprin? Not even Petya, though one doesn't expect much from that boy. No one's been near this place since they came for her. You'd think I suddenly had leprosy."

"Do you know where they took her?"

She shook her head. "I can't get about. My legs are bad, And I wouldn't know where to start looking. If only the major would call. He's never stayed away so long."

Tears started trickling down her fat cheeks. Rip sat down opposite her and firmly held her hands. "Who's this major? What's he got to do with Hanne?"

She tried to explain, though it didn't make much sense to him. But one thing was plain, this major probably knew where she was and might be the key to getting her out.

Rip had no idea how to start looking for Hanne or the major, but he needn't have worried. The Russian officer was waiting for him, leaning against his jeep as became out of the apartment building.

"You are looking for Hanne Goldschmidt? Let me introduce myself, Leonid Kuprin, major. We may be able to assist each other."

Rip looked him over suspiciously. This man was a little too smooth for his taste, and he was in no mood to play games. All he wanted was to find Hanne and if this was the princess's mysterious major, too bad. Personally he neither liked nor trusted that type. "Where is she?"

Major Kuprin ignored the balled fists. "Moabit Prison. Not a bad place, really. Not Siberia, by any means."

"Is that supposed to be funny?" Rip found that he was in a rage.

"There's nothing funny about Siberia," the major assured him blandly. "Leave your jeep here. We'll take my car to go and see her, and we can talk on the way."

"I had no intention of having her arrested, Sergeant," Major Kuprin began when they were under way. You forced my hand. I couldn't risk her running off with you before we got the statement out of her."

"Exactly what charges are you holding her on?"

"We have enough on that poor girl to lock her up and throw away the key. But we have no use for her. All we want is a simple confession pointing a finger at Paul Karinof. She's been reluctant to implicate him, but it was only a matter of time—'til you barged in and forced us to act."

Rip swallowed hard. "If she gives you Karinof, you'll let her go?"

"Certainly. I take it our interests do not conflict."

"I want her out of jail—and I don't care what you do to Karinof. He's no friend of mine."

The major gave him a thin smile. "That's hardly surprising. For such a handsome and charming young man, Karinof seems to have very few real friends. He is perhaps not a very likable person."

"Look, I don't care about him one way or another."

"But he is the one we want. Persuade that silly girl to give us the statement and sign it for us, and she can walk out of the prison before the ink dries."

Moabit Prison was gray and gloomy, and Rip waited in the visitors room in a silent rage. How could they do this to her? How could she permit them to do it to her?

She came in and sat down beside him. At least they didn't have to talk through a grille. She looked pale and tired, and the faded uniform dress was too big on her, but her expression was surprisingly calm and cheerful.

"They're not ill-treating me or anything like that," she told him. "Don't look so angry. After all, I did break the law, so I had to expect something like this. Have you seen the princess? She was terribly upset, and she's so helpless by herself. Petya and Mimi should really move in with her."

He held her hands tightly, loving her, loving everything about her. Here she was in jail and all she worried about was her friend. "I'll try to get hold of them, whoever they are. Maybe Major Kuprin will try to find them."

Hanne looked away. "So you've met him. It seems he was having me watched all the time. In a way I'm glad it's over. I'm not frightened anymore."

"All he wants is a statement from you—that's all. Why don't you just give it to him and get out of here?"

Hanne looked at him as if across an enormous distance. He felt her detaching herself and slipping away. "You, too," she said softly. "I didn't think you would turn on me."

"Not on you, darling, on him. You owe him nothing. He took advantage of you and got you into this mess. What do you owe him?"

"Loyalty, I think. Because I did love him and then I stopped. That was a betrayal. I can't betray him again."

"If he gave himself up, would that be okay?"

She gave a tired smile. "Why should he?"

"Because he got you into this, and I think maybe he loves you."

"I think maybe he does, in his way. But he's not likely to put his head in a noose for me."

"I would."

Her smile was radiant. "I know. That's why I don't love him anymore and I *do* love you. You are a better man, and I've realized that I deserve—that I'm good enough to—I don't have to settle for less."

He put his arms around her and the policewoman turned her back and looked out the window.

"Not quite like Siberia," he said. "But I'm going to get you out of here, idyllic though it be."

Rip encountered the major as he left the visitors' room.

"No luck," the major said. "I can see it in your face—that moony look, but not the air of a man who has won his point. Well, it was worth a try."

"She won't do it."

"Women are amazing, aren't they? After what he did to her...."

"Are you sure he was the one who beat her up?"

"Oh, yes—no doubt about it. But it doesn't seem to make a difference. It's a pity. I'd help the girl if I could."

"You will get her released, won't you?" Rip searched the major's eyes.

"In due time, but not 'til we've got Karinof."

"There's something you might do for her."

"If I can."

"The old Russian lady—she's worried about her. Can you get someone to take care of her?"

"I imagine so. You do me a favor, too. Don't go beating up Karinof. You might enjoy it, but it would only complicate the situation."

The next day his papers came through—the furlough, the travel papers, the Russian transit visa, the letters—the whole bundle of them. If you had enough bits of paper, it seemed, you could do anything.

The timing was right, too. There was nothing he could do in Berlin. At least it saved him from the temptation to find Paul Karinof and smash his face to a pulp.

ஒ *Chapter 18*

Once you left Berlin, there were fewer people who spoke English. Rip struggled along with his few words of German, with sign language, pointing to maps, and chocolate bars as a last resort.

His other advantage, and one that didn't surprise him, was that he always seemed to make people laugh. It had bothered him when he was small, but now it came in handy,

He drove all day and got to Gleiwitz after dark. There was a hotel, and an English-speaking manager, even. Luck was smiling on him.

"A room for the night? Certainly. With a bath? There is a fine bath at the end of the corridor. Hot water extra."

The temporary ration book he had been issued did not seem to entitle him to a meal, but four cigarettes did.

It was a simple meal, for which the manager apologized, pleading hard times. Rip thought that boiled potatoes and a spoonful of applesauce was not too bad a supper. What made it strange was having it served with great ceremony on fine china and accompanied by a splendid red wine.

The manager had disappeared before Rip had a chance to ask about the orphanage, so he went to bed. There was nothing else to do.

Gleiwitz looked smaller by daylight. It had a cobbled square with a carved stone fountain in the middle, surrounded by tall, peak-roofed houses with gaily painted stucco walls. The war had left no scars on all this prettiness.

His jeep was causing a sensation on the square. Children were climbing all over it, and scattered when he came out of the hotel.

"It's okay," he called out to them. "I'll take you for a ride."

They hovered at a safe distance.

"Chocolate," he said. It worked. They came closer. He pulled out several bars and divided them up. Holding up the pieces, he asked: "Convent?" No response.

He handed out a few pieces. "Orphanage?" Nothing.

He shrugged and gave away the rest of the chocolate bar, then decided to have one last try. "Ursulines?"

The effect was magic. They beamed at him. *"Ursulinen? Ja. Die Ursulinen. Wir zeigen Ihnen. Wir kommen mit."*

They all climbed into the jeep with him, more children than he would have believed possible. They overflowed the seats, hung from the back, and straddled the hood, all pointing and shouting conflicting directions. It would have saved a lot of time to walk.

It spite of, rather than because of, all this assistance, he finally found a narrow drive dead-ending into a tall iron fence. At the sight of the locked gate, the children scattered. No one seemed to want to go in with him.

They just melted away.

One small tot hung back, pointed through the gate, and nodded encouragingly. *"Ursulinen."* She had a marvelous gap-toothed grin and a button nose. Against his better judgment he rewarded her with an entire Tootsie Roll.

"Danke," she said, bobbing a curtsy. Then she sat down on the curb and started licking.

He rang the bell and waited for a long time. His small companion had finished her candy bar. She looked at him hopefully for a while, and finally ran off.

He was beginning to wonder if anyone really lived behind that gate when an elderly nun finally appeared, looking flustered. Since she made no move to let him in, he poked his letters of introduction through the bars. She took them and scuttled away.

Rip sat and waited. It showed signs of turning into a long wait, and he wished he had thought to get himself a cup of coffee before setting out. His stomach was sending him distress signals. What's more, he was getting low on chocolate, and a man could hardly eat his passport. Without chocolate, he might never get back to the hotel.

Finally, the nun returned and opened the gate, but with an expression of doom that would have been funny under different circumstances. As it was, Rip felt pretty gloomy himself. He had come on a fool's errand. It was probably the wrong Gleiwitz, or the wrong convent, and most likely no one here had ever heard of Hanne. If it was an orphanage, where were the children?

He followed the nun along the gravel path and into the side door of a square brick building. Inside it smelled like a school, he thought. It had that aroma of floor wax and disinfectant. But children made noise, even well-behaved children. The silence here was deafening.

He was shown into a small, whitewashed room, furnished only with two wooden chairs, a small table and a large crucifix. It was saved from ugliness by the sun streaming through the uncurtained window and the view of the neat garden outside.

There was a rustle behind him and he found himself being examined by a short, squarely built nun with small, bright eyes.

"The mother superior has sent me to try to assist you because I am the only one here who speaks English."

He beamed at her. No introduction was necessary.

Here was the accent that Hanne had picked up as a child, and now he knew what it was—English as spoken by someone who spoke German with a French accent.

"Sister Celestine?" he said.

"Why, yes. How did you know my name? We have never met."

"We have a mutual friend—Hanne Goldschmidt."

"Hanne? Oh, you mean Maria. Of course, she would change it back. The good child—is she all right?"

"Well, to be honest, no. Right now she's in all kinds of trouble. That's why I'm here. I need your help."

He tried to make his story short, but she slowed him down by asking questions, very astute questions. After a while he felt she knew more about him than he did himself.

A bell rang and she started up.

"Please stay," she whispered. "I will return very soon."

Half an hour later she was back, carrying a tray.

"A little bread," she said, "and a cup of coffee—malt coffee, I'm afraid. We have had no coffee beans for a long time."

"I wish I'd known. I could have brought some along." She laughed at both of them. "What does it matter? Drink it while it's hot. It tastes even more evil when it gets cold. Now we must see what can be done for our girl. Is she still so beautiful?"

"She was in an accident, and her face is sort of scarred. Not that it matters. She has the kind of face.... Yeah, she's still beautiful."

"It so pleased me, that beauty," the plain little nun said dreamily. "So few people are such a delight to the eye. Her mother, they tell me, was the same—a very beautiful girl. But of course what Maria—I mean Hanne—what she has is better. The spirit shines inside."

He nodded gratefully. It was going to work. He had found his ally.

"What I need is all the information about her family, and I have to get it in writing. How many people can you think of who knew Hanne's parents and her grandmother? I don't suppose I can get her birth certificate but...."

Sister Celestine clapped her hands. "But we have her birth certificate!" she said briskly. "It's all in our files. Of course, it will take a little time to dig it up. Our school is closed down, no more children. The Russians thought we were a bad influence, and they set up a new orphanage. I'm afraid all the records are locked away, but we can open them up."

"So that's why it's so quiet."

"Sad, isn't it? Especially for the ones like me, who love to teach. Perhaps in time I will get transferred to another community. I am useful only as a teacher. But at least this means I have time to help you. We owe Hanne a great debt. I always felt guilty about her."

"Guilty? She knows you loved her."

"My poor young man, do you think we never harm the people we love? She came to us very frightened and needy, and we tried to shape her, as her Grandmother Weber wished, into a good obedient child, a child who would forget all about her Jewish father, who would forgive her mother's desertion. In fact we tried to make her over into another person altogether. And that is a sin."

"Is that why she ran away?"

"There was a reason for that—a good reason. At least I think it was a good reason. Now you must go and see the Webers. I have permission from the mother superior to come with you, to interpret. They do not speak English. Meanwhile someone here will look for Hanne's birth certificate."

The jeep delighted her. She sat bolt upright and stared about her with bright, curious eyes. While he drove, she talked. "I am a failure as a religious, you know." Her tone was cheerful and chatty. "If I hadn't been so very plain I might have married. Or if we hadn't been so very poor, I could have gone to the university. I had a choice—housework or factory. And I wanted so much to teach. So I persuaded myself that I had a vocation, but God probably knew I was cheating and punished me by giving me a most impatient disposition—and sending me to Germany." She laughed. "We always get what we deserve in the end, don't we?"

"Hanne has not gotten what she deserves, Sister."

"Be patient. She will."

"Tell me about her, won't you?"

"No, you tell me. Are you in love with her?"

"That's one reason I need all these papers—to get her out of jail and to get permission to marry her."

Sister Celestine nodded sunnily. "She will make a good wife. You don't want a docile wife, do you, the kind of wife who says, 'Yes, you are so right,' and 'How true, how true.' You will have a strong wife, and a loving one. That was one of the bad things we tried to do—thank God we did not succeed—we tried to make her stop hating. Thinking back on it—after all, I am older now—one sees these things differently. You have to be able to hate well in order to be able to love properly."

"Hanne talks just like you," Rip said. "You both start a sentence and keep going 'til you run out of breath. She's a very determined girl. The first time I saw her she was trying to dig up a patch of rock-hard ground to make a garden. She ended up breaking the shovel, and even that didn't stop her."

"You two seem well matched," the nun said with a nod. "You are quite a determined young man yourself, aren't you?"

The Weber's house had a prim, buttoned up look, the front door flanked by two narrow iron benches, every window tightly curtained in spotless white.

Sister Celestine's ring was answered by an elderly woman who smiled uncertainly. "Are you collecting for the poor, Sister? I'm not sure...."

"I *am* collecting," Sister Celestine assured her cheerfully. "But not for money this time, just a few bits of paper. This is Sergeant Tyler."

Frau Weber's eyes slid up to Rip's face, and quickly slid down again. "I will go and fetch my husband." She closed the door behind her.

"Let's sit down," said Sister Celestine, indicating one of the benches. "Oh dear. I don't think this is meant to be sat on. I suppose it's a penance. I often deserve one."

Time ticked by, uncomfortably, until the door opened again. Herr Weber bowed stiffly to Sister Celestine and managed to look around and through Rip. He was a handsome old man, much older than his careworn little wife, and rather elegant in his well cut loden jacket and embroidered waistcoat.

"We are a bit puzzled by your visit, Sister. What is it that you wish?"

"We are here on behalf of your granddaughter."

Herr Weber pursed his lips. "We were informed that Maria ran away from the convent. I don't blame you personally, Sister, but you must admit that there was a break-down in discipline to make that possible."

"We were shockingly careless," Sister Celestine agreed. "Luckily no harm came of it. Hanne is safe and well, but she has no papers. We hoped you could help us."

"No papers?" Herr Weber sounded as shocked as if Sister Celestine had told him that his granddaughter had lost her clothes and was walking around stark naked. One could hardly function without one's papers. He gestured impatiently to his wife. "Lotte, the big envelope in the bottom drawer."

He sat down on the opposite bench. "Maria has been a great trial to us all. She completely ruined our daughter's life, you know. Claudi had prospects—could have married anyone—but that Jew talked her into running off with him—without even a proper wedding."

"They were married," Sister Celestine said, her face curiously closed.

"It was a great mistake. Our daughter was a beautiful girl, and highly intelligent. That Jew...." Herr Weber's mouth puckered in distaste. "So clever, aren't they? They always get what they want. He turned her head with flattery. And then the child...."

Rip did not understand the German words but felt the man's cold distaste and Sister Celestine's controlled fury.

"Exactly," she said. "The child."

Rip had the impression that she was about to explode into a flood of French insults, but that interesting possibility was prevented by the reappearance of Frau Weber, who handed her husband two large envelopes.

He looked at the top one. "No, no, no. Those are the tax records '36 to '38. For goodness sake, can't you read?" He handed the other envelope to Sister Celestine. "That is all we have."

Sister Celestine thanked him. "You will be relieved to know that your granddaughter is doing well. She spent some time with the nuns at the Charité Clinic in Berlin, and has also been working for the Americans—an office job."

"I tried to love Maria." Frau Weber sounded pinched and sad. "You would have thought she would be more like her mother. Claudi was a happy little girl, always laughing and singing, like a little angel in the house. Not that she comes to visit us these days. But Maria... oh, such a gloomy child!"

"And ungrateful." Herr Weber sounded indignant. "After all we did for her, taking her in at a time like that. It was bad enough that Claudi had been so foolish."

Sister Celestine stood up, clutching the envelope to her chest. "We appreciate your help."

Herr Weber inclined his head and sat like a handsome statue. Frau Weber stepped uneasily from one foot to the other. Her hands fluttered uneasily. "We did our best, sister. Everything was so difficult."

"Sometimes our best is not enough," Sister Celestine said, then bit her lip. "Forgive me. I was talking to myself. I have frequently done my best when something more was required."

In the jeep, safely out of sight of the Webers, she opened the envelope and shared its treasures with Rip. "Good heavens, look at this, sergeant! We can now prove that Hanne was inoculated against small pox and had regular dental checkups. And here are all her school reports, even the prize she got in Kindergarten for coloring in a map of Germany without going over the lines."

Rip was glad to get away from the Webers, and pleased about the wad of documents. It looked like enough paper to give Miss Peterson the ammunition she needed. "But what's wrong with her grandparents? They didn't seem real pleased to hear that Hanne is all right."

"Bah," Sister Celestine said. "Just as well you did not understand. I know I lack charity, but those are two pitiful people. How can people live with so much fear and prejudice? Never mind. However they failed as grandparents, they are good Germans, very methodical and with a tremendous respect for documents.

"The only thing missing now is the birth certificate, which I am quite sure will be found, and of course something from a rabbi. For that you must go and talk to our priest, Father Brandstetter."

"Let me guess," said Rip. "He stretches his income by serving the Jewish community on Saturdays and the Catholics on Sundays."

"Close, but no. Father Brandstetter had a rabbi hidden in his attic during the war, and they had many conversations. Of course, the rabbi has left—he planned to go to Palestine—but if an affidavit is needed, I'm sure the father will make a deposition. He knows about the whole Jewish community—all the names. He is sure to be able to vouch for Hanne having been raised in the Jewish faith."

"I can see one major problem, Sister. The rabbi could not have discussed Hanne's family because they lived in Neustadt, which is quite a ways away. It took me almost an hour by car. I'm sure they had a different rabbi there."

"My goodness, you are as legalistic as a German. Do you want that deposition or not? Look at it this way: If the rabbi had known the Goldschmidts, I am sure he would have said about them exactly what the father will say he did."

Father Brandstetter spoke no English, but in response to Sister Celestine's note he escorted Rip across the street to the office of his friend, the judge, who knew two sentences: "So pleased to meet you" and "Lovely weather we're having."

Here the priest proceeded to dictate a lengthy document. The two old men seemed to regard the whole thing as a magnificent joke, and Rip hoped fervently that Miss Peterson would never check up on this particular bit of documentation.

A bottle was produced and the signatures were drunk to, the American sergeant was drunk to, the end of the war, the fine fall weather, the absent rabbi, the future happiness of Miss Goldschmidt—all perfectly good reasons for a toast. Rip found that they all understood each other perfectly. The wine helped.

He decided not to try to drive back to the hotel. The street was buckling under his feet, and the lampposts didn't look too steady. He finally made it on foot, very slowly and by no means by the shortest route.

The hotel manager provided aspirin and sympathy the next morning. Yes, the local wine was very strong. Father Brandstetter and his Honor should have warned him.

He presented his bill with an air of apology. "I hope you will return when we are back to normal. It was a great honor to serve you."

"Thank you," Rip said sheepishly. "My only problem now is I seem to have mislaid my jeep."

"No problem at all. It is parked in front of the Marienkirche—a short walk. I will send my son to show you the way."

There was much bowing, and Rip made his escape.

His folder of documents was bulging. The affidavit from the priest alone comprised several pages and looked gloriously official with its array of stamps and seals. He had everything now except the birth certificate. Sister Celestine had sworn it would be found, and had made him promise to come back to the convent for it.

The gatekeeping nun admitted him without delay this time, and Sister Celestine was waiting at the side door, waving an official-looking envelope.

"I knew we would find it. And now that you are here, we will have a short walk around the garden. I promised myself I would tell you why Hanne ran away."

"You said she had a good reason."

"I think it was. You see, the war was over and her mother suddenly found it convenient to have a Jewish daughter." Sister Celestine scowled. "Whenever I think about Claudia Weber, I find myself sadly lacking in Christian charity. She is one who takes. Whatever happens, she will have the softest bed and the spot in the sun. If other people sleep on the floor and shiver in shadows, too bad."

Rip nodded. "Yeah. I know people like that."

"Hanne is not at all like that," the nun said emphatically. "Hanne would give away her only shirt."

"I know," Rip said softly.

"So Claudia wrote to the convent to suggest to the mother superior that Hanne should come and live with her again. Hanne refused, and the mother superior was most indignant. She told Hanne of her duty to her mother, second only to her duty to God, and that it was not up to her to judge. And so on and so on. She is a very old woman, and so unworldly that she sometimes makes very little sense."

"Poor Hanne."

"Yes. That was why I left the money where I knew she would find it. I thought it was time for her to go."

Rip shook his head, amazed. "You did that deliberately? How do you feel now that you know all the trouble she got into?"

The nun tucked her hands into her sleeves and hunched her shoulders. "Quite content, I assure you. Did you ever read Voltaire's *Candide*? No? You should. Hanne did. I made her read it."

"Has it something to do with all this?"

"It has to do with everything. Candide has a tutor who tells him that everything happens for the best in this best of all possible worlds."

He looked at her, trying to figure out if she was making a joke. It was hard to tell. She was laughing, but there were tears running down her cheeks.

❧ *Chapter 19*

Miss Peterson stared at the bulging file folder in amazement.

"You didn't make it up. The girl's for real."

"Very real. Now, what's next? How do we get her out of jail?"

"The Legal Department will tackle that. You see, now that we have a genuine DP to deal with, it's a brand new game. I imagine we can just request the Germans to hand her over, and then she will have a hearing where I can go to bat for her."

She picked up the phone and dialed with an air of confidence, but after a few minutes of conversation she turned to him with a glum face. "You didn't tell me that the Russian military are involved."

"That makes a difference?"

"Of course. It alters everything. We could have bulldozed the Germans into releasing her, but we have no pull with the Russian administration. The best that can be done now is to try to find out if we have someone they want. Perhaps we can trade. I wonder why they're bothering with her. She can't be that important—politically speaking."

"They're trying to get at someone she's covering for."

Miss Peterson sighed. "And she won't cooperate?"

Rip smiled sadly. "Staunch as a rock."

"I suspect I could get to like that young person," Miss Peterson said. "But she does make it hard for us to help her. Look, you'll need permission to marry from your commanding officer. Have his people call me. I'll vouch for her. Meanwhile, I'll go ahead and process her application for an American visa. I take it you'll give her an affidavit?"

"For what?"

"Just guaranteeing that you'll see to it she doesn't go on relief once she gets to the States."

"Good grief! I want to marry her!"

"Then you might as well sign that affidavit. I have all the forms right here. And you'd better talk to Rabbi Kalb. He was hopping mad when they found his signature on those forged papers. So if you want him to marry you, you'd best go and butter him up a bit."

"Somehow I never thought I'd be married by a rabbi."

Miss Peterson made a face. "Hoity-toity—it's legal. And that's how you marry a Jewish girl. When you get her home, you can do it all over again in your own church."

Rip called the Moabit Prison to find out if he needed special permission to visit Hanne. It was infuriating. He was put through to an official who said he spoke English but seemed unable to answer the simplest question.

Exasperated, he persuaded one of the interpreters to call for him. The man came back looking puzzled. It was not a matter of the language barrier. They weren't talking. No one would give out visiting hours or explain the regulations. It was most peculiar.

As soon as he could get off from his job, he drove to the prison and tried to bulldoze his way in. His papers were respectfully examined and returned to him with a polite shake of the head. No, he could not see Miss Goldschmidt.

Rather than give up, he went to see the princess. This time the door was opened immediately by a woman in nurse's uniform.

"You have come to see Princess Tschernskaya? That will be good for her. She gets so lonely."

The princess looked cleaner and happier than the last time. She was delighted to see him. "You've seen Hanne? How is she?"

"They wouldn't let me in."

"Why ever not? What kind of hospital is that?"

"Princess," he explained gently, "Hanne is not in a hospital. She's in jail."

She laughed heartily. "No wonder you didn't get to see her. We managed to smuggle her out. The major was furious. Serves him right. He tried to have me moved to an old folks' home."

Rip took a deep breath. "Look, I've been out of town. I know nothing about any of this. Start at the beginning and tell me what's going on."

She clapped her hands and her fat shoulders shook with laughter. "Such fun—just when I was so upset. I was almost ready to accept the major's offer. Me in an old folks' home—can you imagine such a thing? Then Paul cooked up this lovely scheme and got her out—just drove up in an ambulance with orders from that Dr. Pankau at the Charité that she had to be rehospitalized for plastic surgery. All forged, of course. And once they had her in the ambulance, they changed back into American uniforms and brought her straight to the American hospital. And then he got me this nice nurse, so I don't have to be alone. He's a good boy, after all. I've misjudged him."

"Paul Karinof!" It was not a question. It was a shout of rage.

She patted his hand indulgently. "There, there. You mustn't be jealous. He has redeemed himself in my eyes. Of course that will make no difference to Hanne, and it shouldn't. He's not good for her."

Rip stood up, unsure of what to do. The princess seemed to be so happily certain that everything would be easy now. He had a hunch that Paul's latest maneuver had completely destroyed Hanne's precarious claim to legality.

"And how does Hanne feel about all this?"

"You must visit her at once," the princess urged him. "I have her room number here—214—that's on the second floor. She's under the name of Lieutenant Ann Brooks."

"Another false name?"

"Well, of course, she had to have American papers to get in, and she's so much safer from the Russians. I'm sure they found out right away she'd gone, and they'd have checked all the German hospitals. They'll never think of looking for her there."

Rip took the slip of paper and thanked the princess. She was perturbed by his gloomy expression and tried to rally him. "Everything will be easy now. You will marry her and take her to America. Major Kuprin can go whistle—old folks' home indeed!"

There were no special visiting hours for the second floor of the army hospital. It was reserved for female personnel and dependents, and few of the rooms were in use. He passed door after door, wide open to display empty beds. Lieutenant Brooks's room turned out to be a lavish private suite, comprising a bedroom, sitting room, and bath. Hanne was sitting in an easy chair, staring out the window.

Her shoulders were sagging and she looked much worse than she had in jail. His heart went out to her. She looked so defeated.

He sat down quietly and waited until she looked up. She tried to smile, but it wasn't one of her really good ones. "I've done it again, haven't I? How do I get out of this one?"

"But why did you do it? Couldn't you just have refused to go along?"

Hanne raised her hands in a helpless gesture. "I didn't know. I thought the ambulance was on the level, that I was going back to the Charité. They had talked about fixing the ear. And then it turned out to be Paul, and he was so pleased with himself. He thought I'd be pleased, too. I'm frightened."

"But what does he think he's doing? He's got you here under a phony name, with phony papers. Where do we go from here?"

"He's got it all figured out," Hanne said without expression. "As soon as I recover from the surgery—he wants me to get a skin graft to cover the scar, too—I'm to get still another set of forged papers and fly to Zurich. I think he's got some more plans after that, but that's all he told me."

"This is crazy. You're not going to Zurich with Paul. You're coming to America with me, aren't you?"

She shivered. "How can I? I am an escaped criminal. They'll never let me in. It was bad enough before. Now it's all ruined." She started to cough, a hard, dry sound, more painful than tears.

Rip gripped her shoulders. "Just tell me one thing: Do you want to be with Paul?"

She shook her head violently.

He started breathing again. "Okay, then it's quite simple. You're not in jail. There's a phone right there, by the bed. Pick it up and call Miss Peterson."

She stopped the hacking sounds, wiped her nose with the corner of her robe, and looked at him attentively. "The social worker? She'll crucify me. Paul said she and Rabbi Kalb were after my blood when the forgeries came to light."

"Paul seems to have this talent for dumping blame on other people—especially on you. Look, he's responsible for the forgeries. It's his blood they're after. Miss Peterson has been knocking herself out getting your papers processed. Legal papers, Hanne, in your own name."

This time the smile was real.

"As for the rabbi," he added with elaborate concern, "he's not so bad. He agreed to marry us. Not in the synagogue of course—maybe in the mess hall or in his study. Will you settle for that?"

"Rip, you're not pulling my leg, are you?"

"Would I lie to you? Yeah, I guess I would. But this is on the level. Now, you see, you've got to get out of this dumb trap your pal has got you into. Call Miss Peterson. She's got connections in the Legal Department. They'll work something out."

"I suppose I'll have to go back to jail? It's all right. I don't mind. At least they called me by my own name."

"Do you want to get your ear fixed? They told me downstairs that you're scheduled for surgery on Tuesday. We might be able to get that done for you—in your own name."

"I don't mind it the way it is. Do you?"

He touched it gently. "I like it. It'll make you fit right in with my folks. I told you about the funny ears."

"A recessive trait," she said solemnly, then laughed. "People have made such a fuss over the way I look. Just like my lovely mother, they used to say. I don't look a bit like her anymore. I like myself better this way."

"I met your grandparents. They're pitiful, Hanne. They're awful. They sure did remind me of the Huckles."

She started to laugh for real. "More relatives?"

"No, ma'am, I should hope not. Huckles are nothing but trash. Why, Huckles put buttons into the collection plate on Sundays. We wouldn't touch them with a ten-foot pole. That Sam Huckle shot Grandpa's best hound. Just because he ate a few sheep of theirs. And you know how sheep are. They practically lie down and ask to be eaten. We never forgave them for that. Not that we had proof, of course, but who but a Huckle would do a thing like that?"

"Huckles, eh?"

"You wouldn't care for them," Rip assured her. "Huckles get up in the middle of the night and move your line fence. Why, they'd steal library books—if they ever learned to read. But before you can turn up your nose at them, as any right-thinking Tyler woman is bound to do, you're going to have to pick up that phone and call Miss Peterson. I can't do that for you. The call has to come from you."

Hanne straightened her shoulders and went to the phone.

The man from the Legal Department was smiling broadly. "That just about wraps it up. The Germans want no part of her. She's a big embarrassment to them. The Russians are playing it cool. Not a word from them about the whole thing. As long as we don't receive an official complaint, we have no obligation to turn her over to them. The fact that she didn't sign anything claiming to be Ann Brooks puts her in the clear with our authorities. Unfortunately she's still the only one who can tie in Karinof with this little prank, and she won't do it. It's infuriating, but we'll get him sooner or later on something else. He's bound to get careless."

"Then she's in the clear?"

"We had to bend the rules a bit, but she's obviously a decent kid, a bit sappy but no harm in her. Miss Peterson's given her a clean bill of health—no moral turpitude. We're going to shuffle her through with the next batch of visas."

Rip stirred uneasily. "Can't you hurry it up? You see, I'm being shipped home. We want to get married before I go. I want to see her safely out of Berlin."

"You can't take her on a troop ship anyway. Be reasonable. Marry the girl. When her papers come through, we'll ship her home to you. Meanwhile, Miss Peterson's lined up some sort of job for her."

"She's scared of Karinof."

The officer made a helpless gesture. "If she won't speak up against him, there's nothing we can do. Chances are, he'll leave her alone now. Miss Peterson's going to keep an eye on her."

"I wish I could be here to look out for her. Karinof's done some pretty weird things. Hanne had left all her clothes behind—all the stuff he'd given her. He got angry because she hadn't taken it."

"Well, so would I. Look, Sergeant, when you give a girl presents and she gives them back, you feel hurt. I would, too."

"Would you make a pile of them outside her window, pour gasoline on them, and burn them?"

The officer looked disgusted. "Good grief! He is a bit unstable, isn't he? We'll have to keep an eye on him."

"Yeah." Rip wished he could get more of an assurance, but that was all there was. Hanne would stay at the nurses' dormitory as a maid until her papers came through. Men weren't allowed upstairs. Paul would not be able to get at her.

The trouble was that Paul seemed to have a lot of tricks up his sleeve, and Hanne was scared to death of him.

❧ *Chapter 20*

It took Hanne less than a week to get promoted from maid to cook at the nurses' residence. For one thing, the director hated to see such a fragile little person, obviously just recovering from an illness, struggling with heavy buckets. More important, she turned out to be what the director, Major Margaret Pim, called "a good plain cook." There was no higher praise in her book. It was just lucky that Hanne had learned enough from Fannie Farmer to be able to produce the kind of food that made Major Pim feel at home.

"She made brown bread for us," the major crowed triumphantly to Miss Peterson. "And what's more, it tasted like brown bread. It was steamed, not baked, and her apple pies are a delight. We're all putting on weight, except the girl herself. Dreadfully skinny, poor little soul. I'm getting her some dried cod. She's going to make fish cakes for us."

Miss Peterson smiled. Major Pim's devotion to food was a byword, and only much exercise and very tight girdles kept that splendid woman from bursting out of her uniform. But she was a magnificent administrator all the same, Miss Peterson told herself sternly, with the kindest of hearts. "I'm glad Miss Goldschmidt is working out so well." Her voice was properly serious. "We've clarified her status now, and permission for the marriage should be coming through any day. Of course, we don't know when Sergeant Tyler gets shipped out. It's all a bit rushed. Would you be willing to keep her on after she's married? It may be several months before we can arrange a passage for her."

Major Pim reassured her cheerfully. "Any girl who could cook like an honest Yankee is welcome anytime. She's a nice little creature, too, though a bit on the solemn side."

"She's been traumatized, and it will take time for her to learn to relax. But I'm coming over to see her this afternoon. I've got a letter and a package for her. Both from female friends, so that's safe enough. I'll bring them over and see if that doesn't cheer her up."

Major Pim expressed satisfaction. She was a mother hen at heart and yearned to see "her girls," as she called them, as healthy and happy as she was herself.

Hanne showed much pleasure at seeing Miss Peterson and her mail. She looked less drawn than the first time they'd met. Miss Peterson was forced to assume that a figure she considered admirably slender would look pitifully scrawny to Major Pim. She thought Hanne looked rather wonderful in spite of the scars. There was a bloom on her skin that hadn't been there before, and the tense look about her mouth was less pronounced.

"Your hair's growing back nicely. It's such a beautiful color."

"It's slow going, but I hope I can get it cut before the wedding. If the ends were even, maybe it would look more like hair and less like fur."

Miss Peterson nodded. She herself thought the furry look was rather fetching.

"I have a couple of letters for you, Hanne. Or rather, a letter and a package."

The big, serious eyes brightened. "A package? Whoever would send me a package?" She tore it open as greedily as a child opening a birthday present.

"Ahhh," she said, expelling her breath very slowly. "I think I know.

She picked out the card from the froth of white eyelet embroidery. "Frau Gerhardt—the dear soul. And look, there are shoes to go with it. Aren't they beautiful? Platform soles—I've always wanted platform soles. Now I'll be tall enough for Rip. Herr Scholte must have made them for me."

She translated the card into English for Miss Peterson's benefit: "I have made a good profit on all the clothes I sold you, Miss Goldschmidt, but this dress, which is a present, gives me more satisfaction than any. Be happy."

"A real wedding dress," Hanne said in an awed voice, holding it up against her. "Isn't it beautiful? I thought I'd have to get married in something borrowed."

"And so you shall," said Miss Peterson. "You need something old, something new, something borrowed, and something blue." She took off a small gold pin, enameled with the American flag, that she always wore on her lapel. "This'll be your borrowed item. Now all you have to find is something old and something blue."

"I don't have anything old. I left all my clothes behind, and Major Pim was so kind—she outfitted me top to toe in army issue, all brand new."

Miss Peterson laughed. "Nothing old? I'll give you a pair of very old white gloves. You may have to mend one of the fingers, but they'll look nice with that dress, or you can just carry them."

Hanne nodded seriously. "For blue, I can just put a ribbon around my neck."

"Very nice." Miss Peterson nodded. "You know, Major Pim is letting us use the dining room, and we can decorate it with flowers and paper streamers. It will be a beautiful wedding. I'm looking forward to it."

"Can I invite Frau Gerhardt to the wedding, and Herr Scholte? He's the old gentleman who made the shoes."

"You can invite anyone you like."

"Even the princess?"

"Of course."

"The letter's from her, I think. No one else writes uphill like that."

Hanne opened it and looked upset. "Oh, dear. This is awful. They put her in an old folks' home."

"Well, from what you told me, she really needs more care than she could get in her own flat."

"But, Miss Peterson," Hanne said, scanning the letter, "she sounds so upset. She writes she'd rather be dead."

"Perhaps we can find a better home for her. Where is she now?"

Hanne checked the address. "Saalburg Heim, Grunewald."

Miss Peterson looked relieved. "Don't worry, then. That's the nicest nursing home you could imagine. I placed a darling old lady there only last month and she's happy as a clam."

"But the princess is miserable. I must go and see her."

"Of course you must. Take her some nice fresh fruit. I'll drop you off, and you can get a bus back in time to cook dinner."

The old folks' home was a supermodern villa surrounded by pleasant pine woods. If it had suffered any bomb damage, it didn't show. The stucco was freshly painted, and the big windows were intact. The general effect was of brightness and spaciousness. Hanne was reassured by the pleasantness of the building, but the tone of the letter had been despairing. It might be an ideal nursing home and still be the wrong place for that proud, stubborn old woman.

She found her friend in the solarium, playing a spirited game of bridge with three oddly dressed old ladies. One was wearing a huge straw hat, and another one was draped in a gaudy silk shawl. The princess's partner was tightly buttoned into a man's raincoat. In contrast, the princess looked quite lovely in a flowered kimono. Hanne had never seen her so sensibly dressed.

At the sight of her visitor, the princess threw down her cards and hailed her delightedly. "So you *did* get my letter. How nice of you to come."

"Play your hand, Excellency," the lady to her left demanded. "Don't try to bamboozle me. I know you overbid."

The princess threw up her hands. "I concede—you have won all my money. There!" She pushed a pile of toothpicks toward the disgruntled opponent.

"The trouble with the princess is that she doesn't take the game seriously," the offended lady complained to no one in particular.

The princess ignored the grumbles, hoisted herself out of her chair, and waddled to the French windows, pulling Hanne along. "Frau von Bülow is a bit cranky. You know how some people are as they get on in years. We must make allowances."

Hanne noticed that her old friend was a little thinner and moved more easily. She appeared to be in tearing high spirits, quite a contrast to the poor, deserted old woman she had described in her letter.

"We will sit here, where we can look at the chrysanthemums. It is very pleasant, isn't it? Although one does wonder why they have planted only that sickly mauve. They come in such wonderful colors—orange and bronze. Such a lack of imagination. But we must not be critical, they do their best. Like with the food—such small portions and a mere scraping of margarine on the rolls. On the other hand, they do make very nice soups. One can't have everything."

Hanne was confused. She had come to rescue her friend, and no rescue was necessary. She handed over the bag of grapes. Immediately the princess attacked them, picking them off one by one and examining them with pleasure before popping them into her mouth.

Hanne watched her, much reassured. "Are you sure you're comfortable here? I thought you hated the very idea of a home like this."

The princess managed to look mildly embarrassed. "I wrote that letter when I first arrived. I was upset, but it's really quite different from what one expects, actually a very decent class of residents. The women I play cards with, for instance, quite respectable. Frau von Bülow is the widow of a general, Frau Director Wederfeld's father had an estate in East Prussia. We have invited Frau Lemmel to play with us because she is a good little soul. She and her husband ran a grocery store, but she has very nice manners and excellent card sense, which is more than you can say about Frau von Bülow."

"I'm so relieved. I was afraid you were unhappy. You sounded so desperate in your letter."

"Well, it was a shock. One day I was in my own place, with a nurse to take care of me, and suddenly— *pfoot!*—out in the street."

"Not really in the street?"

"Oh, yes, literally." The princess gave an angry snort of laughter. "You see, Petya had stopped paying my rent months ago, when business was so bad. I had no idea. Those boys never tell me anything. So Paul was paying all my bills. Very generous, of course, but Petya didn't say a word, which was foolish of him. And when you left the hospital, Paul was annoyed. You know the problem the poor boy has with his temper. So he had me put out into the street, literally into the street. There I sat on a trunk in the middle of the sidewalk. It would have made a more effective picture if I had had a bird cage on my lap. They always show poor homeless old women clutching birdcages. Unfortunately, I never kept a bird. They make me sneeze. Oh, I can joke about it now, but I was very angry. I'm just glad his poor mother is dead. She would have been humiliated beyond words."

Hanne was indignant. "After such a long friendship. To put you out in the street like that. What happened then?"

"The police came and I told them to call Major Kuprin. He was quite nice, too, came and fetched me from the police station and brought me here," Her eyes glittered maliciously. "Of course it wasn't just kindness. He wanted information about Paul." She chuckled. "You have to admire Paul. He has been very clever. They haven't been able to pin a thing on him."

Hanne's throat closed up. "You didn't tell Major Kuprin what you know?"

"And send my own nephew to jail? No, I have to look out for poor Petya, though I must say he has not looked out for me."

"Do you think they'll get Paul in the end?"

The princess chuckled. "Oh, no. He has trusted so few people, and he has always been able to get others to take all the risks for him, He's a clever one. I wish poor Petya had half his brains. No, Paul's all right. No one seems to be willing to point a finger at him. You could, couldn't you? But you won't. Your nice sergeant would, but he has no firsthand knowledge of the operation. Paul is safe."

Hanne nodded seriously. Paul was safe, but was anyone else? She wished she could be as optimistic as the princess about the whole thing. But then the old lady was impressively resilient. She was burbling on about her new friends, all apparently of impeccable social standing, and very respectful toward her.

"Do you get a lot of visitors?"

The princess was silent for a moment. "None of my old friends have come," she finally admitted. "Only Major Kuprin, and those aren't truly social visits. He's after Paul and he hopes to find you through me. Don't worry. I haven't said a word."

Hanne nodded. The major was wasting his time trying to pump this tough old lady.

"Will you come to my wedding?"

The princess brightened. "You are marrying that nice sergeant? Good. Yes, I'll come if someone will order a taxi for me."

"Would you consider a jeep?"

"I would come by wheelbarrow—as long as a young handsome man does the pushing."

Hanne was early for the bus, so she sat on the bench and closed her eyes. The sun felt good. The pine trees smelled lovely. The princess was happy. It was a splendid day. She paid no attention to the car pulling up, didn't even open her eyes, until she was shocked out of her dreamy state by Paul's voice.

"Let me drive you home." He sounded tame enough and looked quite calm and friendly, leaning out of the car door.

She shook her head and shrank back against the bench.

The movement seemed to irritate him. "Stop that! I'm not going to hurt you, Honey, for heaven's sake. All I want is to talk to you."

She looked up and down the street. It was empty.

"Good God! Do you think I'm going to force you into the car? What's happened to us?" He turned off the ignition and came toward her.

"Go away," she begged. "I won't talk to the police about you—I promise. But you've got to leave me alone."

"Just a few minutes," he said. "Right here in broad daylight. Okay?" He sat down at the far end of the bench, making no attempt to touch her. His eyes were sad.

"What's happened to us, Honey? What went wrong?"

She could only stare at him. He looked so honestly troubled.

"Look, I know I lost my temper and slapped you," he went on in the same troubled voice. "I'll never be able to forgive myself for that. But I did try to set it right. I arranged for you to get your face fixed. Why did you walk out on me?"

She was amazed by his inability to face facts. "It's over, Paul. It was over even before you beat me up. Yes, beat me up. You didn't just slap me. You tried to kill me. And now you want to know what went wrong? Nothing went wrong. I grew up. I'm not your little Honey anymore. I'm Hanne Goldschmidt, who is getting married next week."

His face was sad and reproachful. "I always planned to marry you. You knew that. We made such grand plans."

"You made the plans," she said. "I did what I was told."

"I planned it for both of us. It's not fair. I never meant to fall in love with you, remember? You barged into my life and took it over. Then, just as suddenly, you walk out on me. 'Sorry, I don't love you anymore. Too bad.' Is that fair?"

"Not fair. Only honest," she said wearily. He was so handsome, glamorous almost, and he was looking at her with such an air of sincerity. What he said was quite true, and it should have touched her heart, but she felt nothing.

"I'm sorry about your clothes. I was so furious that you left them behind— after all the fun we had picking them out for you."

"Oh, Paul, you should have tried to understand. I have no use for those sort of clothes. And Rip wouldn't have been comfortable to have me wearing them. You shouldn't have burned them. They were lovely. Someone else could have used them."

"Do you really think I'd let another woman wear them? They had your perfume on them. Do you still wear it?"

She smiled faintly. "*Jeunesse*? No, it's all gone."

"I could get another bottle for you from Paris."

"No."

He sat silent for a minute, his hands clenched on his knees.

"I have something you will accept from me," he said at last. "You must take it."

He held out a small jewel box covered in dark green leather. She made no move to touch it.

"Look," he said, opening the lid. "You must accept this, at least."

Against the dark velvet lining lay a locket, an old-fashioned gold case with a gold-flecked blue stone in the center, it didn't look in the least like the battered treasure of her childhood. It was too good, solid gold and beautifully crafted.

Hanne tried to say something, but no word would come out. Paul was looking at her so hopefully, holding out his present. For the first time in all the months she had known him, he looked uncertain and humble.

"I can't take it."

"Please. I'll never bother you again. I promise. It's a good-bye gift."

"I can't."

The cold flash of rage she dreaded crossed his face, and was quickly hidden again. "But you wanted this. I got Claudia to make a drawing for me. She remembered your grandmother wearing it."

At the mention of that name, Hanne's face froze. Paul's mouth began to twitch. "What have you got against your mother, anyway?"

She merely shook her head.

"But isn't it like the one you had?"

"Yes. But I can't take it."

"Claudia warned me," he said bitterly. "She said you were every bit as self-righteous and hard-nosed as your father. She did warn me."

Hanne felt utterly weary. "All right. I'm like my father. I take that as a compliment. Don't you see, Paul, we are miles apart. You'd really like me to be like my mother, wouldn't you?"

"But you are," he said eagerly, leaning toward her. "Or rather, she's quite a bit like you. She's got that style, that ability to think on her feet. I can see you in her."

"I hope you're wrong." Hanne shuddered.

"No, I'm not," Paul said with an edge to his voice. "Right now you're on a pink cloud, but it won't last. Sooner or later you'll get bored—like Claudia did—and you'll come back to me."

"No, I won't. I really won't."

He bared his teeth in a strangely wolfish smile and held out the locket. "Take it. It's something to remember me by. You can't really get away from me, you know. I had you first."

"It's over, Paul," she said steadily. "I did love you, but it's over once and for all."

A spasm of rage and pain contorted his face. He stood up, dropping the open jewel box on the ground. His heel came down on it, crushing it into the pavement.

"You miserable little bitch," he said bitterly. "I can't imagine what it is I see in you. But we're not through, not yet. And don't kid yourself. I'll be the one to decide when we are."

After he had driven away, she picked up the ruined locket. It looked more like the one she remembered now that it was scuffed and broken. She couldn't leave it lying in the dirt like that. Clutching it in her hand, she started to cry.

When her bus came, the conductress helped her up the steps and settled her in a window seat, making sympathetic clucking sounds.

"There, there, miss. You'll be all right in a moment."

She wept steadily all the way back, as if a dam had broken. All the tears she had refused to shed poured down her face. She cried for her father, that kind and clever man; for her stiff, cold, unhappy grandmother who had seen her world turned upside down; and for the small Hanne who had been alone and frightened and hadn't dared to cry. She cried the angry tears, the frightened tears, and the sad tears, and she couldn't stop.

Weeping wildly, she stumbled off the bus and through the gate, and past the embarrassed guard, and stormed into the safety of her bedroom.

❧ *Chapter 21*

"We don't know what to do with her, Miss Peterson." Major Pim's voice sounded strained over the phone. "When you drove off with her, she was perfectly cheerful, wasn't she?"

"Happy as a clam."

"That's what everyone says. She went off all smiles and she came back crying, locked herself in her room, and she's been at it ever since." There was surprised indignation in her voice. "Why, we had *canned spaghetti* for dinner!"

Miss Peterson brushed this issue aside. "She won't talk to you or let you in?"

"No."

"I'll be right over. And please, see if you can arrange permission for Sergeant Tyler to come, too."

Major Pim's voice sounded uneasy. "But men are not allowed upstairs."

"Look, if she were sick you'd get her a doctor, whether it was a man or a woman, right? Same kind of emergency. Try to bend the rules."

Hanne finally unlocked her door and allowed Rip and Miss Peterson to come in. She looked awful. Her eyes and nose were swollen and red, the short wisps of hair stuck to her head with sweat. Her beauty, which could survive hospital and prison, had deserted her. She looked damp, soggy, and plain. Rip took one look at her and folded her into his arms, holding her gently and stroking her hair.

Miss Peterson nodded, satisfied. "You two work it out. I'll go downstairs and try to comfort Major Pim. She had canned spaghetti for dinner!"

"Hey, doll, can you tell me about it? I want to help. And even if I can't help, I want to cry with you."

She raised her puffy face to him. "I don't cry. I never cry."

"You're giving a fair imitation of it right now, And there's nothing wrong with crying. You're supposed to cry when you feel bad."

"Strong people don't cry."

"Of course they do. They just do it when no one's looking. Look, I cried when my cat, Ophie, died."

He sat on the rumpled bed and pulled her down on his lap, where she curled up, her head tucked under his chin. He couldn't see her face, but her tense body started to relax a little.

"Ophie was a real goofy cat," he explained. "I found her in the woodshed, brand new, with her eyes still closed. Her ma had abandoned her. Animals will do that to their babies when there's something wrong with them. Ophie had everything wrong with her. She was missing one leg—and to be honest, most of her marbles. She was the sappiest cat you ever saw—didn't know enough to come in out of the rain. But I didn't know that at first. Mom and I raised her on a bottle and she turned out to be the prettiest thing, one yellow eye and one green, and creamy sort of fur, with whiskers turned up on one side and down on the other."

Hanne lay warm and limp against him, giving an occasional hiccup.

"We called her Ophelia, and she was my cat. She slept in bed with me and kept my stomach warm on cold nights. She also made nests of my socks and tore holes in my underwear. I told you she wasn't bright. And then she got herself poisoned. Fine and fluffy one morning when I left for school, and when I came home there she was in the driveway all cold and ratty-looking. You bet I cried. The vet said it was poison."

"One of the Huckles, probably," Hanne said in a small voice.

"I wouldn't be a bit surprised. Of course, not being too bright, she just might have ate some rat poison, but let's blame the Huckles. Us Tylers always do."

Hanne gave a weak giggle. "You mean you blame them whether they deserve it or not?"

"Well, Hanne, I'll be quite honest with you. I lied. There are no Huckles. I made them up."

She sat bolt upright and glared indignantly. "Don't you ever lie to me. Not even about Huckles and such. I'm so tired of lies. I've told them, and I've listened to them. I don't want to hear another lie as long as I live."

"Not even to make you laugh? I can be quite comical when I'm telling lies—or so they say."

"You are very funny," she said solemnly. They both laughed, but Hanne sobered quickly.

"We'll have to work out some sort of code, so I know when you're telling me lies just for fun. I'm sorry I got your shirt all wet, crying all over it."

He assured her that he didn't mind a bit, and they sat quietly together for a while.

"Is this how it will be when we're married?" Hanne asked dreamily. "So calm and comfortable."

He smiled down at her. "Not all the time, I hope. I reckon we'll have a bit of uproar now and again. I can't promise you perfect happiness. Things can go wrong—and they usually do. But we'll work it out."

She nodded, satisfied, then sat up straight and faced him. "Do you want to know what happened to make me act like this?"

He nodded.

Hanne laid her head against him again. "It was Paul. No, he didn't hurt me this time. He was being quite nice to begin with. Only then he wanted me to take this present, and when I wouldn't take it he threw it on the ground and stomped on it."

"That man does have a way of breaking things when he doesn't get his own way," Rip said thoughtfully. "What was the present, and why did it make you cry?"

Hanne opened her clenched fist and displayed the locket. Rip picked it up gingerly and turned it over in his hand.

"It's like the one you got for your last good birthday, isn't it? So he knew about that. Why didn't you want it?"

She shook her head violently. "I want nothing from him. He uses things to take you over, like buying you. And he's so sure of getting his own way in the end. I hate him."

"Poor guy," Rip said softly. "I never thought I'd feel sorry for him, but you are a good hater, aren't you?"

"Yes," she said fiercely. "I owe it to him not to talk to the police, but I owe him nothing else. I want him out of my life."

"He's out. He can't get back in. Taking that trinket wouldn't have given him any power over you."

"I suppose not, but he won't let go. I just didn't want it. And then he stepped on it. That's what hurt. He couldn't make me take it, so he ruined it, like he ruins everything he touches."

Rip took his handkerchief and started wiping her face. "I wouldn't say that. He hasn't ruined you and he hasn't really ruined that locket. It's a bit scratched up and scuffed, but we could get it mended and put a little chain on it. I think it's sort of a pretty thing."

"You wouldn't mind my wearing it?"

"Not if you let me get the chain. Then it'd be from me, too, and from your dad and grandma—as well as from Paul."

The dining room looked lovely. The nurses had decorated it for the wedding. There were great swaths of bunting draped across the ceiling, in the only colors available: red, white, and blue. They were left over from the Fourth of July and looked a bit odd for a wedding. But the tables had been pushed aside and the chairs arranged in two blocks, just like in a chapel. Rabbi Kalb looked festive with the blue and white prayer shawl draped over his uniform tunic and a white satin skullcap.

He had been uneasy at first about performing this marriage. After all, the girl was not Jewish by Mosaic law, not even by upbringing. The groom was Presbyterian, sort of. Apparently his family accommodated a number of different opinions, and its members followed a wide variety of faiths, seemingly without friction.

Both of them had assured him that they would bring up their children to love God and behave decently but had been quite vague as to what ritual they would follow. He suspected that there would be no ritual. Their religion, while quite sincere, might easily remain a purely personal matter between them and their God.

He could not marry them as Jews. The ceremony didn't fit. But ceremonies could be adapted. A rabbi more orthodox than himself might object to this mishmash of a service, but the Deity, he felt, would understand.

Miss Peterson sat in the front row and glowed. She saw a new American. The small enameled flag she had lent Hanne for the wedding formed a bright spot against the white wedding dress. She felt fierce pleasure. Every day she went into battle against the ugliness and horror the Nazis had left behind. Every day she squared off with the enormous damage Hitler had done. And this once she had won.

Frau Gerhardt and Herr Scholte sat in the third row. Occasionally they exchanged a satisfied glance. The bride was lovely. The eyelet embroidered cotton flared out from her tiny waist, and the bodice rose like a flower stem. It was a dream of a dress, and the girl was lovely enough to break your heart.

The princess, resplendent in her brocaded tent, raised her lorgnette and examined Hanne's profile. She nodded to herself. Yes, the child looked happy with her young sergeant.

"Who gives this woman in marriage?" Rabbi Kalb demanded, raising his head.

"I do," a short, square nun said, stepping forward and taking the bride's hand. "On behalf of her father and the community to which she was entrusted, I give Hanne Goldschmidt in marriage."

Rabbi Kalb blinked just a little, and went on with the ceremony.

One of the guests had come late and stood in the back of the room. He had not been invited. In fact, he had some difficulty getting past the guards. He looked around sardonically at the red, white, and blue streamers that gave the bare room a festive look. Realizing he was in time for the wedding after all, he relaxed. He had been anxious to get there. He had, after all, a very special present for the bride.

In response to Rabbi Kalb's nod, Rip bent down and kissed his bride. The face she turned up to him expressed such utter joy and trust that his heart contracted.

The chaplain gave a satisfied nod and turned to the guests. "On occasions like this, it's the custom to spend the evening with the newlywed couple to join them in celebrating the start of their new life. But normally the wedding reception is just the beginning of the honey-moon. Today, however, I'm asking you to forgo the cake and champagne, the speeches and the dancing. Sergeant Tyler's orders came through this morning. He's being shipped out the day after tomorrow, and the new Mrs. Tyler won't be able to join him for several months. I suggest you all follow my good example and give these two what they need most—a bit of time alone together."

He made a gesture that was halfway between a salute and a wave of dismissal and started propelling the couple toward the door.

Hanne, almost floating on Rip's arm, never even saw her uninvited guest. He had stepped back behind the others who crowded around her to kiss and congratulate.

Only the princess recognized him. She clutched at his sleeve and her lips trembled. "Good heavens, Major Kuprin. You aren't going to arrest Hanne on her wedding day, are you?"

He smiled and shook his bead. "Far from it. Actually I came to bring her good news, but it hardly matters now. Your foolish little friend seems to have found a safe harbor."

"Good news?" She regained her poise and looked at him curiously out of the corner of her eyes.

He merely smiled and offered her his arm. No one really wanted to hear what he had come to say—least of all this indomitable old soul.

He had meant to make a big splash with his news, but this was better. His silence would be his wedding present to the girl—her freedom to start her new life.

She would not be hounded again. There would be no demands on her to do something that conflicted with her loyalties, those stubborn, irrational loyalties. It had all taken care of itself. The woman who called herself Claudia Goldschmidt had talked as soon as they arrested her, had talked so freely that Paul Karinof was already under lock and key. Another job completed.

"I shall drive you home," he told the old woman, patting her fat little hand. "The excitement seems to be all over."

She gave her hoarse chuckle. "Oh, you poor man, do you really think so? I'd say it's just beginning."

Author's Note
My family's history, 1939-1945

My mother, Margot Ilse Dorothea Leyser, was born in Berlin in 1893, and married her cousin Hans Zweig in 1919. They moved to Ratibor in Upper Silesia, which is now Poland.

They had been engaged for four years because my father refused to marry while there was a chance that he might get killed. He fought on the West Front and received an Iron Cross (Order Third Class – the least impressive one). I was one of three children. After my father died in 1930, we moved to Berlin.

From 1931 on we lived with my widowed grandmother in the 3rd floor apartment of Flensburgerstrasse 6, Berlin NW 87. My grandmother, Gusti Leyser, owned the building. It had been a present from her parents, who were dissatisfied with the accommodations my grandfather provided.

Grandfather was a lawyer, and not very good at it, having no talent for law, and being so disastrously honest that he refused to eat black market food during WWI. His dream had been to study architecture. His family, although poor, had scraped together money for his university tuition. In return they extracted from him the promise that he would marry a rich girl and provide dowries for his two sisters.

My grandmother's family was indecently rich. The big apartment accommodated us quite nicely. My mother took over a huge room that had been the salon (the women's drawing room), while my grandmother used the other drawing room, which had been the "Herrenzimmer" (the room where men congregated). There were enough extra bedrooms to go around, although I ended up sharing a room with our governess, Fräulein Hettwer (Wawa), which pleased both of us.

Life in Berlin became increasingly ugly. In 1936, when my sister was sixteen, she went on a trip to England, got herself a job and stayed. Thanks to her efforts, my brother and I also ended up in England – he in 1938, I in August 1939. By the time I left, our family fortunes had declined as a result of the forced sales of two factories. We were down to just two servants, very old ladies who had been working for Oma from the start of her marriage.

When I saw my mother again in the summer of 1946, she handed me a diary she had kept from 1939 to 1942. After I read it she took it away from me and burned it. She said she needed to do that so that she could start her new life with a clean slate. I am afraid I have forgotten all the historical events, the gradual cutting away of all legal rights. The bits I remember are the personal ones.

Soon after the war started the two maids were forced to leave. Jews could no longer have Aryan servants, not even old ones. Also, everyone was issued a ration card. The Jewish ration cards were different from the others. They were good for much less food and could not be used for anything considered a luxury, but it was enough to survive on at first. Jews also had to wear yellow stars on their clothing to identify them, and were not allowed to use public transportation.

This last was especially hard for my mother who had been assigned a job in a war factory. Because she was the only caregiver for my grandmother who by now was bedridden as a result of a stroke, my mother was permitted to take home three days worth of work assignments. She was supposed to repair the soldiers' heavy gloves. Without the use of public transportation, she had to get up at four o'clock twice a week, carry a heavy package to the factory, and another one back. It took two to three hours each way, depending on the weather. She then had two days to get the work done, three over the weekend.

Wawa, my beloved governess, was working as dietitian in the Charité Hospital at that time. Every day, as soon as she was through with her work, she came to help my mother with the sewing. Without her, my mother, whose sewing skills were negligible, could not have kept up. Wawa also provided food from her own ration. This was important because the rations for Jews kept shrinking.

Meanwhile, my grandmother's apartment building had been taken over, and non-Jews occupied the two lower floors. My grandmother's third floor apartment was gradually filling up with other Jews whose homes had been seized. By 1942, my mother's room accommodated her, her sewing machine, my grandmother, and two other old ladies. Every other room was crowded with people. I have no idea how they all managed with one and a half bathrooms. Food was prepared on electric rings. Every room took care of their own cooking. The kitchen was only for washing up and laundry. The refrigerator, Oma's pride and joy, had been taken away.

By '42 the deportations had become daily events. People were told that they were going to work camp. My mother, in her innocence, actually believed that for a while. She and Wawa constructed a sort of pants suit out of old quilts to prepare for that new phase of her life. Soon the reality leaked out, and one of the old ladies who shared the former salon chose to take Veronal rather than report at the railway station when so instructed. My mother also had a supply of Veronal, although she never used it. I still have it.

Soon after that, my grandmother was moved to the Jewish Hospital, and from there to Theresianstadt where she died. A surviving nurse told me that she died of hunger, because she gave away all her food. "Nimms, liebes Kind," she was heard to have said. "Du brauchst es mehr als ich." (Take it, dear child. You need it more than I.) The woman who told me that story was deeply touched by Oma's generosity. Knowing my grandmother, it was probably something other than pure selflessness that motivated her. The food must have been pretty dreadful, and she was a food-snob.

Wawa and my mother had been preparing for Oma's deportation. Wawa took along bits of personal belongings each time she left at night, and stored them in the basement of the Charité. (The women were obviously not thinking too clearly at this point. I inherited more than a hundred beautiful linen napkins that had been squirreled away in this fashion, as well as boxes of bobbin lace Oma had made in her younger days. I managed to use up and give away the napkins, but I still have the lace.)

Wawa bought a fake ID with my mother's photo on it from an SS man. She then purchased a train ticket for her. After Oma's deportation, my mother took off the yellow star, grabbed a handbag, and walked out after dark. Wawa saw her safely onto the train.

The diary only went that far. I pieced together the rest of the story from bits of conversation. My aunt had been living in Fürstenfeldbruck, a small town near Munich, since the twenties. Only close friends, including the local priest, knew that she was Jewish. Pfarrer Brandstätter was a delightful old man who probably saved my mother's sanity by visiting after dark and playing chess with her. The local doctor also knew Mother was hidden in the attic, and took care of her when she got sick. She stayed hidden for the rest of the war, only coming downstairs at night to use the bathroom.

Before making it to the comparative safety of that attic, my mother had a close call on the train. Halfway between Berlin and Munich, policemen boarded to check everyone's papers. The document provided by the SS man was obviously meant to look phony. A policeman asked my mother to get off the train and come to the police station to have her papers examined more closely.

She knew that she had nothing to lose. So this woman, rigidly ladylike and honest to the point of being occasionally obnoxious, with no previous acting experience, put on a glorious show. She stood up, put her hands on her hips and started yelling. "You want *me* to get off the train? Who do you think you are, sitting here at home on your fat arse, while my sons are at the front fighting for the Fatherland?? While you have it safe and easy, my Hannes got wounded and is lying in the hospital. I work in a war factory, but they gave me 3 days off so I could go and see him. I am a good German woman, and what are you? You are a cowardly piece of shit!"

It must have been lovely performance. Everyone in the compartment was yelling at the policeman, who kept looking at the forged papers. Of course he knew that my mother was lying through her teeth. Finally he shrugged, smiled at her and said *"Na schon gut."* (Okay, already.) All the good Germans in the compartment cheered the brave, hardworking German woman, and sneered at the heartless policeman.

I hope there is a special place in heaven for him, and for Pfarrer Brandstätter, and for the doctor whose name I don't remember. I don't worry about Wawa. She needs no intercession from me. The last time she came to visit us, about 37 years ago, she continued what she had started, the education of our daughter. She had already begun German lessons on an earlier visit. Our daughter was surely the best prepared child in her Kindergarten class.

Discussion Questions

❧ How does Paul's own background affect his relationship to Hanne?

❧ Why do you think about Paul changing Hanne's name to "Honey?"

❧ Time and time again, Paul is offended by vulgarity, and seems to want Honey to keep from losing her well-bred manner. What do you make of this?

❧ The book shows us many characters whose lives are altered forever by the destruction of their way of life. (Honey, Paul, Ulrike, Princess Lydia Ivanovna, Fraülein Stulp, Mimi Krall, Herr Scholte, Ingelore, Petya, Ulla Printz, Sister Celestine, Hanne's mother, and grandparents) Who seems to be best at adapting? Who seems most wounded? What traits does the author seem to value most in her characters? What traits seem to aid survival?

❧ What do you think of Paul's gift to Honey of the lilac tree? What is Paul's attitude later, towards the tree? How does this contrast with Rip's attitude toward the tree?

❧ What kinds of gifts does Paul give Honey, in general? What kinds of gifts does Rip proffer?

❧ Many of the characters in the book engage in black market activites. Ulrike won't even take paper money for providing a service, she insists that Hanne fork over a potato. Rip gives away cigarettes and chocolate. What, if anything, is the difference between these activities and what Paul does? Where should one draw the line between keeping law and order, and doing what one must in order to survive? Is it ever alright to break the law?

❧ How does the story that Rip tells about his mother being adopted by the teacher parallel Hanne's story?

❧ Different people tell different lies during the course of the book for different reasons. Is it ever okay to lie?

❧ Is Paul right when he claims that Honey is just like her mother, Claudia? In what ways is she alike, and different?

❧ Looking back, do you think that Paul's relationship with Honey was a mistake or a blessing?

❧ Looking ahead, what do you think are the chances for happiness for Rip and Hanne; an earthy backwoods boy, and a cultured European waif?

About the Author

Nicolette Maleckar, *née* Zweig, was born in 1926 in Breslau, Germany. In 1939, she was sent to England in one of the children's transports arranged by the Quakers. From 1945 to 1947, she worked as a translator and interpreter for the United States Military Government in Berlin, where THE LILAC TREE takes place.

Nicolette Maleckar lives with her husband on a mountaintop in West Virginia.

Bonus features &
Special offers

At the Ben Yehuda Press web site, you'll find video interviews with *Lilac Tree* author Nicolette Maleckar, as well as other special features and the opportunity to sign up for special pre-publication sales on forthcoming books. Visit http://www.BenYehudaPress.com for details.

Share the magic of
the **Lilac Tree**

Check your favorite bookseller, or order here:

[ ] **YES,** I want ___ copies of *The Lilac Tree* at $17.50 each, plus $3 shipping per book (New Jersey residents please add $1.05 sales tax per book). Canadian orders must be accompanied by a postal money order in U.S. funds. Allow 15 days for delivery.

My check or money order for $_____ is enclosed.
Please charge my [ ] Visa [ ] MasterCard

Name _____

Organization _____

Address _____

City/State/Zip_____

Phone _____ Email _____

Card # _____Exp. Date _____

Signature _____

Checks should be made payable to Ben Yehuda Press.
Please return to:
Ben Yehuda Press
430 Kensington Rd.
Teaneck, NJ 07666
email: sales@BenYehudaPress.com
buy online at http://www.BenYehudaPress.com

Printed in the United States
99888LV00004B/73-76/A